The Nocturnal Library

By Ermanno Cavazzoni

Translated by Allan Cameron

Vagabond Voices
Sulaisiadar 'san Rudha

Translation copyright © Vagabond Voices Publishing Ltd 2010

First published in 1991 as *Le tentazioni di Girolamo* © Ermanno Cavazzoni

Vagabond Voices Publishing Ltd.
3 Sulaisiadar
An Rubha
Eilean Leòdhais / Isle of Lewis
Alba / Scotland HS2 0PU

ISBN 978-0-9560560-5-4

The author's right to be identified as author of this book under the Copyright, Designs and Patents Act 1988 has been asserted.

Printed and bound by Thomson Litho, East Kilbride

This translation has been funded with support from the European Commission. This publication reflects the views only of the author, and the Commission cannot be held responsible for any use which may be made of the information contained therein.

For further information on Vagabond Voices, see the website, www.vagabondvoices.co.uk

Contents

Chapter A   9
    Extract: The Whys and Wherefores   14

Chapter B   16

Chapter C   29
    Extract: Giants of the Twentieth Century   35

Chapter D   39
    Extract: The death sentence in America   48

Chapter E   52

Chapter F   60

Chapter G   70
    Extract: Proto-philosophies   76

Chapter H   80

Chapter I   86
    Extract: How philosophers are born   92

Chapter L   96

Chapter M   105

Chapter N   114
    Extract: Retrogrades   121

Chapter O   127

Chapter P   139
    Extract: Hairy women   149

Chapter Q   150

Chapter R   159

Chapter S   170
    Extract: Cycle paths in purgatory   178

Chapter T   179

Chapter U   185

Chapter V   202
    Extract: Twentieth Century, Chronicle of   203

Chapter Z   214

The Nocturnal Library

Chapter A

Midnight chimed as I went through the library's shabby little entrance. To be honest, the door would have seemed more suited to a coal-merchant's than a library, if it weren't for the shiny and showy embossed plate whose letters pierced my eyes and jarred their nerves. It read: *Public Library. Opens at 24.00 and closes at 08.00. Closed all night on Mondays for cataloguing and inventory.* A coated figure sidled up while the bells rang. Although a scarf obscured his face, I could see his feet: he wore a pair of battered slippers and pyjama bottoms rather than trousers protruded from below his coat. I instinctively peered down at my own legs and discovered that I too was wearing pyjamas, but I did have shoes. I then shuddered with the cold, even though my face continued to sweat. By the time they opened, a small crowd was huddled together and well wrapped not only in coats and jackets, but also in blankets that covered their shoulders or their heads. There were even a few who had brought a pillow held tightly under their arms. Pyjama collars, nightdresses, slippers, nightcaps protruded in various directions; they looked like refugees from their slumbers or sleepwalkers in flight from another country. The surrounding throng started to carry me inside, pushing stupidly as though we were entering a bus, while actually we were descending a flight of stairs towards a badly-lit and uncertain destination. We trod on each other's feet as we went, to the shrieks of the barefoot who defended themselves with their elbows. I got one in the mouth that jarred a tooth, and further down the head of a shorter man was being pressed against the wall. Someone else had lost his glasses, and I could hear them crunching underfoot; then he, too, fell and they trampled over him. Carried by the crowd, I stamped on his face, while he tried to bite people's feet, and he must have succeeded in biting those without shoes, because I heard sudden cries, kicks and short but vicious scuffles on the ground. The flight of stairs stretched endlessly and the walls narrowed, so that we could hardly breathe or we breathed the smell of greasy hair, musty mattresses and the stale bodies of the bedridden. A head was pressed against my vertebrae with such a force that I would have been sent spinning down the stairs if it hadn't been for those in front: a man wrapped in a nylon quilt and a bony woman in a woollen turban who constantly twisted her neck in order to stare at me.

I stopped when we finally entered a dim but spacious reading room, like the cork from a bottle, and the other bundles of humanity rushed across the room to occupy positions around the tables. There were plenty of places, but clearly some were more valued than others and arguments ensued. In the shadow of a corner, I saw two men fight over a chair, pulling at it while a third man of considerable girth came running up and sat on it. He held it tightly with his hands and his legs, until they managed to tip him over; they then proceeded to clamber over his face while continuing to tug at the armrests. Especially from the side aisles you could hear the dull sound of blows to wooden surfaces, tables brusquely moved and muffled arguments. One hapless individual was driven away from a chair under a rain of blows, and collapsed like a dead man at my feet. He peered round and, no sooner had he spied a place to his liking than he was up as though nothing had happened, dusting himself off and making himself comfortable in a chair by one of the square columns that held up the low ceiling of the reading room. In fact the room had all the appearance of a cellar, a rambling and dimly-lit cellar with little headroom. Metal tie-beams ran between the pillars at head height. The first thing I had noticed on entering the room was that chickens were promenading on the tables or perching on the chairs. When we rushed into the room, most of the chickens leapt away, while the few that resisted had to be frightened off by waving a scarf or blanket. For a few moments the air was thick with dust, flapping wings and the occasional feather.

Chapter A

Gradually the arguments died out, each person found a place, brushed away the chicken droppings by hand or with a handkerchief, switched on the small table light and sat down. Many of the chickens had migrated to the metal tie-beams, and were noisy and agitated for a while longer, the remainder wandered cautiously between the tables. Finally even the chickens settled down: some sat broodily, others scratched about and pecked at the floor.

I was there by pure chance. I had been in bed for no more than half an hour, when I suddenly awoke with a slight toothache, and remembered that the following morning I had to sit my school-leaving exam. I had to sit it again because years had passed, too many years, more years than the law would allow, without my having gone to collect my diploma. It had therefore expired. This was the reason why I twisted and turned beneath the bedclothes and came out in a cold sweat.

I sat up as this recollection afflicted me, and switched on the light which gave out only a feeble glow, as though the filament was just about to go, or the power was low at that time of night. The card instructing me to attend in accordance with current legislation lay on the bedside table. While I ran my tongue along the aching tooth and gum, I picked up the card and realised that I had not read some of the small print. The letters were so small and the light so bad that I couldn't read the text. I wondered why the letters were so small, like the information sheets that come with medicines. I got up and switched on the main light, which also failed to illuminate the room properly; in fact I saw even less because it was very distant and the ceiling seemed higher than usual. I could only read a few words which were written on one line in bold type. Straining my eyes and holding the bedside light very close, I felt I could just make out *The* ..., followed by an illegible word, and then *of the Twentieth Century*. It was either the syllabus or the name of a course text. I heard the clock on the next floor chime half past eleven. "What if they discover that I no longer know anything?" I asked myself, "not even the basics! The twentieth century?" And so I started to ask myself elementary questions: who invented the steam engine? Who invented electricity and who the internal combustion engine, the aeroplane, the helicopter, and when? How many world wars were there in this century, and what were they called? And what changes did they bring about in mankind, generally and philosophically? Nothing! I was struck dumb, I could not reply. "Kindly explain yourself!" I told myself for practice. "Do you mean that you have not studied for this exam?" And I couldn't answer even this question. I paced the room, hitting my head in a useless gesture, and still straining my eyes to find something else in the syllabus, something easier. I continued to circle the room, as the questions circled in my head: around and around drawing me into a vortex – into an abyss of ignorance. All my thought was concentrated in my teeth, in the form of acute neuralgic pain which ran through them like a pedal-driven sewing-machine.

As I circled the room prey to apprehension and recrimination, I decided to leave it and go downstairs; I wanted to find a chemist's and get a pill to calm my aching teeth. Instead I found the library, in the street under my flat, where I had always thought there was a coal-merchant's.

In the reading room I had entered, most people were seated near the walls and in the shadows of narrow recesses and little crypts. They congregated in large numbers around the darkest tables, while those more in view remained empty. A few people had dimmed the light by covering it with a handkerchief or some item of clothing: a vest, a pair of stockings, a bandage or a hairnet. Others had not even bothered to turn on their light, and were bent over their books or something similar, using the feeble beams coming from their neighbour's light.

The guy who had been trampled on the stairs was the last to arrive. He wore silver and blue pyjamas, and his

Chapter A

hair was dishevelled from the fracas. He held his twisted and lenseless glasses in his hand, and said: "Now, how do I read?" The question seemed partly directed at me and partly to himself. I took the opportunity to ask him about library procedure. "The first to arrive," he replied politely, "get the best places where you can be left in peace. Generally speaking everyone has their own book kept aside and they pick it up themselves. But if you are new, you should ask for one." And he went off to take a seat with an air of resignation.

The silence was punctuated by furious sneezes and sonorous nose-blowing that resembled someone practising the chromatic scale on a bagpipe. I looked around and realised that a library official was standing rigidly to attention and so close that I could feel his breath on my neck. I stepped away as I turned, to avoid my nose brushing against his face. His hat was a moth-eaten mortarboard, and he wore a dust-grey soldier's uniform, so threadbare as to invoke pity. Loose threads, little feathers and indeterminate stains had collected in the creases, and he appeared to have lived and aged within the uniform without ever undressing. His epaulettes barely survived with a faded and unstitched number. A badge pinned to his chest read: "Dr. Accetto, Head Librarian".

I immediately looked for my card and showed it to him, even though it was impossible to read it in the poor light. I pointed to the line that in my opinion read: *Twentieth Century*. He made the suggestion of a bow by a slight forward movement of his rigid torso, and then demonstrated his perfect knowledge of the situation by a generous sweep of his arm. "Is it a book?" he asked, and after I had intimated with a nod that this was in fact the case, he continued: "Of course, but don't be surprised by the question. People sometimes come with the most absurd requests: such as beer or wine, and they start to sing as though they were in a restaurant. This constitutes a disturbance, and we are obliged to throw them out."

"Yes, quite," I agreed, "but I want the book that is referred to here."

"Very good, please take a seat and we will bring it to your table."

"If you don't mind, I am in rather a hurry."

"We will do all we can," he said stiffly.

It all seemed very straightforward, as though experience had taught him to interpret my needs better than myself. Perhaps my case was very run-of-the-mill. This was the most serene and relaxing moment during that long night crammed with troubling incidents that came one after another. I would have happily let myself fall asleep if I had not been in a library. Even the toothache seemed to have receded leaving only a slight sensation of pins and needles in my mouth.

The poor man who had been so badly trampled at the entrance was seated in full view with his desk light on, so I went across and sat next to him. He was sitting up straight as though reading, except that his head was slumped in front of him, and even the folds of his cheeks drooped with the heaviness of sleep that resonated in his nose. He was surrounded by a fog of little moths caught in a dusty halo by the light. It seemed to me that the dust fell from his head to the book like some by-product of sleep, and the insects too had been freed from the depths of his dreams. Every so often, he would twitch his cheek just under his eye, as though he released the sharpness of his dreams from there. I rested my chin on my hand, while I watched a slug slowly climb up his sleeve. Instead of sleeping while I waited for my book, I leant over and seeing the heading halfway down the page, I blew away the ants and out of curiosity started to read.

The Whys and Wherefores

Moreover, at the beginning of the century, there was the case of the woman from Recanati. She was married, even-tempered and extremely sensible, but on occasions she

Chapter A

was unexpectedly assailed by a sense of loss that knew neither limit nor reason. Her face became quite white, as though her blood had ceased to circulate, she stiffened and stared in front of her with glassy eyes, suddenly ignoring her household tasks, the water boiling on the stove, the taps gushing water and the laundry yet to be laundered. She would stare at her arm in anguish and repeat to herself, "Why do we have veins?" She would stare at her hands and say, "Why do we have fingers?"

This could occur at any time: while she was sewing, hugging herself in front of the mirror, or stirring the soup on the cooker. These queries came from the depths of her brain, against her will, and they took over and froze every part of her self.

She would come to a sudden halt, and stare down at her feet, while her face aged a hundred years, and say, "Why do we have weight?" Or while she was washing the sheets, she would fall prey to a terrible dismay, and ask herself, "Why is there water?" and find no reply. She would then repeat the question a couple of times in a lower voice. She would look at the soap, the scrubbing brush; she would look at her hands, her veins. Finally she would let the question drop, or it would simply evaporate from her mind, and she would return to her washing, serene and unaware, or continue to stir the soup.

Chapter B

Before I could finish reading two heads came up from beneath the table. They looked around and studied the face and expression of my neighbour very carefully and for a considerable period of time; one of these persons waved his hands in front of the sleeper's eyes. He then took the slug and placed it on one of those eyes. In the meantime, his companion had sealed his nose with sticking plaster so that he would have to breathe with his mouth open, and now that mouth was inhaling and expelling great clouds of small moths and other flying insects: hymenopterans, dipterans, crickets and, it seemed to me, even a few fireflies which went off leaving a trail of suggestive phosphorescence. The two men were delighted with their handiwork and proceeded to inspect the inside of the sleeper's mouth; it seems that they went about this business in part because it was simply a job that had to be done, in part out of natural curiosity and in part to satisfy some private whim. They were both wearing faded, rumpled and threadbare uniforms of the kind worn by errand boys or lift attendants. Then suddenly and without saying a word to each other, they bent down and pierced his neck with a needle; he jumped, writhed in his chair and forcefully exhaled. The slug fell from his eye, and the two men hunched their backs and hurried away to where they became lost amongst the tables. His breath on the book stirred up another cloud of insects and dust; there were even flying ants. The hen perching nearby started to peck and call the others which arrived in a great rush. I noted that the sleeper's eyes were slightly open and he was looking at me through the narrow fissure. One of his eyes was glued up with the slug's silvery slime, so the eyelids were not equally apart, and at the same time he was massaging the puncture to his neck.

"It was not me who woke you," I said.

Chapter B

"Eh!" he said. "I should be in bed at this time of night, don't you think?" There was a silent pause while both eyes looked me up and down, and then he resumed, "Listen, I have the opposite complaint: insomnia. The back payments of sleep I am owed are so colossal that at times I lose consciousness. You know, this could be dangerous; I could fall and break a bone... Clearly you don't know."

"But I do. I do know," I said, "or at least, I can well imagine."

To which he responded, "For me a bed is full of needles: if I lie down on it, I start to jump all over the place, as though I've got grasshoppers in my blood. That's why I come here – because we're seated, time goes by and we're slightly less aware of it. Except on Monday, when the library is closed. Then night-time becomes a torment; I wander around this neighbourhood, rest my head against a house and close my eyes, but it isn't like sleep, it's ersatz and carries the risk of injury from stray animals, thieves and drink-drivers."

"This evening I couldn't get to sleep either."

"There's only one cure. Do you know what it is? ... A fiancée! Do you have a fiancée?"

"I have had one on some occasions."

"I've had one too, and when I was on her, that is on my fiancée, I perhaps came very close to shaking off my insomnia; she was the only one who could make me sleep and even sleep deeply, although not regularly. In other words, I was fond of her because of these advantages that accrued from our cohabitation, and this was a slightly more normal period for my repose – until she eventually got tired of me."

And he continued to tell his story in a hoarse whisper, while waving away the swarms of midges that entered his mouth and entangled themselves in his words.

"I went on dates with her more dead than alive, because of this unrelenting insomnia; the bags under my eyes were red and blue, and swollen with ink like a squid. She didn't seem to mind: she said I looked like an actor, that I had the grim stare of a thicket of thorns and my bulging eyes were beaming a hypnotic ray. So on meeting up, we would immediately embrace – she had an expansive personality – and I would take advantage of this to have my first lovely little nap standing up with my head on her shoulder while she indulged in her customary effusions. This decongested my nerves and even my eyes calmed down a bit and became less swollen. Then, wrapped around each other, we went for a walk in the park; she would tell me all about her day and the innumerable things that would result from it and, except for my legs which had the job of maintaining forward motion, my body became drowsy just like when you listen to a lullaby and experienc the overdue delight of the gradual but irreversible approach of blessed slumber. So we would abruptly collapse on an isolated bench, and under a moon whose light filtered through the foliage, we would cling to each other and I would let myself go completely: I slept unrestrainedly with my head across her chest and cushioned in her forearms. In fact her breasts were formed in such a manner that it seemed to me that they had a substratum of plush stuffing sustained by excellent and, I would say, first-class springs, as though they had been designed anatomically to responds to requirements of deep sleep in particular and relaxation in general. Their conformation was well suited to the articulation of the neck, so that the head was lifted just enough to avoid stressing or twisting the vertebrae, thus lessening the danger of stiffness. And we all know that poor-quality sleep is highly detrimental to one's bone structure and one's health.

"These were certainly beautiful moments, even though I was not in any condition to assess them. While I slept, my expression was one of rapture and devotion, and it really did seem that I was purring, while in fact my nose and my now relaxed pharynx were quivering involuntarily. So there you have it: I was on those occasions most authentically myself; there was no pretence and she was my perfect complementary substratum. She talked and talked, being

Chapter B

of a communicative disposition; I never understood what she was actually saying, but my wonderful sleep was the equivalent of a yes, an unconditional agreement on every question and all questions that might arise in the future, and I expressed this all-embracing consent through the weight of my head which made my presence felt. When, however, her chatter took on the tone of a direct question and my neuro-vegetative apparatus detected this, I would then utter the suitable words of reply and I believe I did so without moving. I would say, 'Yes, Emilia (she was called Emilia), yes, Emilia, so very much and for always.' Or I would use suitable adjectives and adverbs in accordance with a simplified grammar governed by my spinal marrow which, in order to defend my slumbers, took personal responsibility for these conversations and ingeniously managed to prolong them as far as it was humanly possible. For example, I used to hear myself calling out her name during a few moments of vague consciousness, like a lovesick sleepwalker: 'Emilia, Emilia, Emilia...' I would also say, 'yes, yes, yes...' but to what I do not know, and yet she felt she was understood, which for her was a source of untold gratification. It was a breathy and whimpering 'yes' that did not involve my higher faculties, nor did it necessarily imply wakefulness. All this was down to the spinal marrow, which kept our exchanges going and even operated my facial expressions with contractions full of love and understanding without in any way disturbing the sleeper's repose; indeed, that marrow stood watch over it.

"But after a while, this was no longer enough for her. She wasn't even happy with the interjections, 'oh, ah, eh' which emanated from my mouth, and all the respiratory vocalisations that were supposed to signify the temperature of my sentimental ardour. You see, this Emilia was a youthful spirit and this kind of conversation could only raise her expectations, so that by dint of repetition she eventually became rather prickly: 'You don't love me any more. You don't love me like you used to. Natale, tell me you're still crazy about me!' Natale, that's my name, and I started to awake on hearing my surname reverberating in my ear, because these questions of loving and not loving were too complicated for the poor vegetative soul. So I would then sigh meaningfully and my embrace would tighten two or even three times so that some notion or other would be sparked off and appear clear and distinct. And what next? Well, I would be off once more with my deepest slumbers. Now let's be clear about this: I was not being selfish; I did this out of a survival instinct, and I did it for us, for her, and for our life together. But once a hour or two had passed with her incessant talking, I would suddenly hear her berating me, pulling my hair and knocking on my head as she might a door, and saying: '... who are you thinking about? You've got another woman! I'm sure you're thinking about her. Who is she?' And I would come to, and say a few reassuring words so that she wouldn't change her position, which was comfortable and perfectly shaped to hold my head and body – in a manner that you could never expect of a bed. But once she was on her high horse, there was no getting her off it, although it has to be said that these disturbances and impediments gave a potency, or shall we say a heightened and more passionate intensity, to those brief moments of sleep between one interrogation and another. To mollify her, I intuitively pointed to the sky or the moon, if it was out, with the air of a dreamy lover expressed by the arch of my eyebrows, and then return instantaneously to my blissful sleep. But by this stage, she was complaining unrelentingly: 'Why don't you say something? What are you thinking about?' and she shook me. I was unconsciously discharging replies: '... our tiny, tiny star up there, way up there, can't you see it...' But she was not inclined to listen. She shook her shoulder and her chest, so that my head tumbled off it, and she came out with some words to indicate her annoyance with the sky, the moon and the bench; she did this loudly and in a tone of voice that completely woke me up. Then again, it would have woken

Chapter B

anyone and everyone – not just me, but even the hard of hearing.

"So there I was once more, sleepless in the middle of the night, when all the living creatures of this world – humans and animals – enjoy their well-earned rest, each in the place Almighty God has allocated to them: the ox in its stable, the sheep in its fold, the dog in its kennel, and so on in accordance with what is appropriate and sacrosanct for peace of mind and allows all living beings to close their eyes in bliss. Everyone but me, and I would feel my eyelids swell and stiffen like a sausage skin; my eyes became confused by magnetic luminescence, and on the northern corner of my cornea I saw an aurora borealis emerge in all its brilliance and then die back. It was insomnia, my insomnia, an insomnia that never relented. I sought my only remedy, I tried to lay her out and remove the lumps caused by her discontent. I pointed to the moon; "Look at how she looks down on us serenely!" I said as I levelled her out, put her on a slant and tucked up the protuberances of her chest. 'Emilia,' I would say, 'Emilia, you know that I love you!' But no, there was simply no means to placate her; I had no idea how to lay myself down – straight, on my side, face up or face down. I begged her, 'Emilia, hug me, get yourself comfortable, hold me on your breast forever.' But instead of encountering that wonderful pillow, all I found was some huffs followed by intricate questions: why didn't I take her here, why didn't I take her there, why didn't we go dancing, why didn't we go on trips?

"'Yes, everything you say, Emilia,' I would reassure her, 'we will do it all,' but then she wanted to have dates and places. Were we going to the seaside or the mountains? In train or by car? These were such exacting questions that we needed to be well rested before we could possibly decide, I told her, while in that particular moment I did not feel that I was up to it; I would have made a false step, I would have got it all wrong. However, I could think about it, and to do so, I needed silence and time. All she had to do was relax and stretch herself out, and I would concentrate on these matters and assess all the pros and cons. To avoid any unnecessary distractions, I would close my eyes. A waste of breath! She just went on: 'Where? When? The date? On our own or with friends?' There was nothing for it, we had to turn it into an argument. So I would say, 'Come off it, Emilia, you're never satisfied!' This was followed by her tears, the poor dear, during which she finally started to soften and become more accommodating, and I would zealously get down to the business of positioning her for maximum comfort – in other words, slightly on a slant and a little concave, so that I could wrap her around me if it got a little cold and damp towards dawn. At last she set off on her long and uninterrupted reply: about who we were, about what I meant to her and the way she felt in my company, about how easy she was to please, and about many, many other things that I could no longer hear, because from her very first words I suddenly felt released and could fall asleep happily like the lord of the manor laid out on cushions and covered with warm blankets. Yes, I really loved her in those moments, although I could not have been aware of it. It is true that her oration did occasionally require her to shake me, slap my face, cover me with kisses or spray from her nose, all of which I was vaguely conscious of. And sometimes I would feel my mouth closing as a minor adjustment to my position caused me to sigh. 'Be quiet, and listen to me for once,' she would say while I continued to indulge my blissful slumber. When the sun came up, everything became clear and there were no more disagreements. She was sweetness itself – kind and understanding. I would yawn as I stirred and felt myself well rested. 'You're tired, poor dear,' she would say, and I would leave her at the door. She would be tired and her voice hoarse, but I would be buoyed up and ready to get on with my day."

While this Natale was speaking, the slug had climbed up almost as far as his shoulder, and his book was teeming with midges.

Chapter B

"Then she left me without me even noticing; who knows what direction her constant chatter took that night. We were once again at our bench and everything was proceeding as usual. Maybe it was even better. I fell asleep as I was walking towards her, and I just fell into her arms as though I were dreaming, and after that I didn't hear another thing, such was my joy. I could not say what we were talking about, nor what happened between us: perhaps she reached the point of an irremediable disagreement as she chatted to herself, perhaps I raved in my sleep and emitted noises similar to discourteous replies, perhaps my face irrationally took on ill-mannered expressions or she thought that I said no and was against her. Who could possibly know? I found myself awake and alone, lying on my back on the bench, and she never wanted to see me again. I desperately sought her out and asked her for an explanation, because I thought that I would at least get some sleep while we were sorting things out. But it was all to no avail. I tried lying down outside her door, but as there was peace, silence and no interference from anybody else, I just lay there with my eyes open to keep watch over my sleep that never came, under the cover of an inanimate doormat and my monumental tiredness. I began to wander around the cafés, and I could only drowse or sleep for a bit if I could find someone to have a conversation with. Staring ahead and propping up my head with the palm of my hand, I occasionally uttered a few words about sport or politics to encourage my companion to carry on talking to me. But political sleep was not a pleasant one, as my head kept dropping suddenly, and sometimes I would follow it, so we would end up on the floor next to the bar, while the insomnia would fiercely go on the attack again. I would never again sleep with such rapture as I did on top of Emilia. That's why I miss her. I have spent my nights in cafés in search of someone to replace her, but without success.

"At the time, I was working as a teacher, but as you can imagine, I suffered from such oppressive tiredness in the school that teaching was an eternal nightmare. After vainly tossing and turning under the sheets through the night, exasperation would drive me from my bed long before dawn. I would try to wash my face, but while putting soap on it, my head would fall on the tap, and sleep was making me sway so wildly that my centre of gravity would go beyond the critical point and I would topple. Then I would find myself standing with my cheek squashed against the wall or buttressed by my knees against the bidet and still swaying dangerously, or perhaps with my forehead against the mirror, so that when my legs suddenly gave way, I would be restored to my incurable insomnia whether I liked it or not.

"Thus in the midst of these alternations, it came to half past seven; I would run to the bus stop, and if the bus came late, there was the danger that I would start to sleep there, with the consequences we can all imagine: I could collapse on top of someone who would get very angry, I could squash a child in my fall or knock over an old person, or I could have simply tumbled under the wheels of the bus. In any case, I used my strength of character to resist, and generally I succeeded by walking and jumping incessantly. I only lost consciousness in those brief moments of stasis when the motory nerves were not engaged. On one dramatic occasion, I got on the bus only to find that I couldn't sit down because I would have gone on to the end of the line, or perhaps the depot when the bus had run the line for the last time that day. But I couldn't stand holding the grasps either. Such was my sleepiness that I slept wrapped by the pressing crowd, as though they were all mattresses, duvets and pillows, and I was carried by the wave of people without any awareness of this on my part. Inasmuch as I was lucid, I attempted to position myself so that I would be pinched or trapped by the automatic doors, which acted as a kind of alarm clock recalling me to my duties when they shut upon a knee, a foot, my neck or my chest. I shouted as they woke me at each bus stop, and the people were rather disturbed to see

Chapter B

my suffering, particularly because of my puffy eyes red with insomnia and my crumbling face. This was the only method that provided a reasonable chance of getting to the school, even though it meant arriving crumpled and beaten. But that was where the veritable pitched battle commenced and was fought hard against the terrifying obsession with sleep. Those who have not experienced it can have no idea.

"To tell the truth, I believe that I have never been entirely awake, and if I have, never for more than four or five minutes. Of course, I fought valiantly to keep my eyelids open and the weighty cranium held high, which was of the utmost importance when teaching. I would say such things as, "Somebody read from the reading on such-and-such page," and just the act of saying spread like a sleeping pill through my brain; I would lift my eyes to the ceiling as though I were about to listen and reflect, but in reality I was in that instant entering that total absence of mind that resembles sleep but is actually insomnia. However, I always maintained a thoughtful demeanour that was appropriate to the dignity of my office. Indeed I would define my behaviour as pedagogically orthodox, because it did inspire a degree of submissiveness. The class would look at me dumbly and await the thorough process of my thoughts. They hung from my lips so firmly that one after the other they were all mesmerised: first to go was class leader, then the more conscientious pupils fell asleep, followed by the mediocrities and finally those whose results were poor. So gradually the entire form was slumbering in unison, including the dolts, the donkeys and the generally distracted, unresponsive and stupid, who, galvanised by the others, also dutifully started to yawn. Then you could hear one thud after another as they started dropping on their desks: some hit their foreheads on the tops while others hunched over an exercise book or used a pen to prop up their heads. All were snoring gently with great perseverance and application. I did not actually witness any of this; I merely inferred it.

"Just to mention one of the absurdities, there was this janitor who was in the habit of eavesdropping from behind the door so that he could report back to the headmaster if there was any insubordination, singing or public vilification of the teacher's person in the class. Yet all he could hear was an exemplary silence, which led him to believe that I was adopting some new experimental method that involved not an iron glove but some inner self-discipline. Indeed he declared that in three hours of listening at the keyhole, he had only heard an occasional and intermittent humming sound, which must have been of flies. Nor could it be said that time was lost in chatter, empty words, scolding or threats. And when he saw through the keyhole that one schoolboy was continuously bent over his desk, the janitor became convinced that there must have been some continuous and exacting written exercise taking place in that class. He was so delighted that after several hours of careful observation he collapsed against the door as though under the effect of a tranquilliser. That is where they found him, cluttering the exit like a sack of turnips or potatoes. Thus I gained a reputation for being a severe and modern schoolmaster.

"My health benefited slightly from this ability of the mind to absent itself, but the resulting repose was neither profound nor sufficient, because as soon as the class had achieved unanimity in its slumber and I too could have stretched my legs and turned on my side with my coat stuffed between my head and the back of the chair – or, in other words, when the classroom turned into a kind of dormitory – I was once again struck down by insomnia at its most virulent. Then I would rise to my feet like a phantom and wander unsteadily between the desks, occasionally waking one of the children to have them read a passage so that I could doze off once more. So I never got any real sleep in the class, and while I worked as a teacher, I continually suffered from an oppressive tiredness.

"One day, things got so bad that I fell unconscious on the floor: the pupils who were still awake kindly placed me

Chapter B

in my chair, and for five whole minutes I slept there like a dead man in paradise. As can well be imagined, no sooner had they made me comfortable with a folder acting as a cushion under my head and some newspapers as blankets, removed my shoes and lowered the blinds to darken the room, I unfortunately succumbed to the following thought: 'Yes, I can now sleep forever,' and these words woke me up briskly. So much so that I immediately said: 'Everyone at their desks! We will now have a test!' You could hear the janitor wriggling behind the door, and then he briefly stuck his head round it, as though to give me support. I was seated and had now opened the register. 'Abate!' I called out. Up stood Abate, who had a vacuous expression and spoke in a whisper. I managed to articulate a question, but I failed to grasp the last part, as the first syllables plunged me back into the land of nod. I was frozen in a severe and resolute pose, so that no one would be in any doubt: I was not going to be giving marks away easily. I cannot know what followed; I only know that when I regained my senses, I found the whole class had collapsed once more into deep sleep, and Abate was lying on the floor and moving his lips as though he was dreaming of answering my questions. The janitor who had looked in was now obstructing the doorway and appeared to be not asleep but dead. 'Lucky them,' I said to myself, and fully awake I stood there, staring at them full of envy.

"I still remember some afternoons when there were parent-teacher class committees, educational meetings and marking sessions at the headmaster's office, in which I would indulge myself in a silent, surreptitious but very determined slumber, which resembled fervent agreement with the points of view expressed, because my head would nod some excellent and very convincing 'yeses' and I assumed a thoughtful and circumspect countenance. To tell the truth, many of us were expressing our consent, and I suspect that insomnia was widespread, much more widespread than is commonly thought. All around, there were red eyelids, noisy yawns and a general desire for one's bed, and I believe that even those who were holding forth were in their heart of hearts indulging in a pleasant sleep. I therefore came out of those parent-teacher class meetings feeling a little rested, but not sufficiently for my needs."

Chapter C

At that moment, I saw the chief librarian marching up with his black mortarboard on his head; from a distance it looked like one of those exercise books with a ribbon hanging from it. His walk was stiff and dignified. Behind him came the fellows who had pricked Natale's cheek, like two hotheads on holiday who snoop and sniff around in every little corner. They were his retinue.

As Natale had been gradually lowering his head since the start of his long oration and had eventually articulated its later stages with his cheek lying on the book, the head librarian took off his mortarboard and slapped in on the table, which produced a loud and sharp crack, like a grenade going off. Natale instinctively raised his arms and covered his head, as though one of the beams or even the whole of the library's ceiling was coming down. Many of those close by, who had been either reclining or completely stretched out, jumped to their feet and looked at each with eyes wide open and alert and a hand on their beating hearts. One of them had the flushed face of an apoplectic, and constantly repeated: "But what was that? What could have fallen?" The attendants, who were carefully inspecting a reader's downy and almost bald head heavily bent forward, were somewhat shaken themselves, and immediately ran over looking quizzical, as they felt it was something to do with them. One of them set about purposefully examining the point on the table where Accetto had inflicted the blow with his mortarboard. Indeed, there were several squashed ants and a dazed wasp that continued to buzz noisily. He waved a colleague over, as though to indicate an incident of some considerable moment, and, following some carefully planned manoeuvres, they managed to deposit the wasp in a small box, which they closed warily. They then got back to the business of snooping around and inspecting the books and readers, while handing out advice and assistance. I saw them whispering in someone's ear and that someone was saying no – but I don't know to what – and putting his fingers to his ears. Another reader had inadvertently slipped down from his chair, and they were helping him to get back up and seat himself once more in a decorous manner, but it appeared that the man did not want this and tried to wriggle free. His pyjama, which was a single garment made of some elastic material, was slipped over his head and hid his face. He continued to struggle like a weasel in a sack that the hunter has closed off with rope.

Accetto leant down towards me: "Is this the book you ordered, sir?"

Overcome with contentment, I thanked him, and he placed it in front of me. I attempted to open it, but its pages were still uncut, even though it was dusty and in bad condition. The pages were like an accordion.

"You'll have to treat the books more carefully," he said, "don't breath on them, don't fold them over, don't be rough with them."

"All right," I said, as I looked for the title, but there was no cover – just a discoloured handwritten label. "This is not the book I requested," I added quietly. "It has another title." He was standing to attention with his mortarboard held on his head by an elastic, but he was refusing to answer. Looking for some encouragement, I glanced at my neighbour who was listening with both eyes open, although they were tired and the midges were giving them bother. He nodded at me discreetly as he sat hunched at the table. "This is not the one," I repeated to Accetto, and showed him the label on the spine, *The Natural History of the Twentieth Century.*

"Yes, it may not be exactly the one you requested."

"You'll excuse me: it is not a matter of 'may be' or 'may not be'. This is not the book I asked for; it is completely different. You have made a mistake." I held it out to him, but he did not seem very keen to take it back.

"The label," he said, "can occasionally be misleading. I may well have made a mistake, but I can assure you that it

Chapter C

is an authoritative work, and if you start to examine its contents, you will probably have to admit that I haven't got it that wrong."

"Listen, I do not have a lot of time, and I asked for a specific book, as stated in my reading list. Would you please get me what I need?"

He just stood there and had no intention of giving in: "You know, finding a book is not an easy matter. This is only the first time you have come here, and you may not be aware that this library is very old and its collections have not been properly sorted out. It is difficult to get hold of the exact book that has been ordered. Sometimes the book is missing, because it has been moved elsewhere, perhaps not very far, and we would have to look for it. Do you understand?" He waved his hand towards the people crouching on chairs with their faces resting on the armrests and their eyes closed by the uncomfortable sleep of those who are resigned to their fate. "Do you understand? All those people are waiting. If you're in such a hurry, wouldn't it be better to make do with something that approximates to what you wanted? Why would you want to sit there with nothing to do but stare at the ceiling? But let's be very clear about this: if you want that book of yours – if you are absolutely determined," he looked at me doubtfully, as if he were giving me time to admit to my own doubts and adapt to the circumstances, "if, for you, it has to be that very book, then you can make a reservation. You are quite at liberty to do so. In the meantime, I would however suggest that you do not give up the one you have in your possession. What is it exactly that has disappointed you? Is it the missing cover? Or is the fact that it is covered in dust?

"It is not the cover," answered dryly, "nor is it the dust."

"Then what have you got to complain about?"

"It is not the book I wanted." I was looking at Natale as I said this, but he was leaning over as though to hear better, but I could not see his eyes.

"Take a look at it first. How can you be so sure? It may not be the right one, but I can assure you that its pressmark is very, very similar, and even the title isn't that different. If however there has been an error, I am the first to apologise of course, but it has only been a very slight mistake. You should not be so severe and punctilious with people who are just trying to do their best. I could have brought any old thing: there are, for example, some enormous atlases. Would you be interested?"

"No, no," I said, "I'm not interested. I'm not at all interested."

"There are globes, which don't resemble a book in any fashion, and yet I did not bring them. There are some red-leather, folio editions that contain no writing at all – just herbs and flowers. Herbals, they're called."

"But I don't want them, and I never asked for them."

"Now you understand! I didn't just pick up the first book that came to hand, the most conspicuous one. I made every effort to please you. If you continue to reject this book, as you are fully entitled to do, I can certainly change it! That is what I am here for."

"Well then, do me this favour."

"However, I should point out that if you are not going to be a little more accommodating – if you refuse to meet us halfway and fail to allow for a margin of human error, you had better make a reservation and come back in a few days. Don't you even want to take a look at this one? It is after all a book. What makes you think it won't be interesting?"

I was left with very little choice. I was prey to anxiety and uncertainty, particularly as my endeavours were hurried and haphazard; besides I wanted him to go and perhaps I would then have managed to get something done on my own. And so I reluctantly accepted the book as a kind of experiment just to bring the matter to a close. At the same time, the idea of the exam was turning my blood to ice and to fire.

"But I need a paperknife," I said.

Chapter C

"Now look, you need to put in an application, if you want to cut the pages, because there's an office that deals specifically with the right tools."
"You don't need much, just a paperknife. I assure you that I can do it myself. I am skilled at it."
"I have no doubt that you have done this in the past and, I do not deny it, done it quite successfully. The problem is, you see, that at the moment you are in a state of impatience, and impatience makes people do things badly. Moreover, I am not authorised to hand you over the responsibility for cutting the pages, and in all honesty, I must confess that I would be doubtful about doing so even if I had the authority, now that I see you in such a hurry and, if you don't mind me saying, so casual in your approach to the whole matter. In any event, I would want you to do a trial on some paper of lesser value, which would not constitute such a great loss. You know that it just takes one little nervous twitch and the knife is out of control!"

I could feel time flying by, and heard a clock striking the hour far in the distance – in some other part of the city. It was one o'clock.

"What if I put in this application?" I asked in the hope of expediting the business.

"It takes time to make the application, and you would have to come back another day. Nothing is improvised here, and in my opinion, although I might be mistaken, the entire procedure is neither easy nor undemanding. I can tell you that in certain circumstances, it could prove impossible."

"But what do you mean?" I said spreading my arms in dismay. "Have you seen the state of that book?"

"You said it. And do you want to degrade its condition even further? Do you know what dangers it is exposed to every day of the week? – what damage it has already suffered because of insects, which, as you can see defecate continually? – and because of mould and light? – and because of unforeseen events, such as earthquakes, frosts, floods, tidal waves, hooliganism and insurrections?" Here he stopped pensively, as though he had been talking to himself, and he adjusted his mortarboard to a horizontal position, as the elastic and the increasing vehemence of his words had shifted it to the back of his head. He appeared to be thinking of terrifying disasters that were imminent, even of meteorites, because he had lifted his eyes slightly upwards. I also looked up and there was a small window with an iron grate. I thought I could see moths and fireflies flying together.

"I have an exam tomorrow – tomorrow morning at eight o'clock, so I can't. If I were to submit this application, I would have to wait and all to no purpose." But why this book? Now my hands were tied; how had I let this happen to me? I thought to myself. Perhaps I should have sent it back and then continued to peep across and read my neighbour's book, given that he was now leaning over on his side with head hanging down, almost touching me.

"Having considered your inadequate state," Accetto started to speechify, "and your pressing requirements..." he lent down, "you show me the page you are looking for, and we'll do what we can, meet you halfway, so that you don't take up a seat for no useful purpose."

"Just the one page?" I asked.

"We have to keep the damage to the absolute minimum; if however that is not to your taste, we will consider the possibility of cutting another one."

Who would have thought it – such a complication! In order to reach some kind of decision, I started to peer into pages I could separate by a few centimetres. As I did so, all manner of things slipped out: yellowish sawdust, dried insect cocoons, spider skins and a black sand, which must have been the aforementioned's droppings famously produced by invertebrates. Then, to speed up the process, I pointed to a spot in the middle of the book, where I could make out the title of a section. He then proferred this huge and quite monstrous nail on his little finger, slipped it between the pages and cut them with just two strokes,

Chapter C

which, I have to say, were both bold and masterly. And so the book opened up in front of me. I lightly but sceptically blew away all the animal remains, while the toothache started once more to make its presence felt.

Giants of the Twentieth Century

According to Geoffroy Saint-Hilaire, giants lack energy, are slow in their movements and unsuited to work. Whatever they do, they are immediately tired. In other words, they are weak in both body and spirit.

Garnier tells us that at the Giants Café, where they attracted much attention, they could be seen around 1852 dragging themselves around lazily with an obtuse and idle expression on their faces.

According to Virchow and the scientific literature, however, people suffer terrible agonies in becoming a giant. They just keep growing, and on reaching their maximum height, they fall into a state of suicidal slothfulness. They look at the hills of on the horizon and mistake them for sleeping friends. So they just stand there and melancholically close their eyes.

In the Gorgonzola countryside, a married peasant nicknamed Pulcinella suddenly became a giant in 1905. He started to experience a sensation of exhaustion in his lungs and noted that his hands and feet were growing. Then he developed rheumatic pains in his bones, and squeaking noises came from his cheekbones and indeed the whole of his face. His eyes began to bulge and he was frightened that they would pop out. At the same time, he was growing in height and girth, so that by the end of the month his clothes would no longer fit. He was just about to turn twenty-six. He felt pain close to his joints, which grew hot because of the excessive friction. He ate huge amounts of food and was always thirsty. He produced a very liquid and volatile sweat. There was a bony outgrowth on his head that resembled a tortoise shell. He swayed on his feet and took fright, because he was afflicted by vertigo. So then he would lie down and take up two beds.

He was very credibly described by a veterinary surgeon. He gave the impression of an oversized sickly baby who could not stand light or water. On inspecting his tongue, it turned out to be inordinately large, flaccid and a little tarry, and his voice was hoarse like an ageing castrato. His memory was fixed on a single point: he asserted that he had albumin in his blood, which needed to be cleansed, and he would endlessly repeat this idea, without ever moving on to other matters. We detected a widening of the nose and lips, which swelled up and merged into a single protuberant proboscis. His sexual torpor was absolute: if you brought his wife close or placed her underneath him, he remained entirely unmoved by her breasts and venereal attractions. He would lean on three men as he walked; he weighed 190 kilos and was over two and a half metres in height. If they asked him: "What does it feel like?" he would reply, "I feel that my head is a long way from my feet."

By then this Pulcinella's only activity was to lie down, overcome by sadness. Only occasionally and in the evening would he look out of the window and appear to grasp, however tenuously, some philosophical idea, and then he would tell his doctor of his concerns about the force of gravity, which one fine day could suddenly increase. Half of the giants are spiritually incompetent, and the other half do not have the strength to stand up or lift a bag. Doctor Marro, the director of a hospital for the chronically ill, observed twelve giants pulling a rope in the garden, and claimed that, if it weren't for their deadweight, a fit porter or nurse could have pulled all twelve of them over with a single tug.

A few rare giants do actually have enormous strength, which increases as their body grows larger. Gian Piero of Monticelli was of normal size until he was thirteen years old. Everyone in the family was well built, but by no means gigantic. But then he started to grow; his muscles, feet, hands and bones all started to swell, and his stature

Chapter C

became imposing. Even his hair became thicker, and almost resembled *tagliatelle*. He said he could feel his legs being pulled because of their length, and his voice increased in volume until it became an indistinct roar, like that of a river. He drank enormous quantities of water straight from a muddy swamp full of tadpoles. This might have been the cause of his typhus. But he never stopped growing, and when he worked in the fields, he displayed the strength of five horses. At the end of the day, the others would sit around and watch him undeterred as he uprooted roots, straightened the poplar trees and happily carried a cart with its load of stones.

One day, while lifting a shovel, he felt a pain in the intercostal region of his back, and he had to sit down in a state of breathlessness.

From that day he started to shrink rapidly: his bones crumpled like sheets of papers, his spinal column shortened as though it were a spring and he became a hunchback with three or four humps. His neck could no longer hold up his head, and his legs could no longer keep straight. His thigh-bones bent into extremely fragile arches and his feet became wide and squashed as though they were bread dough. To look at, he seemed to be an enormous piece of meat weighing down a spongy and inert skeleton, and his head a cast-iron globe attached to an elastic stalk. Once a giant, he now became rickety and something more resembling not so much a man as a piece of meat wrapped up in greaseproof paper. If we laid him out horizontally and pulled him into position, he still measured two metres and forty centimetres, but standing up he would bend and sag all over the place, and it didn't matter how many times we shouted, "Stand up straight!" His enormous bulging eyes shifted on his limp head and looked towards the bed, while he boomed deeply by way of apology and self-justification. Eventually we got round to measuring him, because he was continuing to sink in front of our eyes: he was now a metre and eighty centimetres. But two days later, he was a metre and sixty-five. His highest point was his back, and he looked like a willow because his head was touching the ground. This is the fate of all giants who can no longer hold themselves up.

Professor Peter, an expert on gigantism and macrosomia at the University of Leuven, argues that giants are born as such, and it is not how tall you are that matters, but rather the hide or slough. A true giant is born very rarely – about every ten or twenty years – and the preferred location appears to be Germany. He can be recognised immediately, because he has an adult face – hideous and austere – with jet-black eyebrows and bags under the eyes.

In antiquity, they thought that this sporadic race of new-born babies were ogres, and there was much speculation about their tastes. Today we know that they are not cannibals, although it is true that a few of them can be dangerous: they end up as state employees, some of them as the heads of ministerial departments and others as the headmasters of old-fashioned secondary schools.

In 1935 near Koblenz, one of them was baptised with the name of Proserpine. He was slightly larger than normal, but had a pasty and grimy complexion. His expression was one of silent disapproval; on seeing him appear the midwife took a step backwards and the entire family felt cowed by his countenance and his ugliness. But like all other members of his race he had little need of comforts and indulgencies: they often abandoned him to the sun and wind, and he would shrivel; they would leave him in the sea, and he would float and become swollen and cyanotic, but always retained that same obstinate expression. Then the waves would drive him to the shore. Yet all these inclement conditions failed to weaken him and only served to create an epidermis of vellum and his characteristic impassiveness. He did not speak until he was three years old; nor would he settle for ungrammatical babbling devoid of all meaning. He waited until he had sufficient wisdom and something significant to say. One day he enunciated a very specific question in his deep voice and addressed it to his aunts, close relations and family members all gathered around his highchair: "Is it possible to be more ignorant than you people?"

Chapter D

"If you already know exactly which book you want or need some advice," Natale was whispering in my ear, "just go and look for it. Have someone go with you; it is your right. Have yourself taken to the right place, where they have the shelves of specialist subjects; otherwise they will just continue to make fun of you, or worse."

"But what subject is this meant to be?" I said. "It's not history, not mathematics, and I don't think you could call it philosophy either. What kind of book could it be?"

"That fellow – can you see him?" Natale said, pointing to Accetto who was wandering amongst the desks like an invigilator, "he's a shirker. He is so pedantic, always with that ridiculous hat of his – and with his assistants. Have you seen them? How they like to give themselves airs and graces – such authorities on literature. But they're just two thugs, two vicious bullies – them and their master. Books, as I discovered some time ago, are things they never go to look for. He keeps a few hidden immediately behind the door, and then pretends to go who knows where, to the inaccessible and remote rooms in the building, and to carry out investigations on the highest shelves that require acrobatic skills and some risk to his life; this is what he claims. But as soon as he goes through that little door down there," and Natale pointed to a door that was difficult to see, "he immediately sits down in a kiosk he has there, close to the radiator, and commences to indoctrinate his assistants on how to simulate friendship while actually harming people. When the appropriate period of time has gone by and everything appears to be in accordance with the regulations, he then picks up one of these books, of which there can be no more than three or four, if we're lucky. He thinks he is taking the most suitable one, but you can easily imagine how little a man without learning can understand of these matters, and off he goes with that cantankerous expression; you've seen that face and you've seen that hat, and heard his sophisms and heard his false arguments to persuade readers to keep books they do not want. He considers readers to be fusspots who are impossible to please, and pedants full of pedantry and fanaticism who come here just to abuse the books. But if you state that you don't want that book and insist, then he will change it. True, hours or even days will go by, and don't think that the situation will improve: he will choose another one of those close to hand and say that that is the best he can do and that another in his place would have done much worse, another would have refused, because, according to him, everyone in here is an illiterate who couldn't give a damn. He goes on talking until he has convinced the reader by setting out the impossible obstacles and petitions to the director, the supervisory body and the arbitration tribunal.

"But they're not even happy with those who make no demands on them. Take me, for example: they are always coming to disturb me because they think I don't read enough and consume the books, the chair and the table to no particular benefit. I know it's them, even if they behave deviously when I am confused and dejected by the vice-like grip of my insomnia. 'Leave me alone!' I tell them. 'I am a teacher and know what I have to do. I am not bothering anyone, I make few demands when it comes to bibliography and I'm no troublemaker; I always have the same book, and there is no need to look for it. You have it placed on the table, at my usual place or wherever you like, and I will not disturb you again.' I reread it again and again, because reading tires me and calms the nerves in my body; it's like listening to my fiancée. The words turn around in my head like a wheel; I don't remember them but they cradle my mind and perhaps rock it into its dreams. It's a cure for insomnia; it's my medicine, otherwise I would need another woman at the very least."

I was rapidly reflecting on all this as he spoke: I pulled out the reading list for the exam and waved it in the air. When Accetto came up, I demanded to be taken to the relevant section of the library. "I want to go there in person," I said.

Shortly afterwards without any further problems, although a little timorous and driven by my throbbing teeth, I was walking towards the shelves for the twentieth century. Or at least this was what their reassurances had led me to believe.

We were walking close to a wall where the ceiling came low and we had to be careful not to bang our heads or trip in the dark. Accetto was by my side or a little further ahead; I could hear his two assistants scuttling along behind me.

"Listen!" Accetto turned to address me, "I don't know what that Natale has been telling you, but he isn't a teacher; he likes to say he was and look the part, but he was only an occasional supply teacher, until he was suspended. They found him sleeping everywhere. Insomnia! You've got to believe it! That guy slept standing up, sitting down or while he was walking. He even slept while he was talking; if other people spoke, he would fall to the ground unconscious in the most undignified manner. In his classroom, it was a constant scandal, because of the example he gave, and just the sight of him was generally a disincentive – it took away all vigour, commitment and will. He was occasionally called upon to pacify the more turbulent classes with that enervating appearance of his. Isn't this the truth?" Accetto turned to ask one of his assistants. "He got like this because of a prank, a terrible prank in which he was involved, and since then, he has never been the same. They played a joke on him during an exam, and it made such an impression and so unhinged his mind that he has stayed like that ever since. Everyone knows this in here."

"At an exam? A prank?" I started to show interest.

"Precisely."

Meanwhile hens were scurrying off in all directions as we passed. It must seem strange that they were living in the library, but no one was taking any notice of them. I could also hear wasps flying close to my ears, and that troubled me.

"Yes," the first assistant broke into our conversation, "it was the exam for a permanent teaching post. He – this Natale guy – was very nervous about the exam."

"Well, did you hear that? He can tell you what actually happened," Accetto said and pointed to this assistant.

"Yes, I can tell it all," said the assistant, and he and his companion elbowed each other. "He hadn't been eating for a month; he couldn't sleep and he just studied. He studied from morning to night, and during the night he kept his book under his pillow so he could repeat it in his head all night long. When he got stuck or something slipped his memory, he would take a peek with his torch and start repeating it all over again, sometimes reciting it backwards as a mental exercise, and sometimes asking himself unexpected questions to throw himself into a state of panic. And then he would go back to his studies under his sheets, so as to be the more cosy – like being inside a tabernacle. Then he would stretch himself out calmly, but this did not stop him from listening to himself until morning. He was the one who told me all this, because at the time I was his friend.

"At mealtime he placed his book on top of his soup bowl, and as its contents slowly cooled down, he breathed in their perfumed vapours for so long that he ended up thinking he had actually had his soup. Consequently he wasted away. He lived on sugar, tea, caffeine and tranquillisers. His mother and sister occasionally managed to get him to ingest plain rice, chocolate or eggnog without his being aware of it. They got some diced boiled chicken down his throat; he chewed while loudly reading out the passages he had to revise, and he swallowed while turning the page. By the time the exam was imminent, his behaviour had become manic: he switched from one book to another and read uninterruptedly except for the spasmodic and desperate cry, 'My God, I don't know a thing.' And all the subjects were churning around his brain and,

Chapter D

according to him, leaking out all over the place. At times, he wanted to sit the exam immediately, but at others, he would claim that he needed another year or two at the very least. 'If I think about the exam,' he would mutter, 'I just lose my head, my legs give way, my throat strangulates itself, my stomach rumbles and my heart suffers from a sharp pain.'

"Seeing him in this state, his friends sought to comfort him and make him laugh. 'You need a few distractions,' they said, 'this will calm your brain.' But he only wanted them to test him: 'I want a few trick questions,' he asked gleefully, and to keep him happy, they would pick up a book, open it at random and proclaim, 'Page eighty, line four,' but then read a line backwards from another page. He would leap with joy: 'That's not how it is!' and he would recite page eighty, summarise the book and end up so satisfied with himself that he would become so calm and self-confident that he would eat a plate of pasta, drink a glass of wine, and joke with his friends about himself and his exam. 'If you were my examiners,' he would say, 'I would have no problems.' And they said, 'We can give it a go; that way, you'll get used to the exam and calm down.' He laughed, 'Of course it would be a great system; you lot feed me the questions and give me such a hard time that the real exam will be a piece of cake.' His friends winked, 'Don't you worry. You just have to relax. That's the important thing.' Natale went home grateful, happier and even a little refreshed, but as soon as he picked up the study programme again and thought about the fast approaching date, the examiners' faces and his own foolish and paralysed expression, he took such a fright that he was once more poring over his books, memorising passages to be recited and posing himself terrible questions in an imaginary exam. In accordance with a private superstition, he placed his open notebook on his head in the hope that some of its contents would filter down into his brain, and sang it like a psalm while striding from one room to another and around the whole house.

"When, according to his calculations, there were still three nights and two days before the exam, the doorbell rang and a courier brought him a notification rubber-stamped by the Ministry of Education that the exam was in fact to be held the following morning at nine o'clock. He looked up at the fellow and then fell semiconscious on the ground: he still wanted to do a complete revision and in that moment his head was in chaos – an inferno in which all things were blazing and nothing could be brought under control. When he finally pulled himself together, his face was still pale and gaunt like that of a condemned man, and he thought, 'This is my ruin; I'll come across as inarticulate and lost for words, always supposing that I manage to turn up.' Then he reread the notification: the letter 'n' had been drawn by lots, and as he was called Natale, he had to go first. 'It couldn't get any worse!' he thought, and his bowels felt like they wanted to release their load, and his stomach was shrieking with terror. Then he looked at the messenger who had lifted him up and was fanning him. He had the large black beard of a regular jinx, two enormous, overstated eyebrows, a beret pulled down on his head and a uniform so tight that it could hardly be buttoned up, as though it weren't his. He looked him more carefully in the eyes, and had the feeling that the man was secretly laughing at him. So then he became suspicious, re-examined his notification and reread all of it: at nine o'clock in such-and-such a school in classroom x before the examining panel, etc., etc. and all the pompous and ridiculous names, which surely someone must have invented – Mr Terribile, Mr Suggerimenti, Mrs Bucato. He then looked at the rubber stamps, of which there were a good number, and all fresh and clearly defined; he reread the document yet again and it seemed to him that the wording did not ring true; there was something overstated about it. So he said, 'You are supposed to be the courier?' 'That's right,' the man replied. 'And that beard of yours is really yours?' 'Yes,' he replied again, 'is that a problem?' Natale could easily tell that the man was laughing behind

Chapter D

the big black beard and using it as a hiding-place, and started to understand, or so he believed. 'Who sent you?' he asked abruptly. 'The educational sub-committee,' the response was that of someone reciting a part. 'And do you all have such beards? And are you all so expert with your rubber stamps?' The question unsettled the courier and he took a step backwards, but Natale had seen through the prank, guessed at its authors and purpose, and he stopped. His bowels relaxed, his heart slowed down, and his memory returned to his brain.

"The following day he turned up for the exam with a smile of mocking good humour. The panel had gathered in the gym, and when he entered, he could see them seated in a semicircle at the other end of the room on makeshift and rickety benches. They were waiting for him. He crossed the entire oversized hall and thought to himself, 'Clearly they couldn't find anyone better to put the frighteners on me.' He nodded his head to suggest a bow, and he thought that he could recognise his mate Fischietti dressed as a lady with an abundant bosom, and another friend in the part of a wrinkly, pipe-smoking professor: it was just that he was wearing a bald wig made of shiny pink rubber with a few loose hairs around the ears and the back of the neck; even the eyes had been made up to look like someone else's. They politely asked him to take a seat. He just succeeded in suppressing his desire to laugh because he had just noticed that the chairman was in fact the greengrocer's wife, Mrs. Sifone, albeit in jacket and tie, and amazingly slimmer and more masculine. So the exam commenced, to his great amusement and a prodigious display of knowledge. They asked very difficult questions in turn, and he replied effortlessly. He even went beyond their questions with references to questions not covered by the course, and at the same he felt that all this was a very useful exercise. He studied the other two examiners at length – a man and a woman – but he just couldn't understand who they were, so effective were their disguises. But when another supposed professor came up with a question about Euler's formula, Natale almost laughed in her face, because he recognised her voice as that of the barman at the Puccini Café, wearing lipstick and 15-denier tights, and affecting a French 'r' so perfectly that you'd want to wet yourself. And yet in order to get some practice and play along with his friends, he replied and went into great detail, quoting from memory. Contentment invaded his heart, as he felt calm and confident with all his faculties working in perfect order: if it were the exam, it would have been the greatest performance that anyone could humanly have wished for.

"When they said, 'That'll do!' he demanded, 'No, no, ask me another question.' 'That's enough, you can go.' But he insisted, 'Come on, just another little question, just one; so far this has been a piece of piss.' 'How dare you!' one of them shouted in a high-pitched voce, 'Get out of here!' At this stage, Natale could resist no longer and overcome by laughter, he dragged himself from his seat and grabbed the woman who looked like Fischietti by the hair. It was indeed a wig, as he had expected, but underneath appeared an indecipherable creature who very probably was a woman, but completely bald. He looked at her in confusion and tried to speak to her: 'Fischietti, is that you?' The other four examiners jump to their feet. The examinee Natale could no longer understand where the joke was going and who was doing it, because closer scrutiny revealed that she did indeed have facial hair and a downy upper lip that had just been shaved badly and covered with face powder. He was having difficulty in determining who she was, and so he stroked her face to find out and muttered weakly, 'Tell me if you are Fischietti in hiding.' In the meantime he wanted to see if there was anything else that was false – that could be disassembled: he tried her nose, her chin, and eyelashes, which did actually come away in his hands, together with a tooth that bounced out of her mouth of its own volition. Then he lifted her dress and peered underneath to see what was going on, while all around there was shouting, and this creature he was manhandling was screaming herself. But he wasn't getting anywhere

Chapter D

with his investigations, because under her clothing there was just complete darkness and a terrible smell, so he let it fall and started on another professor by attempting to remove from his face the skin that looked as if it had been glued on. Failing at this, Natale tried to detach the professor's hair and ears, which resulted in a violent scuffle, and he didn't know whether to laugh or cry, and repeated incessantly: 'Peppino, the game's over. I've had enough.' But unfortunately the man wasn't Peppino, and really was Prof. Suggerimenti, and Fischietti was not Fischietti, but actually Bucato a professor of Greek appointed by the Ministry of Education in accordance with all proper procedures. The fifth professor was short, in fact tiny, and the last one Natale attempted to divest of his disguise, but even he could not recognise him however many times he turned him around or from whichever angle he studied him.

"When Natale was finally obliged to give in, he simply muttered, 'I was sure it was Fischietti, I was sure it was Fischietti.'

"So it was said of him that the exam would have been magnificent if an artificial and overly protracted calm, together with a poor state of health and lack of sleep, had not suddenly caused a lesion to the optic thalamus and impaired his ability to perceive distinctions. And from that moment, he no longer distinguished between sleep and wakefulness, and called sleeping insomnia. This is the truth, please believe me; I know this because I am his old friend Fischietti."

On hearing this talk of exams and almost identifying myself with the description of this unfortunate case, panic compounded my cold sweat: I desperately needed to read more and find something reliable and weighty which could come to my assistance.

"All right, all right," I said, "these matters do not concern me. Please do not complicate the little remaining time I have. I too am like a condemned man; give me a book," I begged, "give me a book on the twentieth century." I had heard the chimes for two o'clock and all my teeth had come together in a chorus of excruciating pain. It felt like I had nails in my mouth and a hammer was banging them into a knotty piece of wood.

"If you're in such a hurry," Accetto said more deferentially than before, "we're already in the right area." And indeed he was back again in a flash with a book, if it could be so described, that was in a worse condition than the previous one. It resembled a collection of papers gathered up from the floor, somewhat haphazardly piled together and bound by a string attached to a cross. Perhaps it had once been a book with a title, but now the spine had been gnawed at and you could have no idea of what it was. There were pages in a different format, some smaller and others that were sticking out. I knew very well that this was one of the books that he fobbed off on anyone, particularly the ill-prepared. And he did say, "This book is in great demand, and can be found in every reading list. Please, make yourself comfortable here." He gave me a higher table than the others and even a bigger chair. No one was seated there, and although the difference was one of just a few centimetres, it dominated a large part of the reading room.

The pages were not in order and the numbers were entirely random. There was one page, upside-down and more yellowed than the others, which clearly came from another book. Who knows if by some fortuitous chance this was not exactly what I was looking for? In the absence of anything better to do, I put my faith in fate and took a look at it, a little nervously.

The death sentence in America

A serial killer called Joss was informed of his death sentence in prison. He was a large and effeminate man. He immediately became very pale, and even his eyes dulled.

Chapter D

His expression was that of a deaf man who, although he can hear nothing, can vaguely guess at the meaning of words from movement of a person's lips. "What?" he said and at the same time turned up one of his cards.
Then something inexplicable happened to him. He started to shudder and they thought he was sobbing, but it was actually some kind of convulsive laughter, so acute that his flabby face trembled and he had to steady his solar plexus with his arms. He got his breath back and started to writhe with tears in his eyes and the resonant spasms of someone guffawing and enjoying himself. He looked at the upturned card during the brief moments of respite, and then that terrible laugh would take possession of him again; it had become a cough with exhalations that seemed to say, "What? What?" Believing this behaviour to arise from some misunderstanding or that the prisoner really was deaf, the court official reread the sentence, which was very simple and to the point. This only redoubled the prisoner's hilarity and his "What?" After this and a few moments of perplexity, the official took off his glasses and in a low voice read the ruling he held in his hand to himself again and again, as though he were studying it. Very gradually his face betrayed a smile of slight amusement and questioning sympathy for this Joss, who was now bent double and seemed to find the whole thing increasingly hilarious.

At this stage the prison guard, as with a contagion, fell victim to a senseless and sympathetic attack of giggles, followed by full, out-and-out laughter. Thus they were all three in stitches a few minutes later, without any apparent reason, and Joss more than anyone else. And when another guard put his head round the door to his considerable surprise, convulsions resumed with such force and uproar that this fourth man and the fifth whom curiosity had placed just behind him also by reflex joined in the carnival without asking themselves why, and did so with such abandon and perhaps even excessive readiness that they rolled around the floor, slapped each other on the shoulder and leant against the wall like drunkards. The court official cried out "God... God..." between his raucous laughter, and then had to sit down. Now and then he would lift the sheet of paper as though to beg for a brief respite, but this only revived the full force of the exaggerated and epileptic hilarity, even in the two men who didn't know why they were laughing.

Mr Joss was bent double with his forehead resting on the metal table no longer conscious of what was going on; occasionally he would beat his fists on the table and wobble like a gelatinous pudding. Then they saw him lift his eyes and look around. He was not red, but pale and puffy, his normally sleek hair dishevelled. The others were still prey to their unjustifiable laughter, but already showing signs of delirium: the oldest guard had the twisted expression of someone suffering a stroke and his left arm was struggling to stay up in the air; his colleague was at the climax of an asthma attack, but could not stop laughing; and the third one, also gasping for breath, seemed on the point of losing his senses.

It then appears that Joss noticed the official lying back on his stool and wheezing, the court ruling lying on the floor, playing cards strewn across the cell and, who knows, the cell door open, as well as the washbasin with its hand towel, his unlaced shoes, a few obscene words written on the wall, a cigarette butt in the ashtray and then the ash; taking in all these muted mundane things in a flash, he felt himself once more within that vice of convulsed hilarity, but this time he was fighting for his last breath. His crumpled throat emitted two hisses searching for air, setting off yet another renewal of laughter amongst the others; on the third cavernous hiss – a furious paroxysm of despair – he was suddenly stilled, strangled by the final, fitful regurgitation.

Of the three guards, one was left with a damaged lung, and the other two even more obtuse and sullen than they had been before. The court official never recovered: his career ended there, as he himself asked for early retirement. From time to time, he would suffer a fit of

Chapter D

trembling and enfeeblement that had all the appearance of soundless laughter.

They never came up with a rational explanation for this case, nor did they identify any similar psychic developments. Joss ended up like a dead man with his head resting on the table and the two of spades clasped in his hand, but completely unconscious and unresponsive to any stimulus. Given the vegetative state in which he lived from that moment, his execution was postponed *sine die*. His brain had burnt out, and his laughter appears to have acted like the visible signal of a high-voltage electric current. It is difficult to say what was the initial trigger, because the expert called in by the court was able to ascertain that the words used in the ruling were completely devoid of any hint of humour, nor was he able to identify any symbolism or some ironic or comedic element in that playing card: the two of spades.

As for the guards, one was retired for reasons of partial disability, and the other two were transferred and demoted. However they both justified themselves by repeatedly claiming that there was something powerful in the air, something truly inexplicable that you breathed in as soon as you went into the cell. One said that it was an odourless laughing gas that Joss was letting out, and the other that there was a fast-acting virus or spore or, in any case, micro-organisms of some kind that were lying in wait on Joss or his various possessions and furnishings. Supposedly these micro-organisms were disturbed and stirred up by the reading of the sentence, just as though they were sneezing powder. Always supposing that this was not simply the effects of the very idea of the electric chair on minds already inclined to irrational euphoria and merriment.

51

Chapter E

While I was reading awed and heated because I saw this as a portrait of myself, I was also involuntarily witnessing another spectacle that was uninterruptedly taking place around me. One of the two attendants was slowly inserting a chicken feather into the nose of a reader who was propping up his head with his hand and his elbow on the table. He was quietly snoozing away in the position of someone who appeared to be reading. So, as one tickled him with a feather, the other adopted a jocular air and going up very close observed the man's face and his instinctive grimaces of discomfort. Eventually the poor fellow exploded in an uncontrolled sneeze that sprayed the book and the table. The two attendants bent low and laughed moronically. Accetto came running over and quietly berated him while hitting him on the forehead whenever he let his eyes close and returned to his slumbers. To hit the man he used an ink pad, which between blows was employed in wiping the book dry. I could see the two attendants hiding behind him and using the opportunity for pouring ants down the back of his neck as soon as he lowered his head, so that the ferocious itchiness woke him up and made him scratch the offending area. He would also slap the back of his neck, while Accetto continued to point out each little drop of spit one by one and punctuate this with further blows to his forehead, as though to stamp it on his brain.

Meanwhile Fischietti, having discovered someone else asleep next to him, lit up with an expression of spiteful contentment and knocked away the supporting arm with a sly blow, so that the sleeper's head fell with a loud crack on the wooden tabletop. Now awake, he massaged the painful haematoma on his forehead. On impact, his head must have crushed a Palomena Viridissima otherwise known as a stink bug, which true to its name was giving off a foul and pestiferous smell.

Chapter E

Those two liked to wander amongst the desks like a couple of schoolboy scamps, and torment everyone in turn. They had tied some rope to a chair and positioning themselves a little way off, they started to pull the chair back with its load, a scholar who was sleeping oblivious to it all, until of course a stronger pull on the rope caused the chair to fall, the scholar with it like a pile of rags from which a head rolled out. And the head hit the floor with a sound that would make you think it had cracked in two. The learned man got up on his feet with some difficulty, rubbing the back of his head as he did so. He lifted his chair while all around those woken by the creaking noises and the crash checked out their own chairs and swung them backwards and forwards to find out whether they were solid or unsafe.

But the two tormentors had already moved elsewhere to persecute other people, and as I was seated higher up, I could see them and could not take my eyes off them. Like two shadows, they squeezed glue into a sleeper's ears and covered his eyes with adhesive paper. They worked together very quietly and enjoyed every moment of it. Then they placed a strip over his mouth and a clothes peg on his nose. The fellow became red in the face and desperately struggle for air, unable to hear, see, breathe or understand what was happening. Perhaps he thought he was dying or already dead, as he madly tore the sticky material from his face. He might have cut a ridiculous figure, but he disturbed me because no one was safe in there with those two around. A moment of inattention or weakness sufficed to have them around you, while Accetto controlled them from a distance.

I saw for instance that in passing they pricked a sleeping man with a pin and he, wounded in his nightmare, emitted a silent scream: with his staring eyes he looked around and they bowed to him in unison like two good little boys out for a stroll. They struck another on the back of the neck with the sharp edge of a ruler, a torment that in truth was usually inflicted by Accetto himself. They would stop behind a chair and light a match under someone's ear to see them leap from their chairs with a hand on their smoking lobe, unable to understand how this could have occurred. But the pain filled their eyes with tears. This matchstick trick was widely used and very cruel: they also put lighted matches between a victim's fingers and ran off. The unlucky reader would scream, cry and moan for a considerable period of time. Careful not to burn the building down, they chose people with little hair which they then set fire to, causing a sudden bluish blaze that quickly went out leaving bald and blistered skin that seemed still to fry in its rawness. Victims thrashed around and waved their arms; they rubbed the blisters and smoking remains where the final embers burnt out. You could hear them mutter their smarting complaint like babies, and return to their reading with an afflicted soul.

They used noxious creatures that brought out great itchy swellings. They kept them in their pockets in jars which they took out and shook to enrage them, and then they applied them to the neck or the cheek, or they emptied them down a sleeve, the neckline or into the hair. I even saw them inciting a small neurasthenic dog to attack a barefooted reader. The animal took the victim's toes for something hostile and factious. It could be heard snarling and wrestling under the chair, and everyone withdrew their feet in fright. They placed someone's foot in a sack with an enraged cat. I don't know where they got it; perhaps they kept it solely for this purpose. They went on all fours under the table, while Accetto supervised them from a distance, and they lost no time in grabbing the foot and tying it in. The terrified reader fell down from his chair and attempted to undo the laces, while the cat could be seen leaping about and tormenting the unlucky foot with its claws and its teeth.

The attendants had a predilection for feet, with or without shoes, especially if left hanging loose and almost forgotten. For example, they slipped under the table and hit them with a hammer, or I have seen them spread black

Chapter E

tar over a shoe and set light to it. If made of leather or wool, the shoe became a fireball which the owner vainly beat on the ground, desperately screaming for help as the shoe could not be removed by hand. Everyone around was also woken, but I noted that no sense of solidarity existed between them. I have seen the fire spread to the trouser leg burning away all the hairs as far as the knee. Someone who had no laces kicked off his shoe into the air, which flaming like a ball of Greek fire landed on the head or the book or, in any case, in the vicinity of another reader, spraying him with boiling lapilli and causing pandemonium, given that these bomblets landed indiscriminately even on those who had not momentarily fallen asleep. If, however, the fire landed on a book and set it on fire, the reader, irrespective of whether they were young, old, innocent or guilty, was thrown out and obliged to pay for the loss, failing which Accetto would confiscate a coat, jacket or pyjama as security. I have seen him manhandle and insult a reader as though he were a common thief, while his two attendants laughed and fired elastic bands at the wrongdoer. He happened to be a professor of numismatics who had taken a flaming shoe to the shoulder and then seen his book consumed by fire in front of his very eyes. Accetto took away his coat and also wanted to remove his old-fashioned nightshirt. The professor resisted weakly and was embarrassed by the commotion and the fact that he was the centre of attention.

 The attendants burnt a reader's eyelashes and eyebrows with a lighter, and then set fire to his beard, before immediately abandoning the scene. The man was like someone who had returned to the world after a long holiday; he rubbed his cheeks covered in carbonised hair and grumbled in a low voice. But it was with their lighter that these two really ran wild, and you could see the smoke rising wherever they went. Here you could see a scholar with his sleeve on fire and there another's clothes smouldering and producing a dense black cloud if they were wearing synthetic fibres. To avoid suffocation, the reader was obliged to remove his clothes and end up in socks and girdle or little more. And red with embarrassment, given that underwear is never in fashion and never that decent.

I wanted to escape; I was frightened that I might close my eyes for a second or inadvertently lower my head. I didn't want to attract their attention and their determination to keep me awake; my toothache was enough. But even awake I could not get down to any serious study with them about, always supposing that those incoherent papers constituted something that could be studied.

Fischietti meanwhile was seated at the end of the hall in silence with his mischievous face close to a harmless old man in pyjamas whose head was resting against the back of his chair in a finely balanced position. Fischietti put the lighter under his nose and had him breathe in the gas while he slept. At the same time he called over his comrade with a wave of his hand, so that he could assist and join in the fun. Eventually the old man started to wave his arms about to grasp something and then he stood up as though driven by an irresistible desire for sleepwalking and fell across a colleague who looked awake with his eyes open, but was in fact asleep as well. The latter, on feeling that weight fall on top of him and seeing the two attendants on the prowl, instinctively hid himself under the table. This caused his persecutors to cry, "Can't be done, can't be done; you have been provided with chairs for this purpose. You cannot study underneath the table." They took a foot and dragged it, while he grabbed onto the table leg. And as he only had socks on his feet, they set fire to one and the poor man screamed: "Enough! I don't know anything, and I haven't done anything," and kicked wildly with his other foot which the other attendant unsuccessfully tried to catch and obstruct with one of the man's braces that had come loose. "You cannot go under the table," they said, "it is against regulations." "I'll come out on my own," he replied. "No," they continued, "you have to come out immediately." And they pulled as his sock burnt, probably

Chapter E

searing the most sensitive spots on his skin, because he shouted out, "Help, help, what are you doing?" but it was all in vain. When his toenails caught fire, he let go of the table leg and shouting like a man possessed started to beat and blow upon his burning foot. Perhaps they had poured alcohol on it. Accetto came up with a severe and supercilious expression: "Professor, what are you doing down there?" The attendants had let him go and were standing there laughing and elbowing each other. He sat down again at his table and started to cry in the midst of the smoke.

Everyone else in the area was awake, but pretended that nothing had happened. They affected to be dutifully absorbed in their books and their own thoughts. Someone coughed while scribbling away, but carefully wrapped up in his clothing for protection, his collar up at the back, and scarf on his head and feet lifted up for fear of the dogs. Everyone, including myself, followed the attendants' movements out of the corner of their eyes. Suddenly someone jumped up and rushed out, he was wearing a vest and his shoes were in his pocket.

Behind a column a little out of the way but very close to me, Fischietti had discovered someone who hadn't heard all the shouting and commotion. He was completely stretched out on one of the low tables, and smiled in his sleep as though he were lying in his own paradise. I could see everything when I leaned forward slightly. Fischietti circled him for a bit, and his expression had his colleague running over. He took a small box out of his pocket containing a bee and opened it just in front of the blissful reader's slightly parted lips. When he breathed in, the bee went in too and started to buzz about: he must have stung his tongue or palate, because the man of learning woke up with a start and the grimace of someone strangled by pain who cannot scream. The bee was already away, and he pressed his hands against his mouth. The attendants looked on with an air of surprise and attentiveness, as though to ask him what could possibly be wrong and whether they could assist in any manner. He shook his head to say no, there was no need of anything at all, it was very painful but they should feel free to move on. He really had no need of anything at all. But they insisted, more through signs than words, that they wanted to look inside his mouth; one of them even claimed he was a qualified nurse: "I swear it," he cried. His colleague had brought some medicines along. Eventually they persuaded him or he felt he had to give in as it was two against one. With a great deal of play-acting, they produced a bottle of drops with a dispenser in the top. I have no idea what acid it contained or if it really was a medicine. It gave off the smell of sodium carbonate. When a couple of drops had entered his mouth, a white vapour came out, produced by a reaction with his saliva, and the poor fellow started to make some strange noises in a high pitch, and pinch his lips and gums with his hands and then spit. As soon as one spit landed on his book, without any real intention but just in the blind impetuosity of pain, Accetto came over, stood between the man and his book, and hit the man on his neck with his ruler. The two attendants defended the reader: "No, no; that's enough!" they said to Accetto. "It was not his fault." And they wanted to administer a few more drops, but the man refused emphatically, without however managing to speak. He stuck out a tongue that was as large as a hand; it was swollen and black, but at the same time limp. He attempted in various ways to get a look at it. One of the attendants came up with the pincers he kept in his tool bag, and wanted to convince the man in a well-mannered way to allow him to pull one tooth, because, he persisted, he was qualified in dental surgery and this was now the only means to stop the spread of the granuloma. The scholar said that he did not want their assistance: "No, no, I can do without, thank you," and he clung to his chair. But the second attendant argued that the pincers needed to be applied directly to the tongue and he produced a pair of curved ones, as this would release the black bile. Failure to do this would cause necrosis of the jaw and the mucous membrane. Or perhaps his gland should be lanced to prevent an anaphylactic shock. So they started to argue with each other over whether it should be the tooth or the gland, and while one attempted to demonstrate their arguments to the other, they held the man of learning by his ears and accidentally pinched his chin and cheeks as they attached a washing peg to his lips to keep them apart. One of them had got hold of the victim's nose with the pincers, but the other defended the victim by asserting that the nose had nothing to do with the problem. In their excitement they pinched each other as well. But when Accetto saw that the book was in danger as one of the attendants had climbed up on a chair, he beat them, including the reader who covered his head with his hands while his flaccid tongue hung pendulous from his mouth. Initially the two defended themselves with their pincers, but then they stopped and submissively offered their heads and necks to Accetto for punishment.

Chapter F

When however I attempted to get back to my reading to see if I could obtain some advantage from it, a tiny shrew with the look of one of those Alpine crack troopers jumps out in front of my eyes, sat down and waits for me at the end of the line. Spreading its whiskers, it smelt the sentence and scratched its head. To avoid distractions I tried to take no notice of it, and my eyes leapt over it, but with its nose down to sniff, it ran along the lines behind me, overlaying the meaning and getting me in a muddle; then, quite suddenly, it leapt on a cricket that landed on the edge of the book, and it ate it. "How am I supposed to revise for my exam?" I said and shook the page. I should never have done that! An army of earwigs marched out of a hole that ran down from the middle of a capital "o" probably to the last page, and invaded the whole book. The insects then started to climb up my hands: "So much for my studies! So much for my exam!" I blew hard and out of the corner of my eye I could see the two attendants straighten up and Accetto looking at me. Tiny moths were stirred up with the dust and as they twisted through the air some landed up in my hair and down my collar. One nearly went in my eye and another in my nose.

"You were putting you finger up your nose!" Accetto exclaimed as he unexpectedly towered above me and looked me straight in the eye.

"No, actually."

"But you were scratching yourself. I saw you."

"I was not. It's all these moths and lice. They're everywhere, get all over my face, fly around my head and are a continuous irritation. I was just blowing them away." He looked at me very suspiciously and clearly wanted to thrash me. But he seemed to be weighing me up – me and my words. "How come," I said, "there are all these offensive animals? They are such a disturbance!"

Chapter F

"How come? You ask me. Well I can tell how come, no trouble at all. Take a look!" and he pointed out a yellow mark on the page, while all around known and unknown species of insect continued to crawl. "Take a look," and he pointed to a hair that could have been from someone's eyebrow or ear. You needed excellent eyesight to see it, as it was as white as the paper.

"It's not mine, I can assure you."

"It doesn't matter whose it is; these are the normal and necessary organic by-products of reading. Yours or someone else's, it makes no difference. But this waste material of yours, albeit unintentional, is what these animals feed off and reproduce from. And then you people complain, but you provide the food on which they thrive." My face expressed innocence, and he came even closer breathing his dampness on me.

"You have no idea, because you're a novice still wet behind the ears," he said, "but the pages of a book can contain the most horrendous filth that can be produced by these dirty and hunchbacked beings called readers. A reader absorbed in reading is by its very nature a corrupt and foul-smelling being in its breath and its trousers, on its way to cerebral dystrophy with all the consequences this has for the health and perspiration of its limbs. So you find all kinds of things in books: dandruff for instance! You have no idea of the filth: snowstorms of dandruff and other sebaceous substances, as well as hairs! You cannot begin to imagine the quantities of hair that fall out, and not just from the head! Hairs from beards, moustaches and ears also play their part. And every time someone reads, they pile up and add to our woes, because reading is an act of vandalism, no less. I can show you the most popular pages on which people injudiciously linger; these are pages covered in grease, spots and stuff that is continuously falling from the reader's face, even if it cannot be seen. There is spit which crumples the paper or makes if wavy if produced by coughs, sneezes, expectorations or laughter, and especially when executed forcefully through the teeth creating the kind of unhygienic spray that you are aware of. And then there is the nose! What isn't the nose responsible for when it comes to damage inflicted on paper! The more a person is absorbed in reading, the more good manners are forgotten, and one finger after the other makes its way up into the nose. God knows what it gets up to in there, what foul excreta are to be found and inevitably end up sticking to the poor book. I am only telling you this to put you on your guard, because just talking about it turns my stomach. In any case the fingers of your average readers, especially those who are regular or passionate ones, would be something iniquitous even without the proboscis problem. They are a trap for animal oils, bacteria, enzymes and glandular secretions. What do readers do? They scratch their feet – or somewhere even worse – and then transfer the fetid mucilage to the page. Some of them stick their fingers in their mouths to clean between their teeth, and then proceed to turn the pages, so the corners turn yellow, then grey and finally shiny black. And their ears? Just about everything comes out of them and not just that yellow wax that covers the print. I want to show you that in the long term some pages end up transparent like greaseproof paper, they are so filthy and saturated with oils.

"You'll be thinking that only shelves for general interest books are affected by these torments. Not at all! Quite the contrary, my dear sir. When a book is exceptionally dull, I find not just the usual human waste matter, but also the imprint on every page of readers' foreheads, cheeks and noses, after they have given in to that heaviness of the head and bent double across the table."

"Bent double?" I repeated a little disgusted.

"Yes sir!" he said, "and sometimes there are superficial oily shadows, but at others there are the products of hours of sleep, and you must know how we sweat, exude liquid from our tear ducts and toss and turn incessantly, and the head is worse than an ink pad and a rubber stamp; it prints deep deep down from one page to the next. If we are

Chapter F

lucky there are no suppurating pimples or ulcers, given the mania for scratching oneself and picking at scabs during the period of reading and drowsiness, because if there are, then the poor book is little more than a gauze or a bandage that covers a leper, and becomes a kind of repulsive and, might I say, stinking shroud, on which I can recognise the eye-sockets, the chin, cheekbones and all the wrinkles of that delinquent, that philistine who used it as a pillow."

I tried to interrupt him, but he ignored me.

"You are naive, my dear fellow; you are an idealist if you think that people in here use their books correctly. This place has just turned into a nocturnal nursery school, a public dormitory, where people snore loudly and rest their sleepy heads on the books, resulting in considerable damage to our library stocks and literary heritage. I would have such persons wear a nightcap at the very least and use cushions. Do you think it gives a good impression to have a renowned library full of people fast asleep with an open book in front of them? What, I would like to know, does this say about reading? And then there is the smell! Have you noticed it? You see, during sleep the body has to free itself of all the gases produced by fermentation – not only through the principal meatuses but also through pores and the nose, so the air becomes thick and there is obsessive convulsed coughing, and then there are the ravings generated by dreams and the screams because some people are troubled by nightmares, not to mention all the other base and scurrilous language that sleep brings with it. I wander amongst the desks and bang on the table to make a noise. I bring along paper bags which I blow up and explode close to the ears of these bogus readers. When I clap my hands, they stir and sway about for as long as I am in the area, but if I turn my back, their faces fall flat on their books as though their cheeks were made of honey. Just imagine the state in which a book can be returned to me: I lift it up with two fingers and I would gladly hit them over the head with it, rain down blows on them and throw them out of the library, because our books have become a breeding ground for viruses, diseases, herpes, brucellosis, scrofula and myasis. Do you understand?"

I stood up and started to walk away, to flee. He followed me and whispered his ideas in my ear. I was unable to block them out.

"My honourable friend, even if none of this were true and all the readers had gloved hands and masks over their faces, our books would still end up covered organic residues and effluent; and do you know who would be the primary culprit? The print worker! Do you know how filthy and unscrupulous print workers are? They grow the nails of their little fingers very long;" and he showed me his own one, "even longer than that. Out of sheer badness and in order to harm the owner of the print works who has failed to grant them a pay rise or a coffee break, they insert the nail deep into their ears and dig around very conscientiously and with their air of achieving God knows what, they flick the balls of wax amongst printing paper where they become long translucent splotches as they run through the drums. I have worked as a print worker and I know these things; come and see, if you like, just how many you can find in a single volume. This is their vendetta against society.

"Now listen to what happens, because I would see this every day with my own eyes; the boss would call them over and say, 'This book is full of earwax; who is responsible?' The faces of the print workers, true to their way of doing things, expressed their incomprehension, and they said, 'What? Whose ear?' The boss pulls out a copy of the book, leafs through it to show the great quantity of blotches and stains, and said, 'This is not a book but a *mortadella*.' The print workers bend over the book to inspect it, they raise some doubts and they say that generally this is the fault of the paper mill or rather the workers in the paper mill, who are repulsive: such blacklegs and so intent on their work that they never bother to blow their noses; what can you expect of people so deeply in thrall to their employers. Besides that stuff doesn't come from ears, but, in their

Chapter F

opinion, from noses. There ensued a long debate, they looked at the pages against the light and someone summoned the shop stewards' committee which decreed that the offending substance definitely came from a nose. The boss however counted on his long experience and said, 'No, I know earwax when I see it. I'm not a fool.' And looked at all those long nails on little fingers and saw them as an open challenge. This stage in a dispute rarely resolves anything: one side says nose and the other side says ear, and you would have to have the marks analysed by a chemist to establish the real answer, and then by a biologist who could identify the DNA and therefore the guilty party. These are all procedures that are long and very sensitive, and require calm and common sense which are never present in real-life situations.

"So the owner, who was enraged not so much by the damage as by his workforce's slyness and trickery, and by those provocative nails they flaunted as a symbol of their resistance, decided to hide in his office and spy on the production process. From his position he could look at the rotary-press operator from the side, and was able to ascertain that that nail got just about everywhere, and was put to the most base and vile services. It was a receptacle for all kinds of secretions and scabs, starting at the operator's head and working all the way down to his toes. He found this incredibly irritating as, in his opinion, you should work at your workplace and not scratch yourself, and a clause to this effect would have to be included in all future agreements between the union and the company management, for reasons of hygiene and clean air: corporeal grooming, whether carried out with instruments specifically designed for that purpose or with improvised means adapted for the same, is expressly prohibited; and this prohibition shall also apply to delays incurred by self-gratification relating to an itch and similar time-wasting phenomena... And look! All of a sudden, he saw the worker sticking that nail into his left ear and move it around in a vorticular motion, while the drums of the rotary press started to turn and move the paper. He therefore prepared himself to leap out at the critical moment. The print worker, however, appeared not to want to stop, and he prodded and turned his hand and little finger at different speeds without a care for the printing process and all the imperfections that could arise if the machinery was not properly monitored. He stood there as though enjoying this long auricular operation, and the owner quivered with rage. He would have liked to rush out with a cane and cane that hand; and then take an axe and cut that finger off at the root to display it as a warning and a threat to all that gang of miscreants. His contempt was at boiling point, and he too felt a certain itch inside his ear, which he blamed on the unpleasant scene he was witnessing and its contagious effects. While he was scratching it, he thought up another regulation for the workers' statute to protect them from excessive noise and the resulting risk to their hearing: Earplugs must be used in all parts of the print works in order to seal them off from the external environment and prevent noise and foreign bodies from permeating an employee's auricle to the detriment of his or her long-term health, as well as ensuring no outward movement of any by-product...

"Then a printer worker came along – a younger man – and he too had his little finger inside his ear already hard at that obscene exercise. Then a third worker and fourth turned up, and on seeing the others those who were not already engaged in this business soon had their fingers fiddling away in one or other of their earholes as an act of solidarity or sedition and with such vigour and surly arrogance that the owner leapt out and started to scream that he had found them out and caught them red-handed. 'Doing what exactly?' said the ringleader. By way of reply the owner grabbed him by the little finger and thrust it in the air; he summoned everyone in a loud voice, even from the offices and including the foremen and the time-and-motion experts. 'This is earwax,' he shouted, 'and no one can tell me that it isn't.' And he wanted everyone to look at

Chapter F

a kind of yellow polenta under the man's nails and, all the office staff agreed, it was something repellent and you wouldn't want to go near it. Well, with cynicism and insolence worthy of a gaolbird, this leading print worker and all the others around argued that it was indeed polenta, and that polenta is certainly not extruded from one's ears. But it so happens that we all end up with a little under our nails, particularly when we're poor and have to tighten our belts, while other don't even know what polenta is: under their nails you'd only find fragments of capon and roast veal. 'Show us your nails,' they shouted at the owner, and he replied, 'This is not polenta, my friends! I too know what hunger is, whatever you think. I know all about it.' 'But now you only dine on chicken,' they shouted from all sides. 'Not at all, but I do know all about ears, and I caught you in flagrante, as we shall see,' and he wouldn't release the ringleader's little finger. Indeed there was a scuffle. 'Bring in a chemist,' shouted the owner, hoping to use science to prove the entire shop stewards' committee wrong. There followed an endless exchange of insults: 'But you too were cleaning out your ear.' 'Give me a break! A chemist, call in a chemist!'

"A clerk stepped forward: 'I'm not a chemist, but I have some expertise, because as a child I was very keen on experiments.' The owner showed him the leading print worker's finger and long yellow nail: 'Are you capable of telling me precisely what is the chemical composition of this substance? And clearing up whether what we have here is wax or polenta?' The clerk thought for a moment, while everyone stood with a sceptical expression and their arms crossed, and then said, 'Well really, it's not that difficult: at a pressure of 0.76 bar, wax liquefies at a temperature of 66 degrees centigrade; if placed close to a flame, wax will liquefy, whereas polenta will carbonise.' He should not have said that; in a flash the owner had pulled out his lighter and was attempting to burn the print worker's finger. There was a universal roar of indignation: 'This is an attack on the workers' movement!' 'It's proof, scientific proof!' exclaimed the owner, and once more he tried to burn the finger. 'Where are we? In the Middle Ages? This is barbaric,' and it would all have ended up in violent brawl if the counterfeit chemist had not imposed his will with a screechy voice, 'One moment, gentlemen, just a moment!' Everyone stopped and was willing to listen. 'I suggest we take a sample; some of this substance should be placed over a flame.' This appeared to meet with general consent, but when the owner gave the order to proceed with taking the sample, there was a widespread reaction of disgust, and amongst the office workers an obstinate refusal, 'This is not one of our duties; this is an outrage, an abuse of power.' 'Let's have a volunteer,' the owner shouted, still holding on to that notorious finger. A little print worker stepped forward, pushed by the others, 'I'll do it,' he exclaimed, 'my name is Zante Padovani.' Everyone applauded. The boss was suspicious, but in the absence of anyone better, he agreed. A little fire was started with some rags bathed in diesel, but just as they were preparing to take the sample, the owner caught sight of Padovani attempting to remove the remains of his last meal of polenta from his teeth with his own nail; unquestionably this was for the purpose of tampering with the evidence. With a sudden movement, the owner grabbed hold of his little finger too, and held it tightly with his left hand, shouting, 'You swindlers, I saw what you're up to!' He tried to drag them both towards the fire so that he could put the indicted fingers over it to have them cooked. At this moment there was a unanimous and righteous trade-union protestation against this unprincipled persecution of a supposed plague-spreader and the end of civilisation as they knew it. The commotion was indescribable; the owner lost control of the two culprits because he unintentionally stepped on the flames, and instead of setting fire to their fingers, he lit the bottom of his trousers which smouldered, creating a great deal of smoke and a great deal of panic. The sequel was a blur of running hither and thither and a furious trade in defamatory aspersions: 'warmonger',

Chapter F

'swindlers', inquisitor', 'enemies of culture and the nation', 'profiteer', 'bunglers', 'parasite'!

"Then the print run came to an end and the machines automatically closed down. A printed sheet was removed and everyone crowded round to have a look. And the owner gave out a cry, 'Dandruff! Who is responsible?' It was at the time of the great social conflicts, dear fellow; I was in the midst of it all, and every day or even twice every day, the same old stuff was repeated off pat. The truth is that printed paper is a trap for all kinds of filth, even pus, scurf and secretions."

Chapter G

We had walked as far as the other end of the hall, and I could hear three o'clock being chimed out very clearly. "That's enough, please!" I told Accetto; I could have cried, I wanted so much for him to stop talking. He had been so taken with his own story that he had gone much further than he thought and found himself quite outside his usual stamping ground. Who knows where that itinerary would have led, because he had already resumed his diatribe against exocrine glands and the habit of reading too close to the page. I was quite willing to admit that he might be right, but I could not dwell on such matters. "These are important questions, I do not deny it, but I cannot discuss them now because my head is not big enough for them, and they leave no space for anything else; tomorrow I have an exam and I know less and less about my subject." I had pulled out my reading list, but it seemed to have grown smaller and more faded just lying in my pocket.

"Oh well, if that's it," said Accetto indicating a door a little way off and hidden behind two columns, "then there is the reference room. In there books are catalogued by argument – at your disposal." He consulted his attendants in a whisper and then said, "I leave you in the capable hands of my assistants, Fischietti and Santoro; they will assist you and give you suggestions, should it prove necessary."

"Don't disturb yourselves, please," I said, "just give me instructions and I'll look up the books myself." I was a little frightened of those two mischief-makers; I might have fallen asleep and prey to their attentions. But there was nothing for it.

Initially they stayed close to me and examined my feet with interest. Then they lifted the flaps of my brown smoking jacket and held on to it laughing, as though it were a train and they my pageboys, but they behaved more like my drivers or carters. This went on for some time, and

Chapter G

I said, "Enough!" and they said, "Yes sir, Mister Jerome." That's what they called me, as if it were an epithet, but actually it is my name, as recorded on my birth certificate. "Yes sir," they said, "we're here to follow orders," and they pulled back on the flaps as though they were reins and obsessively urged me on. "Ever onwards, sir, ever onwards," but we made little headway even though I tried as hard as I could and started to sweat from the effort. Then they started to shake my jacket because, in their opinion, it was full of hairs, insects and dust. Santoro was beating it with an egg whisk and saying, "Excuse me sir, you take no notice." In actual fact, they were producing a great cloud of dust and insects were flying of it, which they tried to kill by clapping their hands and hitting the air with the egg whisk and a small potato-peeler. This was not, of course, any help, and did not assist me in revising for my exam. "You have bumfluff, Mr Jerome," said Fischietti, "would you like us to depilate you?" "Enough!" I said again, "leave me in peace." He was playing with a lighter, which he was continually lighting and putting out. He wanted me to look at it while he held it steady in his hand. "I know how it works, thanks," I said, "so don't go to any trouble." He wanted me to look at where the gas came out, "Look in there," and I said, "That's an old joke and not very funny." But he persisted so much – and his companion Santoro was asking, "Shall I hold him still by the hair?" – that in the end I looked and Fischietti immediately released a high flame that burnt my eyelashes and other hairs with a powerful smell of singeing. They both sniggered and wanted to apply alcohol, but fortunately for me they were distracted.

Having only travelled a few metres over a very long period of time, I finally got to the reference room, which I entered in a sweat as the door had proved incredibly stiff. It wouldn't move on its hinges, and in my efforts to shove it, a piece of plaster fell on my head.

There was a woman barely visible up on a walkway where she was sorting out some books. There was just one person at a very long table, and just by the door behind shelves running into the room and under a label in large lettering, "Philosophy", were two attendants, one squatting and the other kneeling, both playing cards but with tiny travel playing cards that looked like postage stamps. They studied the cards for a long time before playing them by throwing them on a small makeshift table. I watched them for a while, so as not to interrupt them. They were talking quietly about Accetto; I caught a few sentences, although I would have preferred to have concentrated on my exam.

"Did you hear about Accetto?" said one of them, the taller of the two. "He's got a son who was taking celery."

"Taking celery?" I heard the other man say.

"Celery!"

"But celery's not a drug."

"Have you ever tried it?"

"Of course! I often eat celery in my salad."

"That doesn't mean a thing," continued the first man. "His son was drugging himself with celery and no one could understand how he was doing it."

"As far as I'm concerned, it's impossible."

"Me too, but you should see the state of him: just skin and bone, and his complexion is bright yellow."

"Didn't they take him to the doctor?"

"Yes, but doctors won't do anything but run some tests. Do you think they're the kind of people who believe in celery?"

"No, no, of course not. You can be sure of that. But in my opinion, no one believes in celery."

"That's just it, exactly as you say. No one believes in it. But in the meantime what are they going to do? You can't just let the poor lad go to ruin."

"Well, take him off celery!"

"Aha! Yes, you too, so it's true? Do you agree that young people are in the greatest danger?"

"What do you want me to say? I'm not a doctor."

"And that's your good fortune. The things these doctors say! All words, and in the meantime this poor boy is getting

Chapter G

worse and becoming increasingly withdrawn. I always ask him when he comes here with this father: Is it celery? You can tell me; I promise that it will be our secret. But naturally he denies it all. And I ask him again, Is it celery? If you have this weight on your mind, then just offload it on to me. No one will know anything about it. I tell him that because it's a cure, this need to confide in someone else. His father never talks to him – he is that kind of man – and our children grow up in the midst of things today, with this weight on their mind that they need to unburden."

"But who says it's celery that's causing him harm?"

"Saying it? Well, no one's actually saying it. We all like a quiet life. He denies it, because he's stubborn like his father. But you should see him – he doesn't look well!"

While I was listening to these exasperating inanities, Fischietti came along and flicked an elastic band at the ear of the one squatting down, who was mightily offended and leapt up ready for a boxing match. He raised his arms to the correct pose, but I interrupted, "Just a moment! First give me at least one book." I had seen that the other man had also stood up and wanted justice: to grab hold of Fischietti and return the elastic band by the same method. Fischietti was hiding behind me and continuing to provoke them by waving a straightened finger. At the same time he was pushing me so that I would fall on top of them and crush them, or alternatively so they would see me as their real adversary. "No, no," I said, "everybody stop. I don't have time for this at the moment. For God's sake, I just want this particular book, which is here." And I mentioned the twentieth century, as I showed the card. Everyone ran around me to take a look. Santoro also wanted to smell it. One of the attendants took out a magnifying glass and examined it for some time as he turned it over in his hand, even though Fischietti was trying to put his finger in the man's eye and set light to him and the piece of paper. Santoro told him off and as his did so, buffoonishly impersonated Accetto, and put the flame out with his saliva. I was worried about the card and held it tightly.

Eventually the attendant stood up straight and looking at the others rather than at me said, stressing each syllable, "The Philosophy of the Twentieth Century. Abridged Version. Do you want it?" I wasted no time in saying that I did; it seemed something clear and reasonably plausible. I felt sure that he had chosen a title at random, and I also noted that the magnifying glass was not a magnifying glass but one of those salad spoons made of transparent plastic. Indeed he was now using it to drive off Santoro and Fischietti who sought refuge under a chair.

At this stage, the one who had supposedly carried out the task of decipherment and was also the taller and thinner one, picked up a stool with steps and climbed up to a shelf, further than was necessary because he had to bend down with his head against the ceiling. He looked along the shelf for another eternity pretending to look and leaf through some pages, and then said, "The book is not here; do you want the nearest one?"

"What do you mean?" I said, "does it seem like the same thing?"

"Listen, for me books are all of equal worth; it is not for me to judge whether someone asks for one or another. I am asking you this just in case you want it, to make it easier for you, so as not to make things difficult for you. But if you're going to get offended, you know what I'm going to do? I'm going to come down and the book can stay exactly where it is."

The shorter attendant, seated on the first step, said that I shouldn't be apportioning blame to anyone. "Here there is carelessness," he continued in an amenable tone, "a devil-may-care attitude that you would find hard to credit. It is very unusual for a book to be found; indeed, you might say that in practice they are never found. But if you want my advice, given that I have considerable experience of this place, take the book next to it. You've got to believe me! Even if it is not exactly the one you requested, you should realise that perhaps someone else was looking for this one we're offering and they couldn't find it; and perhaps

Chapter G

tomorrow this actually will be the one you are looking for. I'm telling that you will look for it in vain and you'll regret the arrogance you're displaying at the moment."

"But I wanted the abridged version that you referred me to."

"Yes, of course. Indeed we have no objections, but have you considered that someone else, perhaps only yesterday, might have had the abridged version you're on about in his very hand, and out of mere superciliousness rejected it. Do you want to make the same mistake?"

The man at the top of the steps repeated for my benefit, "I'm coming down; he doesn't want the next book? Is he sure? Is he rejecting it?"

His colleague down below was still trying to persuade me, "Perhaps you are new to the library, and don't know these things, but arrogance is the greatest vice. An arrogant person is never content, because he loses every opportunity. He doesn't know how to enjoy life and develop his ideas. In here you find books when you're not specifically looking for them. That is the moment to take them and not let them go. So why are you being so stubborn and intractable? If you behave like this, you will never have a thing and you'll be alone with your ideas and your absolute demands. And in the end you will only have regrets. Think about your future."

I listened to his argument and was not insensitive to it. I was arrogant, it's true; never happy and full of disdain. Why did I want what wasn't there? That was stupid; besides the hours were passing and my teeth were there to remind me. So I gave in and said, "Bring me it, then. I accept."

He brought me a shapeless pile of paper, all riddled with wormholes. There were even scales from a grass snake and the margins had been gnawed by rats. I sat at the one, very long table. I opened the papers where they weren't stuck together with a slight sense of hopefulness. A little way away, there sat the distinguished-looking gentleman in a dressing-gown whom I had already noted. He was possibly deep in his thoughts or possibly, like everyone else, asleep.

Proto-philosophies

There was a famous sect in the West that boasted the weakest thought of them all. This is how it came about: one of their number, whose name has remained a mystery, was extremely weak-minded – beyond all our descriptive powers – and so weak that he could think of only one thing to do: to cluck like a hen.

This then was taken as the founding proclamation. His followers gradually learnt the new philosophy and, according to where they had risen on the ladder of knowledge, would go "cheep cheep" or "cock-a-doodle-doo". They held many conferences, which however always ended in fierce arguments. On one side, a faction went "bow-wow" and on the other their adversaries predictably went "meow meow". Then the doyen of clucking, who was chairing the proceedings with various feathers stuck in his hair, would start to cluck and cackle into the microphone, "co... co... co... cockaday, co... co... co... cockaday", thus resolving the dispute and guiding the conference towards an agreement. But on occasions, the arguments only got worse, and there would be someone who would stand up from the floor and point their finger while reading a typewritten sheet, "quack, quack, quack," and trigger a whole henhouseful of protests and insults. Some shouted "cheep cheep", others "baa baa", "grrr grrr", "chirp chirp", so that all the chairman's "cockadays" and "co co cos" were in vain.

Any attempt to define the specific questions and controversies would be a trivialisation of the movement's postulates and credo. But it was clear that there were leading figures with greater authority, and when they spoke the howling of the crowd was abated. One man in particular stood out for his brief maxims, which were so weak that everyone held them in admiration. He asked for

Chapter G

permission to speak with a grave and dark expression, then he made a sound resembling that of a dumb duck, a kind of "hhhhh", and then after a long interval yet another "hhhhh", but this time measured, like a ferocious warning. And so in relation to that "cockaday" which might have been defined as the manifesto or programme for the entire school, this "hh" so curt and thoughtless was acknowledged as a great leap forward.

This philosopher of the "h" was however very modest in his appearance, in spite of his great fame. His feet were flat and wide, and he was in the habit of going about barefoot. His forehead was almost non-existent and his cranium flattened at the top. His hair was straight and swept back over his head with oil, and was entirely waterproof.

So we can say that up to and including his teachings was the classical period of this philosophy, and thought had been retrogressing until it practically did not exist, getting close to its mythical roots. But then came the populist turning point. One day at one of the plenary meetings, something quite unheard-of happened. There was a certain fellow who had only recently joined the sect, and was an assistant to a thinker, weak-minded like few others and also a little bit deaf, but nevertheless at the height of his career. One day he stood up and without any introductory remarks said, "Good morning... good morning... my dear colleagues... the purpose of our meeting... primarily philosophy... so let's move straight on to the voting." As in the face of all sensational innovations, there was a little turmoil, a little tension, which meant of course that they flapped, fluttered and pecked at each other, and there were those who wanted to challenge him and go back their ancient ways by neighing and braying and repeating "eeeeh... eeeeh..." but, all things considered, he displayed a great deal of common sense that paled beside the weakness of the other fellow.

So the new philosophy was acknowledged as a revolution, and everyone started to speak with the alphabet and put about their argument and give speeches. People came in huge numbers to listen to them; initially due to excessive formalism there was only a specialist audience, but then just anyone could not understand them. Indeed, there was such weakness about that, it could be argued, this philosophy became so widespread that it governed everything anybody said and was almost a companion to every everyday action.

...

As for the East, we know that in the Indian region of Tamil, every house has an outside shed that acts as a lavatory: it sits on four poles a metre off the ground and has a hole in the centre. The excrement falls through the hole to the ground in a pen where a small black philosopher lives and runs across to eat it.

A traveller happened upon a home where the householder, kindly as they can be only there, apologised for the defective hygiene he was able to offer: his philosopher had escaped six days earlier by furiously breaking through the wooden palisade, probably because something had disgusted him. Out of regard for their guest, they had tried to replace him with a Madras pig, but the animal was shy and recalcitrant, and during the night it gnawed away at the supporting poles so that the whole thing would collapse.

Keeping a philosopher for this purpose, although an ancient custom, is now less common. One reason is that they are less loyal and diligent in their duties – even less impartial and going so far as to take a dislike to a member of the family or some passing guest who they categorically refuse to serve. The reason is a psychological one: you can see them through the hole as they grub around and look upwards. The lavatory user and the philosopher stare silently into each other's eyes. Not to mention the habit of a philosopher rushing over as soon as he hears a guest's footsteps and putting his face and ears through the hole. Once he has got into this habit, it becomes not only embarrassing but dangerous.

These philosophers escape when they get to a certain stage in their lives. They become prey to a wild and ill-

Chapter G

defined frenzy, and they long for the rivers, open grasslands and a life on the run in savage bands as the enemies of man. They wander about usually for a few weeks and if they are not recaptured, they get very thin and become even smaller, blacker and more disorderly. Some of them develop rather watery tastes and take to the marshes and the meanders of rivers like terrapins. Others go high into the mountains as far as the snowline, where they live in a hollow tree trunk or on a spur of rock exposed to the four seasons. Yet others – the majority – become ferocious wild animals with their bristles sticking up and prickly like those of a porcupine, slightly poisonous teeth and curved nails like a claw, which they use for scratching and hanging off branches.

If however you manage to recover them shortly after their escape, they will return to their simple and useful duties after a few days of resistance and stubborn refusal, albeit without spirit or enthusiasm. Superficially one might say laziness. But when they look up and stare at you through the hole, you feel that you are looking at a sleepwalker whose eyes contain a faded uncertainty about the meaning of this fragile existence.

Chapter H

I have to admit that this was not an easy text to read. Partly because it unsettled me: was this all the much vaunted philosophy was about? But of what school and what era? Was this the latest scholarship or was it all invention? I was a little distracted by the young woman talking to the seated man, who was however immobile and giving no signs of life. The young woman was on a walkway where she was dusting books and putting them back on the shelves. Her voice, which was pleasant and very attractive, overlaid my philosophical reading. I heard her complaining about the infestation of animals. If it had only been a question of insects – even, she said, moths, bed bugs and so on – you'd only have had the stench or itchiness; they would have nibbled away at the corners, which, when you think of the damage caused by fire in the past, is almost a good fortune. But the fact is, she repeated several times, that much larger animals have been seen wandering around; some people have seen monkeys. "Not myself," she admitted, "but my colleague in hall no. three and corridors thirty-one, thirty-two and thirty-three, Mrs Beltrami, saw several of them leaping over her head while she was looking for a pressmark at the highest shelf and was at the top of the ladder. Well, that could only be called a health-and-safety risk."

The gentleman down below looked as though he were being cradled, while the pencil held by three fingers was on the point of slipping from his hand. The young woman continued to chatter and ask him for his own opinion.

"Don't you think that we should be covered by insurance?" she said "And not just for falls or landslide of books, but also for bites, because Mrs Beltrami in hall no. three says that the monkeys grabbed her by the legs and started to scream; they scream when they want to bite. She thought they looked like undersized baboons, and the red they have under their tails wasn't really red but white

Chapter H

streaked with red. What do you think?" This last question was also directed at me, given that the other guy wasn't saying a word. "It must be because of the lack of sunlight. A baboon's face is very similar to a barking dog, but they were tiny, tiny, just like dwarfs, and they ran along the shelves; there was a whole pack of them, that much was clear, and who knows where they came from. Because they never came here in such numbers, as the rooms are badly heated and in winter they're freezing, and these monkeys are used to Morocco, where it is as hot as a boiler room – forty degrees, the boiler-man told me, or even fifty. So these monkeys, when they saw the ladder and her standing on the ladder, God knows who they took her for? Perhaps they were looking for bananas or imagined that in nature trees were just like her. They grabbed hold of her legs and pinched her, she says to taste her or maybe bite her. Then they sat on the books she was holding, as though they were palm leaves, and when she tried to put the books away, there was already a monkey sitting on the shelf between the books just where that pressmark was meant to go. And if she tried to put the book in its place, the monkey stood up and deliberately stopped her by pushing with its hands and revealing its teeth. If she persisted and tried to frighten it off by waving the book around, the monkey became incredibly agitated and screamed until all its comrades came running over and leapt on the volume. They would bite into the binding and her hand, and with indescribable yelling they would run up her arm and if she hadn't defended herself by hitting them and sweeping them away with her other hand, they would have scratched her face and eyes, and put knots in her hair that would have to have been cut to unravel. She had to give up what she was doing and leave the books scattered where they fell. She was lucky she didn't fall, and there is a terrible mess in those sections and no one wants to go there. And do you know what they're saying?"

The gentleman was saying nothing, nor did he make any disagreeable noises. In my opinion, he was sleeping, but that may not have been the reason why he was not hearing. "You know what they're saying," she continued, having decided to ignore him and speak only to me, "they're saying that there is even an orang-utan in the hall with the globes, which is always damp and warm. They only send Mrs Bucato there, when it is absolutely necessary. She doesn't have to go there, because she's not an attendant but a teacher."

I interrupted, "You mean Mrs Bucato who teaches Greek?"

"Yes, do you know each other?"

"I've heard of her."

"Well, she's the only one the animal is in awe of. It abducted her, the first time, and took her to its nest, because it has a nest just like a bird's nest, but much much bigger. Mrs Bucato wasn't at all frightened because, she told us, it didn't look like a monkey, but made her think of a solicitor, as its fat, baggy cheeks were identical to those of elderly solicitors – according to her. She says it was covered with long ginger hair and had a beard, a great bushy beard, and it just watched her continuously but never raised its voice or got physical. She says that even its eyes did not have a ferocious expression, that they were the eyes of a solicitor, by which she meant completely lacking any opinion. So she felt relaxed, even there in that nest with someone she didn't know. She would have liked to have known its thoughts, because it continued to study her in silence. She's a bit hairy too, but being a woman not excessively, and she bleaches her hair so that it doesn't show. But it studied the hair without touching it, and it looked over the whole of her. She says that it appeared undecided; deeply affected but undecided. She was dressed as she usually was, because she had never thought that one day someone would abduct her and she had never heard of an orang-utan. But in any case she is not in the habit of changing her clothing, because she has only one dress, one pair of tights, and also just one pair of slippers – very comfortable ones, she says. So the orang-utan scrut-

Chapter H

inised her untiringly for an hour or so; it was well past midnight and it studied one of her brown warts covered with a whole lot of hairs.

It was fascinated by the hairs, and went around her back to study the other side. Her back is not very striking, and actually very similar to her front; perhaps, she thought, it is trying to work out what is her front and what is her back, so as not to make any mistakes. She stayed there the entire night, and the monkey never stopped brooding; basically it seemed rather inexpert and troubled by many uncertainties. The abduction had been a moment of madness, and certainly not motivated by hunger, because all orang-utans are strictly vegetarian, and now that its yearning had been calmed and there was more light, it probably felt the weight of its responsibilities. Mrs Bucato told me that she would never have taken the initiative, even though its eyes did make her feel a little sorry for it. After all those hours nothing happened; it looked at her sheer tights and her legs, which are a bit bony but there's nothing wrong with them, and its reaction was to scratch its head in an entirely inconclusive manner. The sun was up when it left its nest, and Mrs Bucato followed it down. She saw it look around with a crestfallen expression and set off down the corridor, according to her, in search of shoots and ants which are its food. Since then, Mrs Bucato has always been the one to go to the hall where they keep the globes, and when this orang-utan hears her coming, hears her slippers padding along and the key in the lock, it runs to the highest shelf and lies flat in a corner. It observes her from a distance and respects her."

"Excuse, young lady," I said, "but what's your name, should I ever need it."

"Iris."

"Mine's Jerome, even though nobody calls me that during the day, as it is no longer fashionable. In fact, I generally forget that I was ever called that, but it that's how I was baptised."

"I like it. It suits you. Sounds like a saint's name – the patron saint of books."

"Really?" I was a little incredulous; it was flattery but still pleasing. "Iris is better: the name of a flower and it clearly suits you because it resembles you." Then I didn't know what else to say, and nor did she. I thumbed through those dusty and tattered pages infested with mites, with a pang in my guts over the time that galloped by without my making any progress. But this sensation was now joined by another of frenzied desire that affected my bowels. It was caused by the young woman's attractions.

I could not fail to notice Accetto's assistants who were seated on the ground and had got out a roll with salami. There was just the one, so Fischietti shared it out by eating the salami and leaving the bread and skin for Santoro, who started to whine and wanted to recover the salami from Fischietti's mouth. Fischietti bit his finger and held it in his teeth like a dog with a bone, while the other tried to extract it and hit him in the face with a shaving brush. This would have gone on for some time had an inattentive hen not wandered by and come so close that they grabbed it. They held it still with its beak open and fed it the pieces of skin. Then they made it eat the paper the roll had been kept in, once they had screwed it up into many little pellets. Fischietti occasionally gave one to Santoro, who was happy with this and drew the hen's face close and muttered something to it.

When they started to pluck it, Miss Iris heard the rumpus and came down to sort it out. She said some just and very sensible things not only about the hen but also the fact they were disturbing people. She looked at me, only me and not the others when she said, "Some people are trying to study here, move along." "We're the attendants," Santoro said. "Then let that hen go," and she lifted a book as though she was going to hit him with it. "They're not your hens," Santoro grumbled, "they belong to everyone." But Fischietti obeyed, bowed at her several times and gave Santoro what was left of the paper, which he continued to sniff every time he ate a little bread. The young lady smiled at me, and I would have liked her as my attendant rather than those two tormentors. She seemed very patient and sensible. Then I was affected by her perfume that swirled around her and enveloped me and the bookshelves. I would have preferred to look at her than think about my exam because she soothed me – not only my anxiety of lost time but also my toothache. She wore the loose and slightly wispy clothes of summer, even though summer was still a long way off. She, however, carried some remnants of the last one around with her. I was not in love, but I was enjoying the temptation although, in all conscience, I should have only been thinking about my studies.

The two attendants, Fischietti and Santoro, had started to play cards with the other two workers responsible for that room. But every time someone dealt a card, Santoro cut it to bits with pinking scissors, so that the cards all ended up bevelled but radically downsized, some tiny with jagged edges. The other two sat sulkily and mistrustfully refusing to deal or play, until Santoro cut all the cards in their hands in half with a few sudden lightning snips of his scissors. The ensuing squabble hinged on the legitimacy of such a move. The other two claimed their rules were different, and Fischietti and Santoro replied that they hadn't come to get themselves fleeced by the two idiots in the reference room.

For some time I could no longer read. The young woman looked on and shook her head in sign of her disapproval and forbearance.

Chapter I

This round and well-dressed man suddenly appeared. "It's four in the morning," he said in a low but agitated voice.

I looked at Iris questioningly. "He always comes at this time," I heard her tell me, "he's the arbitrator Pantani from the Board of Directors."

"It's four in the morning," he said again, "can't you see that you're disturbing people? Can't you see Professor Rasorio over there?" and he pointed to the other man who, like me, was sitting at the table. "I will report you to the disciplinary committee, and send a complaint to your immediate superior. Who is he?"

The two who work in the reference room pointed to the assistants and said, "He's Accetto. Accetto!"

"No, we're nothing to do with them. I'm not. He's not," they protested and shrugged discourteously, and the scissors cut one of the other two's sleeve.

Miss Iris also took no notice of this conversation. She gave me an exclusive and conspiratorial smile every now and then, and her behaviour intimated a degree of scepticism in the man she had defined as the arbitrator Pantani and a failure to take him seriously. Santoro threw a well-chewed card almost into the arbitrator's mouth, and then pointed to the other two by way of incrimination.

"You can see for yourself!" he turned to me as I was the only person willing to listen to him. "This is supposed to be a library!" He was also going "ssshhhhhh" and his two open hands pleaded for quiet. I did not feel very relaxed in his presence, particularly because of the difference between his clothing and mine, which was not exactly elegant.

"The people don't deserve such a man. Just look at him seated at his work!" he said pointing to Professor Rasorio. "He comes here every night to prepare his lectures, and have you noticed the lack of respect they show him? He needs to be allowed to think; his brain is an encyclopaedia.

Chapter I

We should keep quiet, and he needs the lights low. That's what a library does: it helps learning and scholarship by providing a peaceful environment. But people are ignorant, particularly in here."

It seemed to me that he was looking at Iris's legs, as she turned and walked away.

"Now listen, my dear sir, to what happens in the world as a result of this ignorance."

A beetle was flying around my head, which I shook to discourage the insect, but the arbitrator took this to mean I was very interested, while I just wanted to get on with my research.

"You should know," he said, "that when we first invited Professor Rasorio to the municipality of Villacuccagna, where I reside during the day, to give a lecture on his latest research into gigantism and dwarfism, which, I might say, has already earned him a place in the history of scientific thought – just think that he is mentioned three times in the *History of Scientific Thought* by the famous, the eminent Professor Materdura, Volume Two, and a fourth time in the notes – yes, when he came to speak at the theatre in Villacuccagna, the entire citizenry turned out to hear him, with magnificent pomp and ceremony. There were all the most noteworthy ladies in the first row along with their respective husbands, all professionals or in the employ of municipal corporations, there were our most gifted intellects with their pupils, and there were the people who generally form – no offence intended – the common but honest citizenry of every town. Everyone was there: how else can we put it?. Even those left outside turned out in some strange way to have already got in, and the theatre, which has six hundred seats, was full with over two thousand people, I believe, and that is not counting those who hid behind the scenes, under the stage and inside the curtain, because there were even people there. This is just to explain the extent of the interest and resulting crush. Professor Rasorio started to speak at exactly nine o'clock and continued for an hour and twenty minutes without notes or a single sheet of paper in front of him, and with such clarity, penetration, innovative tones, balanced discourse and conceptual virtuosity that the whole audience was thrilled. On more than one occasion they would have interrupted him – except that this would have been seen as bad manners – to thank him and express their overwhelming endorsement which they had been wanting to do since nine o'clock or perhaps since the afternoon. When he gave signs of coming to his conclusions by summarising with great tact his concise lesson but having nevertheless amply demonstrated his theory and when he actually concluded by celebrating the new and limitless scientific horizons that had been opened, the theatre exploded in thunderous applause. Applause and not just applause. Endless applause.

"At this stage, I felt a presentiment that all this enthusiasm might lead very slowly towards some form of aberration, as sadly has often occurred in our city in relation to events that are in some way motivated by loftier and more exalted ideals than it can ever aspire to. I too applauded, and nobody wanted, it seems, to be the first to stop. The professor responded with small bows involving a forward motion of the chest and measured nods of his head. But instead of bringing the enthusiasm to an end, this dignified and composed behaviour only rekindled it. When the professor lifted his eyes to the gallery, there was another flurry of universal delirium, and the shouts started. Frankly I could not see a solution in the short term and was rather concerned, partly for the good name of science. 'What a penetrating mind!' I heard the Councillor Paganini saying close to me, as he bowed towards Mrs Peroni. And Mrs Peroni, together with other well-established or younger ladies, continued to applaud in an exaggerated manner in order to attract attention. She was checking on Mrs Bonacci's applause with withering and, I believe, intentionally contemptuous looks, because this other lady in the row behind was shouting in a booming voice, 'Bravo! Bravo!' and thus ourperforming all the other

Chapter I

women and demonstrating herself to be the most distinguished and perceptive expert on the questions so splendidly elucidated. She continued to issue forth these bravos as soon the applause started to subside a little bit, and her voice could be heard very clearly. So then you could appreciate her own knowledge and the fact that she had studied at Pavia under Professor Velluto, who had been a luminary in his own time and one of the greatest intellects when it came to pathological microcephalies – and, what is more, one who had a particular weakness for her, at the time endowed with long and beautiful hair.

"During one of these renewals of the applause, Mrs Peroni fell victim to what I can only define as an insane inspiration, which arose solely in order to compete with the insane 'bravos' of Mrs Bonacci and beat her, given that the word 'cerebrum' had been used not once but twice during the lecture, and so no one, in her opinion, could judge in the substance of the talk better than her who, though not a specialist, alone amongst all the teachers in that lecture hall was famous for her passion for all matters concerning the human psyche or psychology. So Mrs Peroni started to shout, first at a moderate pitch and then warbling fiercely, 'Encore', and she persisted with chanting that implausible 'Encore, encore!' while never conceding any ground.

"Now, I ask myself, how could the mind of a human being who has attained not only a university entrance diploma but also, it appears, a degree, possibly harbour such a bizarre idea? How could you demand an encore of a scientist who, albeit in a populist presentation, had provided laboratory information and conceptual framework that was utterly exhaustive? Methodologically, that was how I interpreted the situation, and I still do. But people gradually started to prefer the 'encore' to Bonacci's 'bravo', and soon they were shouting 'encore' from every corner of the hall, in an unseemly and irrational fashion. I wanted to climb up onto the stage and defend science by asserting, 'But please, what is all this about an encore! Go home.' And yet even the councillor with the environmental portfolio, Ario Soffritti, who was already on the stage and applauding a metre away from Professor Rasorio, was repeating "Encore, encore!" in a very loud voice almost into the professor's ear. But then something quite unexpected happened – something I consider also to be unprecedented: this scientist of ours did not appear to be at all put out or disconcerted; he did not send the audience and the council leaders to the devil for their outrageous behaviour; no indeed, he even appeared to feel honoured and understood at last. Perhaps it was only excessive courteousness on his part. He stood up, went back to the microphone and, when silence had returned, did not say, 'Thank you, I am extremely moved, but now we'll go home to our beds,' but instead he cleared his throat and uttered sentences of his speech exactly as he had just done, 'Kind ladies and gentlemen, to conclude this brief and summary lecture of mine, which, I believe, has demonstrated my theory which I have expounded and illustrated here for the first time, and which from this evening opens up new and limitless horizons to science.'

"Once again the applause exploded with shouts of 'bravo! encore! encore!' People exchanged looks to signify, 'Up with science! Let's go for it! Let's hear a repeat of something else!' and at the same time Mrs Peroni gloated at her victory over Mrs Bonacci. Given that time was going by and the whole business was showing no signs of coming to an end, Councillor Soffritti got his voice heard at the microphone after many meaningful coughs, 'Eminent professor, you must understand that this enthusiasm, which I fully share, is a tribute to you as a person and to your studies. And allow me to say this, your studies are ahead of today and tomorrow, and are in fact an appointment with the day after tomorrow...' shouts of agreement and more applause, '... and as you are here, you will excuse us, we wish to say that true science can suffer no gag or be associated with any particular flag, and because of this we want to make the most of this opportunity and not let you go without hearing once again

Chapter I

and understanding most fully...' but he could not continue because the audience had understood where the circumlocution was going and they overwhelmed him with encores mixed with shouts and exaltations. 'Encore, encore,' was shouted from the gods, and also from the stage. Even the stalls, usually so measured, judicious and rational, were prey to a shameful, exploitative and base frenzy, and was shouting 'Encore!' under the leadership of Mrs Peroni and a claque of mindless psychoanalysts.

"The councillor muttered something to our illustrious guest, who decorously agreed. Silence returned once more, the ladies threw their gold and jewellery, and the professor, sensing the public's mood and propensity not only for the subject but also for his oratory, conceded a slight smile of condescension and said without stopping for breath, 'Not without pride I assert that from this moment there opens up a new horizon for science to examine – something limitless.' For a moment there was a thoughtful silence that hung in the air, because the new formulation was more profound and difficult; we might say that it was more philosophical than strictly scientific with that idea of limitlessness falling at the end of the sentence. Then the unanimous encore was a deafening wave of swooning and enthusiastic zeal, a restlessness. 'It all went so well; it went so well!' I heard the deputy mayor repeating close to me in a kind of euphoric monologue. The chaos was indescribable. The councillor with the environment portfolio wished to get some of the credit and gain in popularity, so he stuck the microphone in front of the professor, and you could hear alone in the midst of that hullabaloo of bravos and encores, his shrill voice enunciate a sound similar to or rhyming with 'limitless', after which the microphone started to screech terribly. After this, the professor bowed and withdrew behind the scenes, while the audience spontaneously organised a kind of chorus accompanied by drumming and tapping of heels on the floor. From the stage there even came the music of accordions and ocarinas, which eventually degenerated into patriotic songs and hymns to culture in general."

"Thank you, thank you, this has been most instructive," I told him, but I could have wept and begged for pity, "I have learnt a great deal, but I have a lot of work to do; I have to sort out my texts." I looked around for Iris to see if she could find some pretext for getting him away from me, but she'd returned to the walkway because of an incompatibility with the arbitrator Pantani. She was a long way off, because that room was actually a corridor, and Iris could be seen right at the end of it close to the ceiling. Pantani also seemed to be constantly seeking her out with his eyes, even when he was talking.

So ignoring him completely as though he were a superfluity, I returned to my pile of dusty papers with the frowning air of a teacher in a full-time position who knows what he wants.

How philosophers are born

One of the most singular and fascinating philosophical causes célèbres that ever occurred was the case of the young but highly regarded philosopher whose head, tastes and lifestyle were precisely those of a sheep.

In public he always showed an unfailing repugnance for all meat, whether raw or cooked, and he would shun it like a personal adversary. He ate pears, apples, chicory, bread and, above all, a type of biscuit from his native town, which his mother would bake for him from time to time. He would only drink water.

He developed a very formal language made up of signs and very few sounds meaning: I'm hungry, I'm thirsty, I'm tired, I want to eat a biscuit. All the rest, he made it clear, was of no importance, and he made it clear by lifting and lowering his head, and rubbing his head against the legs of anyone who came by, as sheep do. When his students argued amongst themselves, he was in the habit of hitting

Chapter I

them with his horns, which meant, "You haven't studied! Do you want to be failed?"

He never wanted to sit on a chair to rest or give his lessons. He crouched on the ground and bleated.

His back, hips and shoulders were covered with a grey and very soft fur which was an inch or two long, with the appearance of wool, but actually rather repellent.

Some mountebanks saw him, and suggested to the rector that he should be displayed at fairs and markets in the area, but in spite of the considerable pecuniary advantage, the rector would not allow it and instead he would take the philosopher to the fields with his flock and occasionally have him sheared.

...

Rumination in human beings, as an organic symptom of methodical thought, still has a very limited case record. Its mechanism and nature are still subject to a question that is *sub judice*. Professor Piva and Doctor Sacco were eminent academics whose personal theoretical positions need to be associated with a very marked ruminative and herbivorous tendency, if they are to be understood.

The former had healthy and robust dentition, voluminous and vertical ears, and swollen and hardened temples that stuck out. His proportions were macrocephalous, and he was covered in very short bristles. The latter, distinguished by a reflective physiognomy and a heavy build, had a large nose, frontal swelling with considerable protuberance and the presence of corneous callosity. His hair covered the entire scaly portion of the temporal area and extended so far that it blended into the eyebrows. Both became very happy at the sight of food, and both had an insatiable hunger. They immediately went for those foods that appeared to have the greatest bulk. They hardly chewed at all. They swallowed enormous mouthfuls, and occasionally ran the risk of suffocating. They often brought their mouth close to the bowl, using their tongue as a prehensile organ. Between one food ration and another, Professor Piva in particular liked to spend a lot of time tearing up grass, putting it in his mouth, triturating it and swallowing it, and it should be noted that were he prevented from doing this, he would not set up about chewing rags, threads, sticks or anything else that came to hand in place of grass. In other words, he was quite capable of distinguishing between grass and everything else, and if it had been dried and was in the form of hay, he still appreciated it. According to Dumur and Liebman, rumination is due to a spasm of the pylorus, from which food is regurgitated to the mouth.

Indeed rumination took place in these two, ten minutes or a quarter of an hour after ingestion of their food, heralded by the same expressions of joy that accompanied the beginning of their meal. A hydro-aerated sound could be heard, which could only be defined as sloshing. This was occasionally accompanied by emissions of gas. You could then see the extension and retraction of the neck, by which the chin moved close and further away from the manubrium of the breastbone. The abdominal muscles contracted, abdominal walls pulsated. Then the throat swelled and the mouth filled with its gastric content. This made it possible for them to start chewing incessantly with sideways movements of the jaw, which they did with a serious expression, very conscious of themselves. Sometimes rumination was very peaceful, at others it was noisy. They could ruminate in any position, but they were most successful when they were left to themselves in the fields, and they felt unobserved and alone in the presence of cattle.

...

When a thinker is born, there are recognisable signs: for example a state of apparent asphyxia. After that, behaviour becomes increasingly different from that of humankind. One of the most quoted thinkers, for instance, walks by jumping with his legs bent in a state of timorousness and tremulousness. He twitches his nostrils and lips to scent the air, which is one of the reasons why he can be mistaken for a rabbit – another being his timidity. When he gets frightened, he bangs his right foot as rabbits do, and if you look at him from below, he sprays your face with saliva and snorts. But as soon as you knit your eyebrows, he flees with huge leaps and goes off to lay down his head in cavernous tunnels in the walls or the burrows he digs in the ground. He goes wild for accordion music, and he delights in suffocating hens if they are the weakest ones. He hates cockerels. Another of his favourite games is to detach putty from the windows and eat it, for which reason he is not beloved of housewives.

During pregnancy his mother had had a dream of which she was terrified, and when the above-mentioned thinker was born, she recognised him with just this difference: in the dream he had white fur and very long ears.

Chapter L

In the meantime I could hear activity under the table and feel my foot being pulled. I bent down and there was Fischietti who trying to tie one of my feet up.

"If someone has an ingrown toenail, I'll medicate it for him," he said as he pulled out a carpentry saw. "If someone has a corn, I'll cut it out for him," and he showed me his screwdriver. At the same time his comrade was sitting on the ground and laughing happily and smugly. "Do you have corns, Mr Jerome?" he stared as he asked the question.

"No, no, I'm absolutely fine."

"Shall take a little look at your feet?"

"There's no need," I said.

"Take off your shoes," Fischietti said, "feet can get gangrenous from one moment to another. You wouldn't like to lose them?"

"Not today," I said terrified, "tomorrow! We'll do it tomorrow," and I saw Santoro widening the jaws of vice by turning the screw in the opposite direction, and already enjoying the idea of applying it to my foot and closing the vice. "I can't at the moment," I said, "I have to study and I cannot be distracted. I can't do pedicures."

"Your health must always come first," said Fischietti. "If you've never had one, then a check-up is required sooner rather than later. Would you like an anaesthetic?"

On hearing these words, Santoro brimmed over with happiness and enthusiasm, and waved his vice in the air, "You should never procrastinate when it comes to corns; they can poison your life."

"That's true," I said, "but I don't have any."

"What does that matter?" said Santoro. "Sooner or later you'll get them. It would be in your own interests to remove your shoes, as you wouldn't want your sole coming away during the operation. You wouldn't want us to tear the stitching. It would be in your own interests to remove your

Chapter L

shoes, leather is never very resilient and it won't last if there's some tough work to do."

They had undone my laces: "Would you like an injection first?" I started to kick my legs around as hard as I could. "Calm down, Mr Jerome, this is a free service provided by the library." As I had stood up, they too stood up, and having grabbed hold of my laces, they pulled on them like reins. To avoid falling therefore, I jumped up and down on one foot and followed the other one. And I would have suffered a proper torment if they had not been miraculously distracted by the sight of Professor Rasorio fast asleep or deep in his cogitations. While I was leaping around I had wandered over towards him and grabbed the back of his chair. One of his hands was hanging down. They let go of my laces, and quickly tightened his hand against the table with their vice, which they turned as far as they could. Professor Rasorio woke with a jump and started shouting and pulling his hand, which had become livid and swollen, perhaps already suffering trauma to the metacarpi and phalanges. The fingers took the greatest pressure, and if he had continued to pull, he might have lost one of them; but because of the pain, he did not have the presence of mind to unscrew the vice. The two attendants were now bent double under the table; I could see but he couldn't. They were prodding that hand with a fork where it was most red and swollen. Fischietti held the fork, and Santoro had a Bakelite pen dipped in ink which he used for pricking the hand. These activities, which had the professor writhing, appeared to delight the both of them.

No one was in the room was doing anything, and yet this was a human being. So I released the vice, and I immediately felt the fork and pen pricking my calves and ankles. They pulled down on my pyjama trousers, but I resisted by holding the string with my hand. It was lowered slightly on one side, as though the elastic were broken, and I felt embarrassed just at the thought of the young lady turning up. Professor Rasorio had now freed his hand and was blowing on it and trying to loosen its joints. It was of course covered in ink scribbles. I was in danger of losing my pyjama bottoms, because they were now pulling with greater force and I imagined the undignified scene, and the shame was increased by the mere idea that I had turned up in pyjamas at all. So I picked up the vice that had been abandoned and used it like a truncheon on something – I am not quite sure what, perhaps a head or a horizontal wooden bar – but I did hear a whimper and they stopped their tugging.

"How can we study in peace?" I said. "This is not a library, but a conspiracy against scholarship. It is a place of damnation." The professor was of the same opinion, and I continued respectfully to vent my anger. "Even the books aren't books, but waste paper," and I showed him the chaotic pile of papers I had before me – full of feather, eggshell, hairballs and even the tiny bones of frogs and lizards. "And then they contain such things that are quite impenetrable. You don't know whether to believe them, whether they are scientific or absurd jokes played by some bibliophile who wants to confuse us – to get us lost and make us fail our exams." He continued to agree with me, and looked at me with approval while flapping his hand in the air to cool it down. I showed him a bone and he said, "There are even bigger ones; in some of the rooms there are giant bones, piles of lower jaws and even whole skeletons, but don't be alarmed." Under the table dogs could be heard chasing cats, unless of course it was just Fischietti and Santoro trying to attract attention. A bird was leaning out high up on one of the shelves; it was not a hen, but could have been a carrion crow. It was looking at me and the nocturnal panorama. "This is a jungle or it was one; it is a siege by demons in animal form."

He reflected for a little while and then, as though he were giving a lecture, he suddenly started to expound with considerable calm, "In actual fact, this library is extremely ancient. It was formed by natural sedimentation, but at a

Chapter L

certain stage, a mistake occurred. And libraries are not immortal: they are made of glue, string and cellulose. Initially this library settled quietly and forgotten, like a tomb. This happened some time ago, when my father was a child or perhaps many centuries before that. It lay in a penumbra covered with a thin layer of dust, and because of a lack of funding it was kept closed. It had a caretaker who, for want of a better expression, took care of it. He had the right to live in the two rooms of his lodge, but as there was no money in the budget and in fact no budget at all or even an entry in some other budget, he was the responsibility of a religious charity for the disabled, which appointed the caretaker from their most needy beneficiaries with a minimum pension. Whether by chance or simply because of a lack of other applications, they chose a blind man to be caretaker. And so it was for the last one too, but then it is said that it has always been thus, that it was an established custom, at least since the library came under state control, and no one knows exactly when that was. The ministry entered into an agreement with the charity for the transfer of the two rooms in the caretaker's lodge, but the rest – that is to say the rooms with the books – was not taken into consideration. This status quo persisted, as the areas in question were inventoried at the Land Registry as uncultivated state lands."

I was thinking that it was getting late; I wanted to interrupt him, but he just went on undeterred, as though he were reading a piece of paper written inside his head.

"This caretaker was there, but he never interfered with the books, never aired the rooms and never touched a thing. His sole duty was to keep the doors closed and not to sub-let or allow a third party to use the rooms as accommodation. Occasionally, he would leave his apartment and wander around the corridors without turning on the light: he had no need, and he listened always for that same perfect silence. Then he bolted the doors, not to stop anyone getting in but make sure nothing got out, but exactly what was never known.

"In those early times, there lived a silverfish in the midst of all that paper, without giving anyone any trouble. It was tiny – no more than a centimetre long and belonged to the Lepismatidae family of the order of Thysanura: flat, shiny, with three tails and very clean in its habits, it was in its own way a very gentlemanly and sober-minded insect that slept during the day and was up at night, because it had little liking for the light. It was joined by a few others and they lived in small communities scattered amongst the books; they drank the humidity where it appeared and gnawed imperceptibly at the surface of the papers and the corners of the vellum, linen, cotton and rayon covers. It was the era in which time had not begun and everything was still in a miraculous equilibrium. There were no draughts, changes in temperature or electric lighting. It was as though it were always six o'clock in a Sunday morning in the early spring, when there was still no light but darkness had already withdrawn, and it was neither hot nor cold: the early birds had not yet got up and the night owls had already gone to bed.

"It is not easy to imagine what happened first – what was the primary fluctuation. Some people say that the origins of time and the current ecological imbalance were the work of the three hens that the caretaker kept at his lodge together with a cockerel, for the simple reason that his pension was small and the hens laid eggs. He allowed them to scratch around in the library as he didn't have a courtyard of his own. He kept them under control with a long lead tied to their claws. They grubbed around amongst the shelves and ate the silverfish: in a way they did good to the books, but they could not avoid defecation, and being blind, the caretaker was not aware. So this led to the appearance of cockroaches. The Germanic cockroach, the American periplaneta, the common cockroach or Blatta orientalis and various other members of the family of Blattidae all made their way up through holes and the

Chapter L

waste pipes. They eat everything, but especially dirt, feathers, cardboard and even printed paper, while leaving behind little faeces that look like commas or exclamation marks without alphabetical significance, but which confuse the reader and ultimately mark entire pages with exclamations. For their part, the hens ate up the cockroaches with relish and grew plump. We don't know exactly what happened next; there is a theory that the contented hens started to lay a great quantity of eggs, which they left around the place, especially on the radiators, where they incubated and hatched. But there is a rumour that the cockerel escaped, and in the attempt to trap it using the hens as bait, the three hens also escaped and in no time they had returned to their wild state. The wild chicken is a proud and extremely enterprising bird, and they soon populated the entire library. On the one hand, this was a boon as it kept the number of cockroaches down, but on the other, it led to the arrival of mice, lice of the liposcelidae family, and then mosquitoes, flies and arachnids, which covered the entire place with spiderwebs. The era of the silverfish and the three hens appeared to have been lost forever. When the library was opened to the public and they brought in that zoological species we call the staff, there were already worms, moths, centipedes, ants and termites: the latter ones, typically light-averse isopterans, emptied the library from the inside of its books, floorboards, bones, ivory and metal, and constructed pinnacles of cellulose and cement. There was no money for chemical disinfestation, so some people used their initiative and imported cats against the mice, and a pair of foxes and a pair of weasels against the chickens. The hens went to live on top of the beams and bookcases, while down below the larvae and insects multiplied out of all proportion. Then, a little irresponsibly but with good intentions, it was unanimously decided to introduce the woodpecker, the golden oriole, the bat, the nightingale and the hoopoe, whose diet consists of lepidopterans, ichneumon wasps, froghoppers, silkworms, crickets, brown-tail moths, grasshoppers and other such insects. These measures were then reinforced by the introduction of green lizards, toads, common lizards, tortoises and chameleons, whose numbers, along with those of the birds grew exponentially and had to be controlled by the introduction of the hedgehog and various species of colubrids, corvids and diurnal and nocturnal birds of prey. Once you have gone down this road, there is no turning back, and to impede the hypertrophy of individual species, they had to introduce the entire zoological food chain. Thus the exuberant and sanguinary confusion of living things, whose remnants you see before you, grew from the inert substrate of books in the semi-darkness of the cellars or the light of a few electric bulbs.

"For the terrible calamity of the red ant, the Argentinean ant and several hundred other species there was no possible solution other than the pangolin, the numbat and the giant anteater, which in turn needed to be controlled by the spotted hyena and the African wild dog. Vultures and stray dogs took on the task of cleaning up the mess.

"Naturally small habitats were created according to the mix of light, temperature and humidity, because the library covers a vast area and many people were moving around it. The climates varied: ventilated near the grates, warm and damp around the radiators and cold to the north, where you could find pine martens and mountain hares. In some rooms there was desert and scorpions ruled, while in others a slight vegetation attracted small herbivores in large numbers. Cherry trees grew in a temperate corridor, and persimmons ripened in autumn. But vegetation was rare, because of the lack of sunlight. During some nights vast expanses became covered with mushrooms and moulds.

At some stage, the staff decided to use snakes against the invasion of mice. Unless you provoke them, it was said, snakes don't bite humans, and if you play a single note on a pan pipes or a bewitching berceuse, snakes can become man's loyal friends. So they introduced the rattlesnake, the

Chapter L

coral snake and the king cobra: clean and spectacular, but who could trust them? Some reckless fool released vipers close to the reference rooms. The humidity was such that tree frogs proliferated, which in itself was not harmful, but they mated so often and made such a noise in doing so that they could be heard everywhere, and this was not appropriate for a library; it was like living at the edge of a pond. However, you could wander amongst the books without danger if you played a piccolo, which made all the snakes withdraw. But as their numbers increased, it was difficult not to step on them. More than one scholar was bitten while he was studying and consequently died. What could you do? Obviously they thought about mongooses, secretary-birds and herons. There were also pigs, because someone said they are immune to poison and the instinctive enemies of snakes. But what didn't these pigs get up to! Everywhere defecation, effluent and smell; they rooted around the lower shelves in search of truffles, or just ate the books. If only, people would say, we could go back to the silverfish age! So the pigs were slaughtered and cut up for meat. What a horrendous thing! The screams in the reading room seemed just like those of human beings. The scholars trembled as they looked at each other. No one could read, no one could sleep; every now and then an attendant would appear, gloomy and covered in blood. Vicious rumours were heard when it came to sharing out the salami. Some people were so shaken that they slunk out and were never seen again. The others noted their empty seats and asked, 'So and so, what happened to him?' Rather unkindly the attendants would say, 'Who cares?' And so legends started to spread about obscure satanic rites and exemplary punishments relating to the handling of books. Nightmares were frequent, as were screams during sleep. People remained seated but always on the alert, which was extremely detrimental to their studies. They strained their ears worriedly: howls, roars and a continuous barking in the distance. The doors were always kept closed to avoid invasions, but every now and then a grass snake would come by, or a swarm of insects, bats, snails or lizards."

By now, I too was rather affected, and asked, "Are there any giraffes?"

"Of course there are giraffes; some people have seen them, but they are dwarf ones. As they are fearful of the cold, they huddle around the radiators. Many animals in here have undergone genetic mutations: there are fierce sheep that bare their teeth, enormous, lanky cats without claws or hair; there are philosophical panthers that yawn and weary of life. There is an elderly lion that is frightened of everything, including the fleas on its back, and there are wild boars that nibble the walls. In a cupboard which should be for brooms, there is an elephant that can no longer get out of the door: it eats paper and cardboard, is pale, bloated and toothless, and it has no proboscis. Some people talk of incongruous animals that breed only in libraries amongst books: tiny hippopotamuses, rhinoceroses that are so ethereal they resemble sparrows, fallow deer made of red powder, and solitary ants without powers of reason that waste their time singing in the company of grasshoppers. There is even talk of self-sufficient wolves that eat their own paws, their tails and very gradually the rest of themselves, until all that's left is the lower jaw which dies of hunger. Yes, this is what people say, but we don't know where such animals make their homes, whether they are inside or outside books."

Chapter M

Then Professor Rasorio returned to his cogitations, and consequently he fell like a deadweight right across me; even his head could not stay up. His hand covered in ink landed on my pages of philosophy and left hand marks that looked like stamps. From there, the hand bounced on to my pyjama and stained it. I took this dead hand and moved it away, as he was unconscious, just like our sleeping Natale. In fact he was completely laid out on top of me. But it was an indeterminate hand because it did not know where to put itself.

Santoro stuck his head out; he had an olive-coloured bruise on his forehead and was massaging it. They had remained under the table for all that time; I had felt ants climbing up my legs and very small and irritating bites, which I had scratched.

"You defend him," Santoro said with an expression both offended and malevolent.

"Yes," I said, "he's a very eminent professor."

Fischietti also stuck his head out; they were sitting on a very low trolley generally used for the transportation of books. Their heads did not reach the tabletop.

"Very eminent is your opinion."

"No, everyone says it." I think he had heard what Rasorio had said and everything Pantani had said, even though they always gave the impression of being distracted and entirely consumed by their minuscule idiocies.

Santoro addressed me from his position down below with his head at the same level as the table. He kept mixing up his words and laughing, while Fischietti wouldn't lay off interrupting him and even sticking his hand in Santoro's mouth to hold his tongue still.

"Yes," said Santoro, "this is how things stand. This here Professor Rasorio is just another professor amongst the many others there are in this world, who go around giving lectures. He had a lecture he was specialised in and they invited him to repeat it all over the place: public bodies, clubs, schools, foundations and that kind of thing, as I'm sure you can imagine. I was his pupil out there in the world, and so I looked after him. Lay off!" Fischietti meanwhile was pulling his lip with a crochet hook. "At the beginning the lecture was well thought-out, logical and in fact superb. I listened to it each time and can assure you that it flowed with wonderful naturalness from start to finish. While he spoke, he wasn't aware of anyone, including me, as though in a state of ecstasy. He wasn't even aware of the environment: he felt neither the cold nor the heat, neither draughts nor inclement weather. He entered this felicitous state an hour before the start of the lecture, and you had to keep an eye on him, because he couldn't hear car horns and his distracted mind could easily have led to his falling down the stairs. I helped him put on his jacket and tie, and accompanied him to the venue, as you would do with a blind man. But when they gave him the floor following the introductions in accordance with local custom, he always delivered an identical, masterful and perfect lecture. He even had a few mild witticisms that he recited with great art as though he had improvised them in that moment. Every time it was a great success, and every time they applauded. Even I, who followed him from place to place and heard him over and over again, was happy on each occasion. As time went on, I too wanted to learn this art, and prepared my own scientific lecture and would have liked to give lectures for the rest of my life."

"You!" Fischietti interrupted him, "pull the other leg."

"Yes, me," Santoro confirmed. "But then something happened. I don't know the reason for it – whether it was a normal evolution of this profession or something particular to a certain kind of temperament. He became affected by a slight lack of self-confidence which manifested itself in a terrible sensation of cold just before the start of the lecture. He would sit thoughtfully on his hotel bed and ask me questions, 'Which city are we in? Where am I going to be

Chapter M

speaking? Are you going to be there?' And then secondary questions, 'Will there be a microphone? Will there be a lot of people? What kind of people? Is it a theatre or a hall? Will I be standing or seated?' I would say, 'We'll find out in due course,' but he still felt that abnormal cold and wanted to know whether there would be radiators or whether he could keep his coat and scarf on. But once he had been introduced and given the floor, he forgot all these worries and returned to his normal temperature, and the lecture went ahead unaltered – that is to say perfect and just as it should have been.

"But it was in the period leading up to the lecture that he had lost his prior nonchalance and calm. He was now already worried while travelling by train and would have wanted the journey to go on forever. 'Let's just stay here,' he would mutter as he looked at the landscape from the train window. The sight of the station terrorised him. 'Why,' he would say, 'doesn't someone stop us from getting off? An order from the railway company: the station is dangerous! Would passengers kindly remain in their carriages. We apologise for any inconvenience, but all trains running today will be returning to their departure points with their passengers.' So we got off the train, and he would whisper, 'If only the loudspeaker would say: Professor Rasorio is not wanted in this city for reasons of public order.' He said other weird things such as, 'Do you think that this taxi-driver might think I'm a criminal and drive me straight to the prison?' That's impossible,' I would reply, and he would mutter, 'Sadly you're right.'

"But the greatest torment started during the hours of waiting in the hotel. 'I have lost my concentration,' he would say feeling the chill under his layers of clothing. Apart from the cold, he was besieged by worries and doubts. He tried going over the lecture again and again, he recited the sequence of the argumentation, the most significant sentences and then looked at me questioningly. 'What's up?' I would say. 'Nothing. Did I get that right?' he would reply. Then I had this idea that he could write two or three key words somewhere – on his hand for instance – to jog his memory. 'Just to ward off bad luck,' I would say, as he looked at me and thought about it, 'for your peace of mind, just in case you suddenly couldn't remember how to go on.' It did in fact happen that as soon as he was on the stage and got on with his lecture, he delivered it seamlessly and forgot all about the notes on his hand and was infused with that sense of calm and method that are the gift of all scientific endeavour. But he was also feeling the need to write not just words but also entire sentences. I could no longer approve, 'These are dangerous games.' I could not tell him why, but I knew it was a bad habit – it was antiscientific. Indeed, he was no longer the same once he had this idea in his head: he would say that concepts have to be well rehearsed; he might let slip some illogical statement, or run ahead of his argument or behind. That was like slicing the ball and the lecture would lose its levelheadedness. He would thank me, 'You came up with a good idea.'

"Then he started to get very upset if he caught sight of someone in the audience he had seen on a previous occasion. I had pointed one out to him so that he would be happy about having such loyal followers. But he wasn't and he only said, 'Who is this person? He'll be someone who wants to witness my downfall.' So he would say that someone was stalking him and hiding in the crowded halls and theatres. I would say, 'It's true, but he is just a passionate admirer.' And he would reply, 'No, that man is awaiting my downfall, for my throat to get blocked and for me to remain speechless as though in a trance.' 'Why would he want to do that,' I would try to reassure him, 'there could be no reason. The lectures have always gone exactly to plan.' 'I know these types,' he insisted, 'they bring bad luck.' And thus his nerves became increasingly rattled. I would look at the audience, and recognise not just one or two, but most of them. I told him, 'But this is normal: they are professors, teachers and even common mortals, with the air of those who want to listen to a

Chapter M

lecture and expect nothing else.' He said that I wasn't expert in lectures, and that it wasn't a matter of one or many or most; they are all like that. They come to see the spectacle, the circus. 'They want to see my downfall. They would like to see me humiliated and reduced to silence.' In the meantime, he continued to lecture going from one city to another. There can be no doubt that he was living on his nerves, and the lectures were being affected. He seemed to be searching for the words one by one, to avoid making a mistake, and in those intervals between one word and another, I too was distressed. The audience took all his attention. He looked at them with a mixture of defiance and anxiety, and the lectures increasingly resembled a brittle rock hurled down on the ground as though to make it crumble, but every time it just became more flattened and worn.

"The disaster occurred at Desenzano on Lake Garda, where he had to give his lecture to a famous club of cultured women and various lecturers similar to himself, some of whom were his personal enemies. That day, Professor Rasorio was beside himself. He paced his hotel room like a caged animal. He said that he could not afford to make a single mistake; the lecture had to be a flawless whole. 'What if I hit an obstacle?' he suddenly asked. 'What if a word – any word, perhaps even the least important word – simply eluded me and I could not articulate it?' 'But this has never happened,' I tried to reassure him. "Why should it happen today?' 'You never know,' he said; 'there are some expressions that only need me to forget a suffix or a pronominal link, and I am like a fish out of water. Last time it nearly happened to me, and the audience were already gloating.' Of course I was worried for him and said, 'Come off it! This lecture has been going for ten years. Are you saying that instead of being perfected, it could all fall apart now?' He said nothing, or rather he simply said, 'You don't understand.'

"I am sure that everything would have gone as it should have, if that miserable and, I say, inappropriate of idea of writing the whole lecture on his hand had not suddenly flashed into his mind. 'That's impossible,' I said, 'there are pores and wrinkles, skin is oily and then there simply isn't the space.' 'No,' he said, 'the hand is okay. It was your idea and no one is aware of it. And I just take a look at it when things start to go wrong.' 'But this is quite unheard of! A whole lecture! It's a scandal!' There was nothing for it: he wanted a pen and wrote half the lecture on the fingers and palm of his left hand. He then insisted that I write the other half on his right hand, which I did – right down to his wrist. He was cold and stiff. His heart was hardly beating. When we got to the theatre, he looked like a dead body still walking. I held him and pushed him up the stairs using all my strength. He held his hands up and waved them around like damp notebooks. I felt that it was going to end badly, because his idea was so unnatural. If he had written something on a few pieces of paper or a word or two on his cuffs, that would have been psychologically acceptable – but relying entirely on his hands!

"He went off to his place, observed by everyone. He was hobbling along very visibly, but I can tell you that he had never been lame. It was one leg that was baulking, that was tugging, that wanted to say, 'I strongly advise you to turn back.' But this was no longer possible, as I would have been the first to tell him. He sat down at the table all tense and looking smaller; so much so that I could hardly recognise him. The presenter introduced him very quickly. He spoke of Rasorio's international stature and what an honour it was to have him there as whatever else, it could never be said that Professor Rasorio had ever made a single mistake, not even a slip of the tongue. The professor himself confided in me afterwards that these were wonderful words and no different from the usual, but more noisy that evening because of his ears, which then shrank into him, and he could also feel his aorta, coronary arteries, ventricles and gastric artery tightening. This had never happened to him before: it felt like he had no blood and the lecture had drained out of him. He stood there in

Chapter M

full view of the people and looked at them one by one. He thought that he could recognise them all, that they had been convened from all the places in which he had spoken. Only one thought was clear in his head: an executioner's axe that was coming down behind him to cut off his head, which would fall on the table and then on to the floor where it would roll amongst the people's feet, and everyone would know that this lecture was not about to take place. Then they adjusted the microphone in front of him so that it was at the height as his mouth, and in that moment the only speech he could have made was an extended my God. He was thinking, hoping that an anarchist still had time to stand up in the audience and start firing a pistol at him from the second row; the first shot would go through his throat, and while he gasped for breath he would try to summarise his lecture in a single word, but the second would shatter the microphone and embed itself in the wall. The third, he imagined, would go astray and hit the presenter standing close by, knocking him to the floor dead or at least fatally wounded. After which, there would be absolute chaos; the anarchist would perhaps open fire on the crowd, emptying two magazines. Or perhaps he would throw a bomb, although his motive would always remain a mystery.

"Instead the scene unfolded much more simply: as though by the chance act of a nervous man stretching his stiff fingers, he opened his left hand and started to read from it in a mannered and metallic voice. And the audience were asking themselves: is he reading? The presenter was asking himself the same question, and peering at the hand, not understanding why it was open and why it was blue. Professor Rasorio lifted his eyes for a moment, and I believe that that was his fundamental error. He perceived a question hanging in the air, and noticed the man at his side leaning forward and displaying surprise, so that the professor's blood suddenly grew very hot and he turned red and started to sweat. Just looking at him made me sweat as well, but he had turned from deathly pale to bright pink.

His hand was now completely covered in sweat and the writing was running. It was no longer legible. The sentences were being erased and mixed together in the wrinkles and folds of his hand, and dripped down his arm into his sleeve. As he had been relying entirely on his hands – certainly not what I had suggested – he gradually lost contact even with the sound of his own lecture, which did continue for a little while. It was a drama that unfolded there on the stage. Rasorio was attempting to hide his hand, but also to blow on it and stop all the writing from being washed away. This just made him more sweaty and restless than before, and the sweat was pouring into his eyes and clouding his vision. He was uttering disjointed sentences which appeared to fall from his mouth, and all around him there stretched the homogeneity of an interstellar vacuum – absolute zero.

"He then drew his hand down over his face, without being aware of it – I think – as he had lost all sense of causal links, and stood there with his face now painted blue in the midst of general consternation.

"Two of us picked him up under our arms and carried him out bodily. We practically had to wring him out, because his hair, his shoes and his clothes were all soaking, and he was dripping like someone rescued from the canal. I slapped his hands. I don't know if he ever spoke again in public or if he comes here to prepare for his second lecture."

It should be said that while he was talking, Santoro would occasionally laugh like a madman and add, "All water under the bridge. Who cares any more? We were all so young." And Fischietti would give him an elbow in the ribs and say, "Shut it. You don't know what you're talking about. Who do you think you are? A professor?" Santoro would then laugh all the louder and between them they started to do those playful punches in the stomach and slaps on the face. While the other was talking, Fischietti had picked up a cockroach from the floor and thrown it in his mouth. Santoro had to interrupt himself to spit it out; he examined the half-drowned insect and then laughed again. There was also an exchange of elastic bands in the middle of story. I didn't know what to believe in the face of this behaviour: whether I should believe it or whether they were just tall stories expressly invented for me. However, it was clear that he was not an uneducated man, or had not been when he was young. Perhaps Rasorio and Pantani had also told tall stories; they were certainly unlikely, absurd and well calculated to upset my nerves, shock me, gnaw my mind and distract me. All of them seemed to be the shrill and malign voices of temptation.

Once more the hour rang out. It was five and my whole brain suffered from discomfort and toothache.

Chapter N

Santoro had put a bandage diagonally across his forehead with a tie and a bundle of paper, primarily with the intention of looking like a pirate and not so much to dress a real wound. They took turns in pushing each other on the trolley at high speed backwards and forwards around the reading room, and tried going under the chairs. It was actually Fischietti who was most interested in getting Santoro to pass underneath with shouts of "Forward into battle, my hearties", but with the malicious intent of making him bash his head on a sharp edge or corner of a chair or table. Santoro, however, seemed to lose none of his enthusiasm and after every collision, he repeated with the tie down over his eyes, "Forward into battle, my hearties!" They tried to get it to go at full speed between the arbitrator Pantani's legs, as he was standing a few metres away from me – I hadn't noticed him till then – and was looking blankly upwards towards Miss Iris, who for her part was up a ladder and apathetically putting books back on their shelves. They got caught up in the arbitrator's trousers and dragged him for a few metres against his will.

In the meantime, I had managed to remove Rasorio from on top of me, taking great care not to stain myself with that hand. I put him back in a position that appeared more professorial, but he had difficulty in maintaining it as he had becomes all droopy and doughy. I propped his head on his forearm and left him in that balancing act to his thoughts.

The two attendants kept whizzing around for some time, and repeatedly passed between the other two who were playing cards, thus creating even greater dust and disorder, and whipping up so much wind that I could barely keep control of my papers. One of them slipped my fingers and flew up into the air, and while I ran after it, the some other papers also escaped. At that moment Fischietti went by, shouting to Santoro: "Come on! Faster, much

Chapter N

faster," so that all the paper disappeared in a vortex. Lacking both brakes and a bearing to follow, they shot off into a corridor to a flurry of terrified chickens, and you could hear the clanking of metal and the rumbling of agitated voices from the ladders. And finally there was silence.

I found myself with the arbitrator Pantani behind me. He was increasingly indignant about the two attendants' behaviour and a rip they had made in his trousers. "There should be proper professional courses for attendants," he said, "and also a degree of natural inclination and a more sensitive approach." He looked at Rasorio with enormous respect and stroked his head.

"You're right, of course," I said, but I would have preferred to have been left in peace, alone with a book and in the hope of finding something.

Unfortunately he had categorised me in his mind as someone to unburden his woes onto. "You'll have seen what's going on! But we're impotent and besides it is easier said than done: we don't have the money for refurbishment; we don't have money for anything: not for pest control, not for re-cataloguing, not for reorganisation, not for the inventory; not even for dusting, sweeping and repairing doors, windows, shelving, glass cabinets, plaster and flooring, which is full of cracks. The lighting and ventilation systems are also in need of work. The fact is," he said, "that this library is not acknowledged by the civil service, and its staff are all here on secondment. When someone is unhappy with their position and their superiors are unhappy with him, because he is irascible or acerbic, they send them here. There is no career for them here. They are left waiting, as though on sick leave, and in a way they disappear from the world of the living. As they are always working nights, they sleep by day and are gradually forgotten – by their old colleagues, ex-girlfriends and all their friends of the past, who discover one fine day with surprise and regret that the dear friend they had lost sight of years ago has in fact died.

"Having said that, we must remember that there are between a hundred and five hundred thousand volumes in here, and perhaps more, perhaps three times that figure. But many of them have been lost, because they are not in their right place. They are buried amongst the others, and the catalogue is pretty much useless.

"It is always a matter of funding: the attendants are badly paid, cynical and do as little as possible. So who can expect them to put back every book scrupulously in its proper place? They put it in the first gap they see. Each one should therefore have a guardian, who follows them, checks on their work and draws up a report to certify the completion of correct shelving of a book. But this would mean doubling the number of staff. To everyone their personal guardian. There is then the question who is going to check whether the guardian is conscientious or slipshod? This is an old question. We have tried it on our more unreliable and unruly employees, but, would you believe it, the result was only scheming of the most invidious kind. I see it all the time on my travels. I had three of these guardians on trial and they were in hiding, one here and one over there in the corridors. They were meant to be taking notes without attracting attention. But one of these three, when he caught a woman making a mistake, would leap out like Silenus and immediately attempt to have sex with her. Given that he was powerfully built, he inspired awe and caused difficulties for the woman, who defend herself with the book which fell apart after three or four blows. The guardian, a certain Tiraboschi, who we unsuccessfully tried to have sacked to rid ourselves of that race, completely lost his temper at the sight of this resistance he considered insubordination, and only renewed his demands for immediate sex. He had a goatee, bad teeth and the smell of the stable, so no woman would ever be interested. He, on the other hand, never changed his mind. Indeed, the more they fled or pelted his head, teeth and groin with books, or aimed at his side with sharp and pointed bindings, the more he lashed out and

Chapter N

sought satisfaction, although in truth this was battle with a wide no-man's-land and the bruises he suffered would cause him elation and gratification.

"After a bit, he didn't even wait to catch somebody out; he would wait in hiding behind some bookshelf, old curtain or underneath a box, and anyone who passed by – were they men, women, young or old, or even old female inspectors – was stealthily followed through the jungle of books, and then at the opportune moment he leapt on them from behind and writhed about like a poor ravenous madman. It was not at all clear what kind of sexual relations he was seeking, or indeed what he understood by the term sexual relations. He made a great deal of noise, rhythmically stamped his feet and wanted to kiss the victim – all manner of confused behaviour patterns like a chicken trying to resist an attempt to pull its neck. In the end, no one wanted to venture into the storerooms, where the danger from the animals on the loose was compounded by the presence of this Tiraboschi. Accetto was sent with a stick to teach him a lesson, because it was said that Tiraboschi's nature had become goat-like and he was now living like a wild animal amongst the books with all manner of mischief in his head. You could hear him galloping along the corridors in an erethistic state and calling out loudly. He appeared at the gallop in public, ran across the tables kicking as he went, and threw himself on the Greek teacher to copulate with her or something similar."

"The Greek teacher," I said, "I've heard of her."

"Yes, the Greek teacher," continued Pantani. "As you can imagine, it was bedlam. Everyone was wary and disturbed by seeing this deranged being appear from the library's recesses and pitilessly and incomprehensibly torment the first old frump who comes along. Even after he had been driven off and pursued with curses, no one could return to their studies, still less concentrate on them. The teacher, red with emotion and shame, and unmindful of her Greek, smoothed out her tartan skirt and kept checking the door from which Tiraboschi had come out and to which he had returned in his retreat.

"So the system of introducing guardians was not a great success, because even the second one was not much better. He had the appearance of a grass snake and was called Bisolfo. His corruption took a different form: he demanded money. Not a large sum, but in return for keeping quiet, closing an eye on careless work. He wanted to be paid at least one *fernet*, an aromatic spirit of which he was particularly fond, and there were those who paid up, principally to get him out of the way along with his bad breath that smelt of cheap alcohol and vinegar. In the event of non-payment of the supposed debt, he attempted to tie up the unlucky victim and hide her away until the ransom was paid. He would drive her down a hole in the floor with his bad breath or steal one of her shoes with a piece of rope, which would be held against payment. He once captured an inexpert attendant and put her in a sack. The ransom he demanded was a pittance, but he still had to lower his price and finally agreed to a few small coins. In vain he kept the poor soul in that sack all night with Tiraboschi, who scented something and saw the jute material moving, while he was prowling the area menacingly and adopting various poses.

"It has to be said that the third one, known as Mr. Guastalamenti, was a more sophisticated little character. He got it into his head that he should check up on the other two, but given the turn of events, he ended up demanding a percentage from one and the right to witness the other's sexual manifestations. Indeed, he induced some of the girls with misleading advice to make mistakes in order to have more scenes to enjoy; just as the trap was set, he would withdraw and out jumped Tiraboschi with an asinine laugh, in no mood for argument but only for punishment, or rather for the imprudent act that his poor mind has classified as sexual intercourse. Just imagine! In the specific case of the attendant held in the jute sack, the third guardian – this Mr Guastalamenti – untied it to enjoy the scene. The terrified young lady made her escape so quickly that Tiraboschi, now at the height of his desire, furious with his ears now straight and pointed, made up for this by hurling himself on his colleague Bisolfo, beating him, inserting his head between some books, and mocking him by removing his trousers that tinkled with coins. To the scandal and dismay of everyone, he then threw those trousers on the head of a professor of ancient music right in the middle of the reading room. This was expressly prohibited by one of the regulations. You can imagine how this reflected on the library and what deleterious effects it had upon our studies!

"So this is what I'm trying to say: a library attendant should have a faith; it doesn't matter which, as long as it is inculcated in him from birth and becomes second nature. He has to be driven by a higher sense of justice in putting a book back in its right place, because when he is alone in the darkness of a corridor and no one is around, only a disinterested love of creation can guide him to make every one of his acts a spontaneous sacrifice, a joy and a desire to do good. This is what my emotions tell me all the time. But in here they are all cynics and scoundrels, who think of nothing but fornicating, stealing and touching each other up. Perhaps good example would be enough, even from a distance, but not threats."

Here I interrupted him with a whole lot of excuses, because he would have droned on all night, whether I was there or not. Seeing that Iris was not far off, I took out the examination card and called her over. She said that you couldn't read a thing and needed a microscope. I said disconsolately, "But my exam is tomorrow morning." Then Pantani, suddenly adopting the gravitas of a mayor or even deputy mayor in a plenary session, tore it from my hand and, holding it far away from his eyes as you would expect of a presbyopic person, he read it or pretended to read it, and solemnly nodded. Iris was laughing behind his back and making eloquent signs not to take any notice of him. Pantani seemed very confident however, and was muttering a series of foreign names as though he were reading them. "Wait a minute," Iris unexpectedly said, "what we need here is Mrs Bucato; she knows about exams and teaches Greek." All that came to my mind was the orang-utan and Natale's misfortunes, always supposing they really happened as Fischietti described them, and I would have preferred Iris's private assistance; in fact I would have prized it. But she just said, "I'm off to get her," and disappeared. Pantani took a birthday-cake candle out of his pocket, lit it and, using this light, he very pompously ran along the books on a nearby shelf, as though he knew just what I wanted. "There's no need to go to all that trouble," I said, but he replied, "For heaven's sake, no trouble at all! When I can be of some assistance..." but the way he held his head and curved his eyebrows gave me the impression he could not see a thing and was feeling his way. Was it all just to make him seem important in my eyes? "Here it is!" he exclaimed. "What is it?" I asked him timidly. "Read this, it will do you no harm." It was a large, very ostentatious box. With grand, ceremonious gestures he placed it on the table on the corridor side and pointed to the high-backed chair that went with it. It was all buffoonery. "I'll leave you here to your work," he said, "I have a few things to do." Off he went sheltering the candle's flame with his hand. I opened the box and, as I suspected, "it was all a joke." There were cigarette butts, ash and a scanty pile of papers carelessly torn from some poor book. Instead of making progress, I thought, things just keep getting worse. While waiting for Iris, I read the title with a sense of unspeakable weariness: "Retrogrades". Well, how about that for a coincidence, I said to myself.

Retrogrades

As with all things concerning humanity, this business of going forwards is just an institution. There are some people affected by the phenomenon of walking backwards: they are retrogrades.

Chapter N

How do you become a retrograde? We don't know this scientifically, because there are very few cases and they are all very different. For instance, during processions organised for sundry and recondite reasons, whether trade-union, some strange cult or a wedding, there is usually something that impedes the regular forward movement. Vociferous arguments can be heard, as can expressions in dialect, and someone says, "But this person is going backwards rather than forwards!" Here is an example: a participant, subject to a sudden inspiration and perhaps oblivious of the setting and his companions in the procession, stops dead still with a question mark imprinted on his face. The others all around him, who don't have any punctuation on their faces, either go round him or into him, with a little altercation between the stationary him and their inertial forward movement. The next thing that happens to him is that the ideas that previously sat firmly and solidly in his head start to go backwards, and consequently he too takes a step backwards, because his intuition tells him that the place inhabited by his ideas is the most appropriate place for him to be as well. However these backward ideas keep pulling him backwards, and he continues to take steps in the opposite direction to the flow, with the consequent chaos of feet and bad tempers and accusations of not being in tune with the procession, as can well be imagined. At this stage, the person in question starts to run blindly like a crab against the flow, because he is anxious about himself and his own thoughts, and creates clashes and intolerant reactions with shouts of "ow" and "fucking this, fucking that, who do you think you are? Where do you think you are?" Eventually he gets to the end of the procession and there's no one left – just a few bicycles, sweet papers and an unmarked police car. Breathless and happy he is reunited with his own thoughts which had stopped under the branch of a tree, where they buzzed and swarmed.

We can only infer from this that retrogrades are not born retrogrades, just as we now know that people are not born progrades: we become progrades because of our upbringing, given that this habit of going forwards has become well established and carved in stone amongst us Indo-Europeans, as well as the Hamitic and Semitic peoples. Retrogradation has been completely expunged from the civilised mind, except here and there, possibly in geographically remote regions during states of ecstasy or somnambulism usually induced by the consumption of spirituous liquids.

When questioned, retrogrades say that it is the other people who are going backwards and that the concepts of backwards and forwards are entirely subjective. They say that we westerners are dogmatic and blinkered, and only see what is a few metres from our noses, an area that we pompously define as "ahead". But the nose, in their opinion, is just a kind of tail which contains an orifice that should be kept closed in the interests of us all.

It is axiomatic that retrogrades can be found in taverns, cafés and streets particularly after dark. For example, it is eight o'clock in the evening, and Mr X is in a café, where he has spent the entire day. He gets up reluctantly and all he has in his brain is a comprehensive "Oh shit!" then he sits back down and gets up as though an idea was entering and leaving his head continually. People can see him looking at his watch and emptying his glass. The owner of the café has already lowered the shutter halfway down the main entrance, and says, "Goodbye then, Mr Artom." Mr Artom, always supposing that is his name, has just thought very emphatically about his mother-in-law, his wife and his five children who all await him at home, and fully aware of his situation replies, "Goodbye." Instead of going towards the door, however, he enters a broom cupboard back first. There is no one around except the owner, who pulls him out with considerable difficulty because his legs are kicking the ground like a wild animal and gaining leverage in the midst of the brooms and buckets of sawdust. From there the owner pushes the recalcitrant customer towards the door with a friendly arm. He lowers his head to pass under the shutter and as soon

Chapter N

as he is outside on the pavement, he faultlessly turns his head in the direction of home, namely to the left. He then aims for the doorway which is just ten metres away, and in his imagination starts quite peacefully to walk forwards, only he is not; he is going backwards. Now you might say that this is due to the slight downward slope behind him, but actually he is the one who in that very moment is inclined to walk in this fashion – initially rather cautiously but then in an increasingly relaxed manner. There is no one on the street, and in no time he is at the bottom of the slope, and crosses the junction backwards. The front door of his home is receding further into the distance and getting smaller as it does so, rather like driving a car and looking at something in the rear-view mirror. He can also see the bar owner who is waving his arms and shouting, but he is now travelling very fast. There is a gate in the wall, and he turns into it perfectly. Exactly how he manages this is not at all clear, because he is practically running backwards and cannot see a thing. There he crosses the garden miraculously avoiding bushes, fountains and worse. This is a distance of two hundred metres over a lawn, and he is moving with the smoothness of a twenty-year-old, while in fact he is seventy-four. Then there is a steeper downward slope towards a stream and he goes down still at his uncommon retrograde speed. We cannot know what Mr Artom is thinking in these final moments – whether he is experiencing some form of exhilaration or nullification, or whether he feels something calling out to him. The fact is, however, that at the end of the lawn he strikes his occipital bone against the branch of a pine tree, not powerfully, but clearly enough for him, because he dies.

One of the observations made about this incident was the following: on his way to the café in the morning, Mr Artom would often expose his head to the sun, which caused it to overheat, and so when he entered the café it was already inflamed to some degree. These sudden changes in ambient conditions inevitably affect the psychological personality and lessen the taboo on retrogradation.

What exactly is retrogradation or retroambulation? We can now assert that it is the entrance to the famous kingdom of the dead.

There is a group of beliefs or traditions spread over a vast area running from the Caucasus to the Carpathians, from Asian Siberia to the Iranic Plateau and the Asiago Plateau, and from Inner Mongolia to Friuli and Venezia Giulia. These belief systems all agree that the descent into hell is always done walking backwards: the dead suddenly get up and are no longer themselves, but unknown beings who retrograde; the back of the head and neck are the new face that moves ahead of itself without seeing and descends the steps of the hereafter. Hell is simply a place in which the dead bump into each other with the terrible and grating sound of bones clattering against each other, because they wander around aimlessly and backwards and all appear to be utterly befuddled.

Thus whoever walks backwards during their life is by analogy in communication with the dead, even the dim-witted man who might as well have been blind as his eyes were no use to him. He wandered the woods, it is said, in a state of torment and sonorously collided with tree trunks. When he reached the end of a wood, he wandered around and often fell off a cliff. There he lay until he woke up again and went back amongst the living. He rediscovered the ability to go forward and using his hands and eyes, he climbed the mountains, crossed the woods and one day reappeared at home like someone back from the dead. From then on he was held in great esteem and considered to have powers of second sight.

We have reached the point in the argument in which should discard all ambivalence: does a land of the dead exist? Yes, it does exist, but not in any particular place. The land of the dead has been put upside down in time, and there everything is going backwards: the grass snakes, cats and geese that live there all go backwards, as do the donkeys, goats and sheep. But trees also go backwards,

Chapter N

given that from dried up they become green and vigorous, then grow smaller and finally become seeds. The rivers – and there are many of them – flow upwards and back to their springs. The rains go up from an enraged sea and evaporate into black clouds, which in turn fly backwards. Even the winds blow in the opposite direction and are like profound inhalations. Night comes before day, and a kind of sunset sun appears in the west and goes back over the hours until it is midday and then morning, dawn, and the first glow on the horizon. Then the cockerels can be heard calling "cock-a-doodle-do", and the dead drink their coffee, shave their beards and leap into bed.

Moreover the dead swallow horrible and pestilential excrements through orifices in their posteriors and then they expel them from their mouths in the form of excellent foods: salami, cotechino sausages, spaghetti, wines from Orvieto and Frascati, roast chicken and boiled fish. At lunchtime, the dead sit down at table and everyone vomits on their own plate and spits in their own glass, until the table is entirely laid out with sumptuous foods. Then the waiters appears – they are also dead of course – and walking backwards they carry all plates and food into the kitchen, where the cooks put it in different pans on the cooker to cool it down very slowly: the fish is then returned to the sea and the salad to the vegetable garden. When the dead talk, you can imagine that first comes the reply and then the question. When they meet, they say goodbye, and then stop to have a chat. It is only at the end that they make a show of recognising each other with exclamations of joy and embraces. After that, each goes his or her own way, still backwards and entirely oblivious of each other.

This upside-down world is neither more beautiful nor uglier than our own one, but it is still more incomprehensible. For example, anyone who has a swollen black finger must instinctively reach for a hammer and a nail stuck in the wall, as a medicine. By putting the affected finger between the nail and the hammer, it is immediately healed, although the reason is not at all clear. But if the nail comes away and there has been a picture hanging on it, this is taken back to the framer who takes off the frame and gives money to the customer.

The dead believe in absolute determinism, and can in fact foretell everything that is about to happen, except things that are too far away or indistinct. On the other hand, they forget every event in the instant it occurs. For example, they are entirely aware of all the people they are yet to meet, but as soon as they meet them, they completely forget them and think they don't exist. For them the past is a land of vague hopes, and the future is perceived as an irrevocable destiny, so they often say disconsolately, "What could I possibly have done in the past to end up as badly as I am going to end up?" they have cities that spring up like mushrooms during an earthquake, but to have them removed they need architects. Amongst the dead, they make it up before they argue furiously, and then they forget everything, as though it had never happened. As for the court system, the general practice is that for no particular reason they serve a period of time in prison, then go through a regular trial, at the end of which they are always released. And in all this process there is some obscure justice, because the accused in the land of the dead spontaneously and secretly returns the stolen goods or, on seeing the victim, removes the blade or bullet, and the victim is cured. Afterwards, the victim and the culprit go innocently on their separate ways, their memories freed of all viciousness.

In conclusion, however, even the dead cannot go on forever: as time passes, they lose cognition of their own future, until they curl up and eventually produce a vagitus inside a leaded box in the company of their poor bones.

Chapter O

Evidently I had fallen asleep while reading. I woke up suddenly with an acute pain in my mouth. Fischietti, seated on top of the back of my chair, had his feet on my shoulders and was holding my mouth open with a hook. Santoro was on my knees and keeping my hands still with his legs, was hammering one of my teeth, the very one that had been causing me so much pain. They had tied my ears to the chair with string, and one had been tied so tightly that the blood could not circulate and was already almost completely deadened. I pulled and screamed in pain; that ear was on the same side as the tooth, so the combined agony rose to my head and thundered in the cavity of my left hemisphere. They appeared happy, as though it were a game, and they invited me in mime and in their exclamations to take part. Fischietti repeated, "How wonderful, how wonderful!" and Santoro laughed, while with every blow of his hammer he would say, "There you are; sir has been well looked after." I roared with my mouth open and I tried to wriggle free, but they interpreted this as meaning that I was enjoying myself – that I was saying "enough, enough, stop it please" as a joke or to make the company laugh. When Santoro got hold of the blacksmith's tongs and started to wobble all my teeth on the left side of my jaw, Fischietti was so overjoyed that he beat his fists on my head. The pain was such that tears of despair were not enough; in fact it seemed that I was laughing as loud as I could, and laughing so much that I had both tears and hiccups. I have no idea how long this torture went on for; three times I heard the chimes for five o'clock, and Fischietti underscored each chime by rapping his knuckles on my cranium and counting them in a loud voice. Santoro happily repeated the number and echoed it with his tongs.

A little door opened and out of the corner of my eye I could see Miss Iris returning with the Greek teacher, just as she had promised. Her reappearance was enough to disconcert my tormentors a little.

"What's going on?" she said and her expression was stern. Santoro stopped, and then so did Fischietti. "Miss Iris!" they said. I now only had the ear that continued to pulse under the knot they had tied around it. I too said, "Miss Iris!" with tears in my eyes and I would have liked to get down on my knees before her. I could smell her fragrance in the air. She smiled at me like an angel sent by our merciful God to free me. Behind her in the entrance of the door, the Greek teacher Albonea Bucato was listening to us. I had heard so much about her that I knew her. She was the thin woman with a woollen turban who had come into the library at the same time that I did. Iris had picked up the volume that was in front of me and was using it to deliver heavy blows mainly to Fischietti, who had fallen off the back of the chair, saying "What am I supposed to have done?" and then she turned on Santoro who had leapt off my legs whimpering, "I was helping him, assisting him – that's all." The pages were flying all over the place, and then the box disintegrated. Miss Iris clearly had authority over them that could not be challenged, and this was more important than the force or weight of the volume. I was able to free my ears. The Greek teacher was now providing backup, and was pushing them away, while assertively flourishing her dress. Fischietti went behind her and attempted to light its hem, but only created black smoke and no flames. Whimpering Santoro started to laugh and wanted to use his tongs. In fact he succeeded in gripping her dress with them and pulling, almost unravelling the whole of it. The teacher rebelled, but the dress was now up to her knees and you could see her suspender belt. Not a pretty sight. Fischietti set fire to her hair from behind, and it went up in a blaze. She just took the flaming hair off, as it was a wig, and used it as a weapon against them, finally driving them away, and their instruments of torture with them.

Chapter O

Then she put out the flames and returned her hair to her head, as the wig was not that damaged. There was only one area where the hair had melted together and looked like twists of wood shavings. She adjusted her tights and her dress, and stayed in the background with the expression of a person accustomed to such things, and interprets them as the sexual vicissitudes that women generally have to put with.

Possibly drawn by the commotion and my screams, the two card players had come over for a closer look, and also two young female attendants who were perhaps just passing by. They had formed a small crowd around me and my chair. They touched my ear to feel its temperature and came out with some very high numbers, almost in admiration. The women examined the Greek teacher's dress and hair. "This library is dangerous for women – and men too," they pointed at me at this stage, "but more for women." I sought out Iris's eyes; she smiled and said yes.

"There are dangers of every kind," they said, "but for us women they are nearly all of a sexual nature."

"I understand, of course," I said, "you shouldn't talk to me about it, as I am not involved. You should speak to the arbitrator Pantani; he is very responsive to this argument." This triggered a unanimous chorus of "Oh yeah, he's just the guy you need!" Even the Greek teacher pulled a face that expressed both commiseration and contempt. The two card players laughed.

So in spite of the confusion of voices and everyone's desire to have their own story heard, I was made aware of the following: when he is close by – at a distance of about one or two metres – this arbitrator Pantani is the perfect gentleman, dignified, respectful and buttoned up. In other words, an upright and moral man, even in what he says. The Greek teacher said that up close he is a real coward. As the distance increases, he becomes more and more brazen. As soon as he is in the far distance, for example at the end of a corridor and believes he can see a woman fifty metres away, he immediately exposes his sexual organs and then maintains that position for hours, irrespective of whether someone is there or not. Given that in here it is generally dark, he carries a candle about and holds it low and close so that it always throws light where he wants it. It seems that he started off on this career many years ago in the country. He was the mayor and at the same time an alderman. If he saw a peasant woman or a holiday-maker in the distance but was able to guess her sex vaguely from her clothing, he exposed himself and stood there challenging her for hours, even when she had gone and there was no one on the horizon. The only thing that concerned him was that the sun should not put his genitals into the shadow as it travelled across the sky. He did nothing else: no ugly gestures or signals, partly because the distance was such that it would have been a waste of time. It would even have been a waste of time to point to his tabernacle and assert that it existed. This habit, they assured me, is often found in arbitrators and aldermen, and goes with the habit of holding rallies and engaging in propaganda activities. While they expose themselves, they shield their eyes with a hand and look elsewhere, towards an ideal point a few degrees higher in the sky along the ecliptic. They remain in that pose as though they had seen an aerostatic balloon and were consequently desirous of getting as must as possible out of it. They do not lean on a tree or sit on a bench; they can continue to stand for very long periods. The value of distance varies according to the visibility: less distance is necessary when there is fog, heavy rain, sleet or a whirlwind or when the sun has not quite risen. During clear days of high wind they position themselves a kilometre away from the houses and look into the air as though there were nothing odd about this behaviour.

As he got older, Pantani naturally found that his eyesight was fading, which put him into a permanent and exhausting state of alarm: he always suspects that there is a woman or something similar that has become confused

Chapter O

with the landscape, and he is there making no use of her, no better than someone who simply goes into the countryside to dig and rake the ground. So narrowing his eyes and shielding them with his hand – for he has no wish to demean himself by wearing glasses – he spends the entire day examining the distance while turning in a circle. If a piece of clothing flaps, he immediately adopts his pose and stays there; equally if he hears a voice at the top of a hill, he thinks that some woman must have appeared on the ridge. He is often wrong. So he can be seen at midday in August, far far away at the end of a newly harvested wheat field with those genitals on display again, static in the windless summer air. He perhaps does not know what is going on; he has the appearance of someone who simply does what has to be done, and doesn't know how to do anything else.

In the end they transferred him to the library, where he is a member of the management board, arbitrator and watchdog. He is not a real danger, but in the long run he is tiresome; it is not clear what he wants, nor what he is supposed to represent.

"Perhaps it is a love of creation," I said.

"Look over there!" Everyone started shouting and getting excited. There was a little light in the distance, a cemetery light and nothing else. Iris whispered to the Greek teacher whose eyes were flashing. The small gathering dissolved.

Everyone rushed off, including Iris, in whom I placed so much hope. "Wait for me, Iris; I need your help," I managed to mutter in time. She turned with her smile, as though it would be a pleasure to give me a hand and perhaps much more. "Come with me," I heard her say before she rushed into the corridor. I jumped to my feet with such emotion that the table jumped with me, and Professor Rasorio, who had his head finely balanced on his forearm, had broken free of his moorings because of the undulatory tremor, and fallen on his side. "Wait for me, Iris," I said while I tried to pull the professor up and rebalance him. He was very heavy and kept falling back on top of me: this was not normal sleep. Eventually I managed to raise him up and prop him up against the back of the chair with his arms hanging down and once more dead to the world. Because of the exertion of lifting him, the tooth that Santoro had been hammering was pulsating once more and I was conscious of the pain.

I entered the corridor, but it was so dark that instead of running, I had to feel my way along, my hand touching the wall and my feet checking out the floor. In the far distance, there was the light of a candle – no more than a speck – and perhaps a human shape. It was easy to surmise, if everything that had been said was true, that there was the arbitrator Pantani in pose and illuminating himself. But you would have needed binoculars. But perhaps that meant that Iris had come by and I was therefore on the right path. "Miss Iris," I called out, "Miss Iris." But the only response was an owl in the distance, and even further away I could hear a donkey braying. I nearly fell down some steps and the trolley used by Fischietti and Santoro whizzed between my legs.

The light became slightly brighter as I slowly made my way along the corridor. Then I got the whiff of something; initially I didn't know what it was – perfume or natural smell. Then I felt a hand taking mine, and a flash of sensation in my nostrils. Full of happiness, I recognised her. "Iris," I said. No answer. She did not a say a thing, but she held me tight. "Iris, is that you?" And she just said, "Sssshhh!"; it was an imperceptible shush. "What's up?" I said under my breath, but she just continued to shush me very quietly and lead me along. "Where are we going?" and she shushed once more, but not to keep me silent, as it was her confidential way of speaking in the dark; words and a voice generally ruin everything, while in some cases a shush and silence make women feel closer and more attached to a man. Her fragrance was particular, and I could not exactly define it. In part, I recognised her splendid and noble perfume, but in part it was new and

Chapter O

more persuasive, as though the number of airborne molecules then unknown to me, raised to the second power, could tickle my mouth and, rising through the mucous membranes of my nose, warm them for me. Not only did they suggest flowers – so much so that I was almost stupefied – but also and more subtly truffle, cheese, pepper, wild quail and hare. They were fragrances that rose up into my imagination and lit my way.

The night, however, was so dark that I could not see a single thing. She held my hand and I went with her, unsure of my feet because of the darkness that covered the floor and the aromatic trail she left behind her, which I drank in with an open mouth. I don't know what was under my feet; it felt as though I was crushing the pages of broken books, but I took little notice. Even my exam had disappeared into a very remote area of my thoughts, where it lingered enervated and locked away together with my toothache.

She too was keeping close to the wall and feeling her way along it, until she found a small door and went up some steps. I would have liked to speak, to ask her: where are you taking me? so that she did not think I harboured any ulterior motives, that I was a hardened playboy who knew how to induce women into temptation with his own particular method. I would have liked to have said something complimentary that signified that apart from the tight grip of her hand to guide me through the dark, I hadn't noticed anything the slightest bit compromising. And therefore we could have returned to our sincere and disinterested friendship. We climbed the spiral staircase without letting go of each other, seeking out the steps with our feet like two snails that withdraw into a single shell. Perhaps, I thought, when we get up there where the stairs are even narrower, I would pull her hand or she would already be close enough, and I would kiss her. Yes, in that moment my imagination was fixed on that one thing: to hell with books; to hell with exams! I was holding one of her hands, and I would have touched her mouth with the other to avoid all mistakes, and in the darkness I would be guided by radar. I would get closer and closer moving in a straight line until I detected the infrared rays that herald the close vicinity of the opposing mouth, just millimetres away. And then what do I do? I asked. I would have drowned, and not just myself, but also my soul in its entirety.

I had to find an excuse, while I was still in time: a perfect sentence that I could offer her, so that she could rest on it without shame, as on a cushion, and allow herself to be caressed by my magnetic wave. Otherwise she might have screamed at the moment of my pulling her towards me, and done so with all the breath in her lungs. Perhaps she would have called me contemptible and exploitative – the kind of person who goes into a library to eye up the women, push them under the stairs and leap on them like a mountain goat. Underneath that air of scholar and bibliophile there lurks a filthy worm lying in wait amongst all that culture, this is what she might have thought. Yes, the kind of person who goes around kissing people all over the place, just anyone who happens along in front of him. Sensing that I was at the top of the stairs and very close to the point where you have to get down to business, I had my sentence ready and waiting: My dear young lady, I would say while squeezing her hand to make a greater impression, in order to meet your desires in part, I now give you all my particulars. I would then declare my surname, registered address at the Office of Births, Deaths and Marriages, and anything else she might have wanted to know. Indeed, I would have said: My dear young lady, in order not to have you think ill of me in relation to... In relation to what? I asked myself. While I was turning this over in my mind, we had reached the room at the top. I lifted my eyes towards a source of dim light: it was a dormer window that looked out onto what must have been a starry night, which however we could not see. Who knows what kind of place it was, as it was still very dark. Perhaps it was an observatory at the top of a tower. I certainly did not think that there was a bed there, given that we were, after all, in a library. But then we actually bumped into one: first her and then myself. I wanted to express my apologies and swear to her that I had not put it there myself: it was entirely fortuitous. Clearly there are some Don Juans around who prepare beds all over the place: beds that come out of the wall or when they pull on a drawer, and they say, "Hey, did you see that? It's a bed." I have often heard that they set them up in the countryside in various strategic spots. They go for a walk with a young woman deep in conversation about studies and the school, and suddenly there in the middle of a meadow they come across a bed. Naturally this is the source of some mirth. "But how could it have got here?" says the girl. The Don Juan laughs along with her, shaking his head as though he knows nothing about it, but is always ready to enjoy the unexpected surprises fields can sometimes produce. He takes her arm in his and says jokingly, "This must have been a house removal or someone has been very careless. Let's take a closer look. Come with me." Sometimes, a Don Juan will put a bed in the shade of some bushes, if he is thinking of going there at the hottest time of day. Another might put them actually on top of trees, in the middle of a wheat field, and in the ditches, so that the girl, guided there by imperceptible readjustments of direction, has a good probability of ending up in one or other of the beds. I did not want to be associated with them or their methods: I went into the library innocent and empty-handed. God alone knows how this temptation weighed heavily upon me and my duties.

Suddenly without any forewarning and without any memory of the obligatory transition involving a kiss, I found myself blindly undoing petticoats and corsets, and removing underwear that at each stage released further layers of aromatic evaporations. And then, I seem to remember, even more intimate, inebriating, silky and lace-covered lingerie. I was kneeling in front of this being I could not see, but every cubic centimetre of her exuding womanhood and, as they say, overly in the areas that matter. And she could have told me no, but instead she was on the bed like rising dough before it goes in the oven. In fact, she, with great heart-warming generosity, came under my hands to let herself be kneaded.

If the truth be told, the exam was still occasionally knocking at the door even in this critical moment, up there in the tiny corner of my brain where it skulked and pulled its painful strings to recall my attention: it pulled on my colon, pancreas, intestine and alimentary tract – all in a state of anxiety – and drew them up towards the throat. For a second I thought I was suffocating. I swallowed, made the exam go silent again and returned to my palpable present – to Iris. She could have sailed on a wide berth – on the horizon of my life without knowing anything of me, as do the beautiful women who navigate the high seas in full view of us all – blonde and the bunting of a full flag dressing fit for a naval review – to the perdition of mankind. Instead she did not say no, she did not say anything and did all she could to encourage me. My heart told me continually to thank her, a compulsion to express gratitude that filled my eyes with tears and emotion.

By now, I had unfastened everything that was unfastenable and sniffed everything that was sniffable, all the while seated cross-legged almost at prayer on that supposed bed, and I was suddenly affected by a mystical spirit, as I imagined her laid out before me like the naked earth. There was no longer just Iris, but a great toing and froing of kindly and obliging young ladies, offering all the temptations that rose through my limbs towards my head and further upwards: beyond my cranial roof, beyond the skylight and beyond the astronomical night. I don't know whether it was heaven or hell, or whether it was simply a case of levitation. I felt a note vibrating inside and what I was experiencing was pure philosophy. I felt like a cloud of pollen that scatters across a meadow on to all those beds and in every place, everywhere there is a secret storeroom in waiting. This is the mathematical law of nature.

Chapter O

She was once more kissing and I had fallen backwards and helpless. The earlier kisses had been sweet, while now she kissed all on one side exactly where my tooth was hurting. I moved my mouth, but she used I don't know what method to keep turning with me, as though she had endless hands, and always insisted on kissing me there, so that I felt the increase in my tooth's swelling and inflammation to be exponential. Even the two or three teeth next to the aching one were now wobbling dramatically. These kisses of hers had a method that resembled an electric drill; I moaned, but not with pleasure. I was now suffering excruciating pain that had spread to my palate, my nose and my face. Perhaps she thought she had found my sensitive spot, my erogenous zone, but they didn't feel like traditional kisses, but rather metal screws digging into my nerves. It was dark and I could not understand her manoeuvres. Was she using her hands or some metal device? I couldn't understand what she wanted with that tooth, until I felt it coming up by its root, as though she were taking it out with a corkscrew. I could stand it no longer and to avoid screaming I grabbed on to her hair at the height not of my ecstasy but of my agonies. The hair seemed to be made of nylon. I pulled a couple of times but the hair came away in my hand.

"What's happening?" I cried. But she had not screamed at all, and I felt her head and it was as hard and bald as the head of a match. Now I was terrified. I touched her ears and they were bristly; I touched her face and there were individual hairs, horrifyingly scaly; her skin was like a cheese grater.

"Iris," I muttered, "who are you?" and all that perfume of fresh bread, hedgerow and marvel of Peru instantly turned into a foul smell. It is not that there had been any chemical change, but it seems that that was the moment I opened my nostrils and smelt what was under the surface: there was the smell of tartar, female orang-utan straight from the zoological gardens, mixed with the scent of sawdust and garlic.

"Who are you?" I said to this unknown being. "Make yourself known!"

"It's Albonea, my dear." It was the Greek teacher, Mrs Bucato. Six o'clock chimed very clearly. I remembered that I had a match. I kept my mouth closed and protected with one hand, and with the other I lit the match. The first thing I saw was Albonea Bucato on a pile of old cardboard boxes and rags, with her wig on back to front. Behind me some mice and other animals must have been scurrying about. Before the match went out, I was able to see Santoro and Fischietti scurrying away themselves. I don't know where they came from, nor when. Were they in collusion with the Greek teacher? Perhaps they were her lovers and this was their way of having fun. Santoro was waving a corkscrew about. Then the light went out.

Chapter P

I hurried away. Or rather I would have liked to, but it was so dark that I could hardly stand up. And to think that I had come into the library to study. It was Circe's cave, and Iris perhaps the unwitting instrument of the Greek teacher – used as a bait to satisfy the latter's sexual purposes. Unless she, cynical and perfidious, was in collusion with Mrs Bucato, for the mere pleasure of bewitching people and getting them to fail their exams. How had I managed to mistake one for the other? And where was I? I followed the bends in the wall with an unpleasant smell clinging to me and the taste of tartar in my mouth. I found a door, opened it, and crossed a small room towards a keyhole through which a ray of light was shining. I knocked and heard someone getting up from a chair and coming to open the door for me.

It was a dirty and dilapidated office with a fifteen-volt light that hung on a long wire. Some of the plaster had come away from the wall and lay on the floor, and I found myself treading on sand, chippings and flakes of plaster. The metal furnishings were all piled up on one side, and mainly upside down. On the other hand the attendant who opened the door was wearing a smart, spruce and light-coloured uniform with stripes on the arms to show his rank.

"Hurry and get me out of here," I said curtly. He came over towards me, courteous and deferential. He studied my pyjamas and wrinkled his nose questioningly. "Quickly, please," I said, "it is sunrise." Courteously leading the way with the suggestion of a snigger, he took me along a corridor in which there reigned a great deal of disorder: the glass cabinets were open and full of nests, and many of the books were scattered across the floor. As we passed, the birds rose in flight and you could hear their screech as they did so. My companion whistled as he spoke, or rather all his words ended with a whistle, like the one we use when we call a hunting dog. At the same time his impudent half-witted smirk had become more pronounced, and I wasn't quite sure whether he had a stammer or his manner of speech suggested some kind of innuendo.

"Just keep going straight on down there," he indicated the corridor and pushed me while adding with another particularly shrill whistle, "Straight down there; it's easy."

I set off in order not to waste any more time, but I was a little sceptical. Outside it was probably getting light, while I was walking in the feeble glow of the occasional light bulb next to the large stacks that divided the corridor in two. I could hear long and short whistles, which seemed to come from the other side of the stacks. It appeared that that person or someone on his behalf was dogging me in parallel and spying on me.

Before a minute had elapsed I heard the loud noise of hooves, like an approaching horse, or perhaps someone with hobnailed boots. Then I smelt the pungent odour of sheep and someone suddenly appeared behind me; it could only have been Tiraboschi. All red and sweaty with his head down, he did not wait to ask himself who I was – man or woman under the pyjamas – and he jumped on my back and attempted to clamber up me as though I were a pole. He was stamping his feet heavily on the floor, sniffing the air and emitting cries more equine than human. I think he had mistaken me for a woman to his taste or perhaps that Greek teacher. He put his hands on my mouth and attempted to open it with a nail, levering it on that long-suffering tooth. He too wanted, I believe, to kiss my mouth, but he was causing me incredible pain as he had touched a nerve. Just at the moment in which he almost succeeded in climbing onto my shoulders kicking his feet as he did so and attempting to bite my ears, out jumped Accetto from behind a pile of books positioned deliberately, in my opinion, in the form of a sentry box or fortified outpost from which to keep watch on the corridor, and he carried a massive wooden batten with which he hit Tiraboschi on the forehead at least three time with a force that would have

Chapter P

killed a human being immediately. Instead the wood bounced off with a deep rumble as if it had hit a hollow tree trunk. Unfortunately one of the rebounds struck me on the cheek close to the corner of my mouth – exactly the spot where Tiraboschi had been attempting to lever my teeth apart with a nail and where Albonea Bucato had been kissing me; the blow shook the tooth and almost removed it. I experienced the greatest pain of the entire night.

Tiraboschi jumped down, but did not appear adversely affected; he had not fainted and still less had he suffered a mortal blow. What had been done was perhaps just sufficient to subdue his irrational and indiscriminate desires. He did in fact jump back on the first stroke of the batten but out of surprise and with no change to his grim scowl as he made a deafening racket with his hobnailed boots by way of a threat. With the second blow he attempted to smash the wooden instrument on its downward trajectory with an upward blow of his head – butting like a goat, but the batten did not break and he was a little shaken and unsteady. There was a slight moan. The third blow must have rearranged the ideas in his head, although his cranium was not the least affected – not a break in his skin. This third blow must have confuted his prejudices and caused him to reflect on the situation. He must have examined me with more discernment and understood that I was neither a woman nor the Greek teacher, even if I did have her odour on me. Unfortunately it had been transferred to me in such an indelible and pungent manner that his error was partly justifiable. I myself could smell it wafting off my feet and legs and all the way up to my head and beyond; it was the smell of bleach and bedbugs. Clearly Tiraboschi was excited by this smell, or it reminded him of other intimate embraces and venereal assignations in the shade of bookshelves, if thus we can define them.

Then there was a fourth blow, which evidently had the task of making him fully aware of the error of his ways and restoring him to his duties as a nocturnal guardian. This was probably normal practice in the library: three blows between his horns to make him desist and a fourth one to enlighten him and reawaken his sense of responsibility as a civil servant. But this final more didactic blow ended up striking the stacks on an upright that was perhaps a little fragile and worm-eaten and the shelves it held up fell devastatingly on top of Accetto and Tiraboschi's back. Behind the stack was the man who had given me directions; it was Guastalamenti. I realised this in that instant, and he fled the scene. An avalanche of books came surging to my feet. In spite of all the confusion, the shouts, Tiraboschi stamping on the floor, the stabbing pain in my tooth, in spite indeed of Accetto's rushing about in the midst of the confusion of books he was the principal cause of, and the stampede of rats, marmots, dormice and lizards, and in spite, finally, of the extremely perturbing swarming of a wasps' nest, I felt recalled to my duties, bent down, opened some of them and read the titles, just in case fortune had decided to smile on me. But I must have been both deaf and blind because before my eyes, Tiraboschi with his gnarled forehead and nose that looked like a bone had mounted Accetto who was on all fours amongst the books, grabbed his collar and acted as though he was at the gallop, while the ensuing pushing and shoving caused another three metres of stacks to come tumbling down and the books were shedding pages in the air like daisies and were trampled by the two contestants who were rolling about in them. There was also a confusion of flying beasties – bats, barn owls and skylarks – whose nests had evidently been made amongst those piles of printed matter and now found their homes had been destroyed. I have no idea what would have happened if the wasps hadn't passed judgement on the guilty party using his smell as evidence. A few of them had approached me, but my smell was not incriminating, or perhaps they just found it disgusting. The whole swam then decided to surround Tiraboschi who ran away like a madman, and Accetto followed to give him his *coup de grâce*.

Chapter P

I looked around: the whistling guy had not fled after all. I spied him partially hidden up a ladder and he looked as happy as someone who has just been to the theatre.

"Listen here," I called to him, as I stood stuck in the middle of that landslide of books. "You must be Mr Guastalamenti!"

"Yes, can I be of any service?"

"I thought so," I almost beside myself. "You were the one with all that whistling that unleashed that colleague of yours on me."

"For starters," he replied, "even if I did whistle a bit, it was not in my power to unleash him. That power was something only you had, if you don't mind my saying so; you can smell it miles off, and you've still got it. All you need is a nose." He adopted an air of amusement and innuendo as he said this. I realised that I had been discovered; I bent down to sniff and turned red with embarrassment.

"Don't be ashamed," he said, "you're just naive." As I stood there speechless, he explained that the Greek teacher did the same with everyone. She had taken some soft and well-sprung boxes to a small room in the basement. From his account, it appeared that everyone knew this. She made sheets with newspapers and occasionally takes the director there. When she can, she takes novices there when they get lost in search of a bibliography. "She is there every night," said Guastalamenti, "and it is not clear what art she uses, because she is incontestably one ugly old woman. There are those who say she knows the books that make people lose their heads, full as they are of double entendres that excite male eroticism. But I know what she uses to get her way: she uses the sexual attraction of pheromones!"

I frowned on hearing this obscure term, "Pheromones? What are they?"

He was happy to show off his expertise, "If you want, I can refer you to the appropriate books, but equally I can tell you myself."

143

"Keep it brief," I said. "You tell me, but keep it short and while we're walking."

But instead he sat down on the remains of an encyclopaedia and obliged me to sit down as well. "There is not a great deal to be said about Bucato, but you, my dear sir, should know that her story contains an unhappy love affair, as always in these cases. She was much younger, only just qualified as a teacher, and a little less hairy, but above all innocent when it came to the question of pheromones. He, on the other hand, was a famous seducer with his own method; in fact he founded his own particular movement. You know, of course, that the males of many species of animal mark their territories with olfactory messages that either dissuade competitors or sexually arouse females.

"In the specific case of this seducer, Tito Sedulio by name, he would walk around surreptitiously disseminating his own waste materials, in which, as we all know, are concentrated the sexually alluring pheromones. He didn't know this scientifically, but answered to the primal dictates in his blood. He felt that all other systems were insincere and unnatural, and posed considerable problems of interpretation for women. 'I want to be clear,' he would say, 'no circumlocutions!' In the evening he would go around depositing his messages on young ladies' doorsteps so that they had time to think about it and undergo the effects of his airborne pheromones. If invited, he would go without further delay to the home of the young lady in question. He entered her flat with the courteousness and correct manners of a real gentleman. He made no hints, paid no compliments and gave no compromising presents. He did not stoop to the exchange of promises or penetrating looks, minor forms of titillation, the use of feathers, hand-kissing or pinching. At the moment in which he felt something for this woman – a definite inclination – he simply stood up, apologised with proper solicitude, and went off to the bathroom to lodge his marriage proposal.

Chapter P

"What he did with Mrs Bucato is now well established fact. He entered her house very respectfully. She was greatly impressed by his *savoir faire* and refined diction. Moreover she felt that he was a paragon of self-restraint. They talked of high-minded things and meanwhile the lady looked at his hands: she liked them, they were slender – those of an educated man. The young Bucato had him sit down and offered him an iced citron squash, which he drank as he had a terrible thirst. 'Another juice?' she asked, and he said, 'Yes, thanks,' because he had decided to make his feelings known. Bucato, it was clear, was deeply affected and almost in trepidation. She stood up to go and get the bottle from the kitchen, and asked to be excused in a voice that could only mean, 'Propose and the answer will be yes.' Thence she left a little red in the face. How long was she away? One minute, one and a half minutes? Just long enough to check her lipstick in the hall mirror, pull up her petticoat that had become crimped, and take in the overall effect of her dress: the zips, hooks, buttons, neckline and maybe a few other things. Two minutes at the most, or perhaps three. Then she returned with the citron squash and there was a smell that terrified her. Meanwhile he was gaping at her expectantly! Later she would tell her girlfriends and colleagues confidentially that he never spoke. The smell did not evaporate, in which case it could have been forgiven, but became increasingly vicious and inexorable. She went red in the face, stammered and could not manage to pour water into the glass. The ice tongs slipped from her hand, and then the ice bucket and the ice inside. And he did nothing. He did not speak; he just looked at her. Eventually tears came to her eyes. She had already been married once but, she said, she had never come across a smell like that. She wiped her eyes with a handkerchief, placed in front of her mouth and looked at him in bewilderment as though he were an executioner and she a child. And yet she was not that young. But the stunning thing is this: he stood up as though he had already said everything, like someone who has already declared himself and awaits an answer. Such eyes he had! Wide open and fired up with passion. Then she thought he had an ailment because of all that ice, and she smiled slightly as though to say, 'It's nothing; I understand.' Sedulio's face lit up and he stood up sure that the pheromones were at work. Bucato also stood up and could not fail to see an enormous lump of faeces between the sofa and the lamp. Now she turned white and pointed to it with her finger. If she had not been in her own home, she would have run away screaming. Sedulio did not even turn. He did not say, 'It's mine.' Still less did he say, 'I'm sorry.' He stood as still as a stockfish, and waited. She had no idea what he was waiting for. After a while, she rushed to the bathroom and shut herself in. Sedulio banged on the door: 'Open up! I have expressed my feelings. What do you have to say?' She did not come out until it was well into the night, after Sedulio had left.

"Afterwards, she suffered his courtship, and her neighbours were all complaining. 'Who is that delinquent?' they would say when they saw him declaring his love in the garden, up the stairs and on the doormats. She knew, but shame stopped her from saying. Nevertheless, she thought about him constantly. It was a fixation, it was love. But being shy and naive, she feared her neighbours' opinion. She stayed at home tormenting herself and dreaming. She never gave him a reply.

"Besides, Tito Sedulio had a polymorphous sexuality, which could not restrict itself to a single object of desire and the resulting lack of variety. At night he went to the courtyard of the girls' upper secondary school and deposited his Easter eggs, as he vulgarly liked to call them, on the steps to the main entrance. Then he rushed over in the morning when the school opened to see the young chicks who recoiled and squealed and said, 'God, that's disgusting! What a stench! What kind of creep could have done this?' Deep in his heart, he cried, 'It was me. It was me that did it. You can see, no?' He rejoiced at having caused disarray amongst that gaggle of geese, because in his opinion it was as clear as daylight what his messages meant, 'I adore you.' He also liked to follow the fate of his artefacts, by pretending to wait at the bus stop opposite the school. The headmistress came out and looked severely at his two or three relics. The girls by this stage had all gathered in the courtyard, talking animatedly and keeping their distance as though the area were a minefield. Others came up on scooters with books strapped to saddle, and were immediately informed of the news. 'You wouldn't believe it. This morning. On the steps!' They couldn't believe it and wanted to see, 'You've got to be joking! Where?' They went over and looked down, 'That's disgusting! That's so gross!' and then they rushed off to comment on it with others and list the names of well-known Lotharios, lovers and boyfriends. He listened to all this in ecstasy. The headmistress called some of the staff; janitors appears, and they too were shocked, 'But who would do this? When? Just now? Last night?' 'Some good-for-nothing, that's what he is!' 'Who let him in?' 'The gate was open.' 'So anyone can wander in and do exactly what they want!' The debate involved everyone, all there in a circle: on one side the grim-faced headmistress and the worried janitors, and on the other, the pupils who didn't want to go near but laughed and enjoyed whispering certain words to each other.

"The headmistress had the faeces covered with sawdust and then ordered, 'Inside!' to the girls. And they shunned the offending material, some with a leap and others by circling round while carefully holding their skirts. From his position at the bus stop, Sedulio observed all these movements and the pile of sawdust under which he felt his *longa manus* could still ogle.

"After this, dustpans and brushes rapidly appeared, and the headmistress oversaw the cleaning and decontaminating operations, so that there remained no trace, no distant memory. However, the pheromones, once released into the air, continue to act in the strangest and most unpredictable manner. For example, the headmistress sits down very gravely on returning to her office, and then she feels a very reluctant and tremulous thought rise up her aorta, squeeze her jugular and flow into her head through the cerebral arteries. She thinks that she is thinking it, but she is wrong. The molecules of Tito Sedulio's pheromones are contaminating her synapses and inducing these thoughts in her brain. The headmistress thinks that she would like to look the author of these abominations in the face. But she doesn't think this calmly, but with a kind of laboured breath. She cannot stand it, opens her private cabinet and, after looking around, drinks a liqueur."

"That's enough. I got the message," I said. Time was passing.

Guastalamenti would not give up, "It has to be said, though, that Sedulio, whether we like it or not, always won the occasional heart, sometimes aiming directly at the target and sometimes bouncing off the wall. Bucato learnt this method from him, to your cost. When she can, she applies it to whoever comes to hand – not to the letter, as she is a woman, but adhering to the chemistry very closely."

I stood up, "That really is enough. I have got the picture: it's all down to her pheromones. Would you let me go now?"

"Don't you want to know about Mrs Bucato's glands, her deoxyribonucleic acid, and those gametes of hers? I could give you a lesson and provide many examples, because I confess to being a little nerdy about this subject. I have done some experiments and statistical analysis, which I will use in a learned paper."

"No, thank you," I was exasperated. "This is interesting, but I am a bit of an outsider. I really know nothing about it; I am just a victim."

"Well then, read this. I am collecting data," and he put a small notebook in my hand. "If you're short of information, you'll find the fundamentals in here."

To indulge him, I opened it, but I did not sit down.

Chapter P

Hairy women

A pretty and plump, thirty-six-year-old German woman from Baden-Baden was in every way a perfect and promising woman, but she had a brown rounded beard which was incredibly long and looked like a broom. She came from a hairy family: her father had hair on his nose and the whole of his face, but it was short like that of a dachshund. Her mother was covered in long, straight hairs, and naked she looked as though she was wearing a shirt. Both parents were born in the same town close to the Baltic Sea, where everyone is even hairier, and the hairs form a hirsute mantle so thick that it is difficult to believe they are human beings. In old age, they become white and resemble polar bears, with the one difference that they are bald in the manner of the rest of us, i.e. only at the top of the head. However, the bald patch has a shiny yellow appearance, like something that has had its lid removed.

This is a not infrequent of endemic hypertrichosis. The Mexican, Julia Pastrana was also covered with a thicket of long, wiry hair. She died in Europe in 1860 after having given birth to a boy with jet black hair on his body and the suggestion of a tail, who would not marry. There was however an amiable and graceful English lady of Greenwich, who at about twenty years of age had a very fine beard of golden locks, four or five centimetres long. She stroked it slowly and softly, like caressing a lover, and she smiled with passive pleasure on feeling a woman's soft hand on her face. It appears that in the intimacy of her own thoughts, she was rather pleased with that lovely ornament.

A fourth observable case is that of a fifty-year-old gentlewoman of Orvieto. Her family were unaware of the beard, as she shaved herself every morning until there wasn't the slightest sign of a single hair. When she became ill and had to stay in bed for several months, the beard, which had been cut for so many years, grew with such vigour that the general practitioner who came to examine her, thought he was in the presence of a capuchin monk.

Chapter Q

I angrily closed the notebook and gave it back to him, saying, "How very clever of you! Congratulations, but I'm afraid I must be off." Such was my desire to get away from those misleading and exasperating follies, I ventured off on my own, thinking that I would eventually get somewhere. I read the subject labels written in a lopsided hand: mathematics, chemistry, accountancy, history of art. I picked up a book and black sawdust fell out. It looked like letters and they separated out like flakes of dry paint. I brushed them off my clothes, and the book was illegible. I opened others: one was an empty box, except for a few newspaper cuttings and insect remains. I tapped on a line of books, and they all sounded empty. Some sparrows flew out of one of them, another was full of straw, and yet another nutshells, perhaps left by squirrels.

These were corridors where you didn't see a living soul, and the disorder just got worse and worse: piles of books on the ground, as though it had been ploughed or was undergoing some upheaval. Table legs, glass, cupboard doors and splinters of wood were mixed up with the paper. It looked like a Pre-Cambrian volcanic eruption, when magmatic and early sedimentary rocks were formed, the earth's crust started to fold, oxygen in the air was below one per cent and it was the kingdom of the prokaryotes. The air was so oppressive and sweaty that you almost felt ill. There was a smell of decomposing wood. Here the books were black; they crumbled like peat if you touched them; they were full of methane and other gases, which made me feel delirious when I breathed them. I would occasionally see the flicker of a light in the distance and thought that arbitrator Pantani must have been down there. I ran towards him in the hope that he could help me to get out, but I just became increasingly lost. There were wooden doors which had been boarded or walled up, and beyond them I could hear growls, hissing, roars, galloping and

Chapter Q

incessant barking. I was afraid that these thin walls of single, hollow bricks could start to crack or that the nails in these nailed-up doors would start to loosen under the pressure of that poisonous zoological maelstrom behind them. I was fearful that the supports would give way and there would come pouring through an infernal jungle of harpies, basilisks, crocodiles, dragons, hernias, weasels, bogeys, herpes, ibises, witches, myrmicoleons, sexton beetles, shadows, peacocks, quadrumanes, suckerfish, satyrs, mermen, groundless fears, foxes and mosquitoes. In a wave of dust, they would have swept away me and my last hopes of finding my way out of that indecipherable and inescapable solitude. I would have drowned in its grimy ferment.

A stray dog came out of a hole barking hysterically, and tried to bite my feet and ankles. Although it was tiny, it was so importunate and snarling that I couldn't get away from it. It had attached itself to the bottom of my pyjama trousers and kept pulling. I tried to kick it away, but as I walked back, I ended up sticking my foot into a slimy hole. It was not deep and only my shoe went in, but I could not get it out and the dog continued to snarl at the other leg, bite it and tear ferociously at the hem of my pyjama leg. The hole contained some kind of sticky tar, a flytrap. The shoe was completely glued up. And there, right next to the hole, was some guy I hadn't previously noticed. He was staring and only said, "Good morning."

"For Christ's sake," I then said, "could you get this bloody bastard dog off me?" I was frightened of losing my balance and falling down without a chance of defending myself and perhaps getting even more caught up in the gluey substance. He had an air of empathy and understanding but he didn't move an inch. All he did was introduce himself by his forename and surname with deliberate and inappropriate courteousness, while I tried to kick in the air with one foot and pull the other one out of the hole. This was the guardian Bisolfo of whom I had already heard so much talk, and hurriedly going through what Pantani had told me, I scrambled around for money – in spite of my other activities – and promised to give him some.

"No, no, don't go any trouble," he said; "just a little small change or perhaps the odd note. It always comes in handy – on the bus or in the bar."

"Hold on, I'll give you some," but the dog was not releasing its grip, and the gluey material was turning into cement. But, God knows how, my pockets had been sewn up. I tried to put my hands in, but to no effect, like when you try on a new suit at the tailor's. "I don't have pockets any more," I said confused and breathless.

"No worries. No worries at all," this Bisolfo replied without stirring from his seat, "take your own time."

In the meantime, by patting myself all over I found a small pocket that I didn't even know I had, suggesting my jacket had suddenly become someone else's. To my surprise, I took out pieces of paper, threads, a brooch, a small comb, bingo numbers, a wax seal and curtain ring. "What is this stuff?" I was saying.

"It's all stuff that could come in handy, you never know. Hand it over, hand it over. Thank you." The dog had calmed down a bit. Then a cork, a nib and a match. "This is useful for lighting a fire," he said, as he took everything, "this is useful for writing, this could be useful in case of need." When I gave him a button and a silver badge, he looked at the badge carefully and seemed happy with it.

"Could you get me out," I said.

"Yes of course, I'll show you how. You pull up hard with your foot, and I'll keep the dog away." I pulled and he blew on a whistle made from dried willow. As soon as the dog heard, it ran off. I persisted with the pulling until the sole came away and that foot was shoeless.

"But where are we?" I asked.

"Eh!" he said, "this is a bad area. This area has slipped out of our control," he pointed to an open door off its hinges, "from here on you'll find nothing and nobody."

I nodded towards the corridor.

Chapter Q

"I don't advise you to go there; there's been a bookslide due to erosion of the load-bearing columns of the stacks. We heard a rumble and then the crash. It was a disaster. All the books in area running for hundreds of metres collapsed producing dust clouds and ruin, and for days no one could get near. The cloud might even be a little radioactive. You never know. Even other rooms at some distance were affected: walls, ceilings, floors, people..."

I looked in the opposite direction.

"I would not recommend going in that direction either," he said. "There is a hole in the ground that goes directly into a sewer. It is not a nice smell, and anyone who slips in out of carelessness will not be coming back amongst the living. Such people adapt to their environment and become unrecognisable – resembling dead people in colour and appearance."

I looked around.

"My advice to you would be to avoid rummaging around amongst the books. There are moulds that when you breathe them cause asthma, hay fever, skin allergies, acne, infections, and even worse. There are moulds that damage the ears and the eyes: they get inside and the eyes swell up like those of a toad; the ears shrivel up and become deaf. If they go in the mouth and the saliva, then these moulds cause hallucinations: for instance one guy believed that the examination committee were hot on his heels and wanted to capture and interrogate him, and the saliva was gluing up his mouth like an adhesive paste, and he couldn't articulate words but only borborygmi and mastic bubbles. As he could not breathe, he fell helpless to the ground, and for a while he breathed through his pores and improvised gills. Eventually he succumbed without ever saying another word."

"But I've got to read something before tomorrow morning," I was sweating.

"I would not advise reading: with so little light and so much disorder anyone would lose heart and despair. None of the books in here are intact, no one knows what they're about, they only contain jumbles of words that confuse people, and whoever wrote them was just trying to put on airs. In fact I would advise against any kind of exertion or labour, and you'll get yourself bitten: dogs that live in the darkness suffer from rabies and can bite. There is no point in playing the part of the hero; you'll just get a reputation for stupidity and you'll be risking your neck if you haven't been inoculated."

"What do you mean? Not even reading?"

"That's right, and I even advise you against opening them. You might have some nasty surprises: vendettas left by other people such as needles for a Pravaz syringe, sharp devices with spring mechanisms, arsenic, carnival bombs and razor-blades with the resulting dangers of serious infections, intoxications, septicaemia and death."

"Does no one have any idea of what's going on? Isn't there anyone in charge?"

"There's a director, but he's not much use."

"Take me to see him, for God's sake!" I gave him a coin no longer in circulation. It was the last one I had in my pocket.

"I can take you there," we set off towards a small door camouflaged in the wall, "although I do assure you that it will be a waste of time. He's not interested in the library itself; he has other interests."

"What's that supposed to mean?"

"This director is called Perbeni; some people think he is a genius, but I am not one of them. He spends all his nights inventing things, perhaps even important things, but in the meantime he is letting the library go wild and it is becoming a danger to us all. Who knows! Perhaps it's better that way. He has gathered together an experimental scientific laboratory in his box room and wants to come up with the great invention of the century, so that his name will live on forever in books and human memory. Accetto's son, who has the unfortunate name of Feltpad, is his pupil and assistant. His father, being a widower, forced him into that career when he was little, so that he could make

Chapter Q

something of himself. Every night he goes to the director's box room, where they keep a camp bed. Consequently, the poor soul has grown pale and thin, because he eats and sleeps very little. You can hear them bustling about all night long. Smoke and vapours can be seen filtering out. Every now and then Feltpad inhales toxic fumes, and when the director does, he swears a lot. He invents at a variable rate, perhaps according to his metereopathies, and when he invents something, he calls for everyone, and they come running in the midst of the racket made by chickens, cats and dogs. 'I've done it, I've done it,' he screams, 'this is the invention of the century!' Even Accetto runs over, beaming with joy because he hopes that a little glory will be reflected on his son and a little also on himself. He runs over with his assistants who lift the director up high in jubilation. As usual they go too far and drop him badly, almost crippling him. In their enthusiasm, they also throw the son in the air, and as he is light, he goes all the way up to the ceiling, where he bangs his head and falls back down semi-conscious stuttering, 'Thanks, but that's enough now.' Then his father intervenes: on the one hand, he is content about the glory that is now for all to see, but on the other, he is a little vexed by the hardly scientific exuberance of Santoro and Fischietti. There are squabbles and protests, Accetto hits out all over the place with his ruler until calm is restored. Then Professor Rasorio is summoned to adjudicate. Do you know him?"

"Yes, I do."

"The fact is that the director Perbeni has so far only invented things that have already been invented. Or so it seems. When Rasorio points this out to him, he immediately flares up, 'Shit! How can that possibly be? I just invented it, this very night!' After having observed boiling water for a long time, given that he drinks about ten coffees in a night which makes him really edgy, he invented the piston and the steam engine. 'This will lead to an industrial revolution,' he declared self-importantly. 'But it has already been invented,' said Rasorio. 'Bloody hell!

When was that?' he demanded to know. 'They invented it two hundred years ago,' the professor said. 'Good gracious! I thought I wouldn't get there in time. But who says this? Could it be unreliable information?' 'I can assure you,' Rasorio repeated, 'it's even in the encyclopaedia.' Then the director generally goes silent and inside him he feels the increasing pressure of a dull anger against the speed of progress, and occasionally he takes it out on Accetto's son, because he sees the anaemic boy lying on the camp bed: 'Wake up, the world is rushing onwards, you layabout!' On hearing this, Accetto also attacks his son, 'You'll always be a nobody! Just like Fischietti and Santoro.' He summons them and to demonstrate how little they amount to, he threatens them with his ruler and then gives the order: 'Laugh! Now cry!' and they laugh and cry. But then they don't want to stop and they try once more to carry the director in triumph, but as he is irritated and in violent mood, he shouts at Accetto to have them desist. There follow very unedifying scenes, particularly for the boy. For the director is a very rational man, but not when he is angry.

"Then he invented something like a helicopter: he did not construct a whole one, but he did the calculations. He collected pieces of tin, measured the air resistance in relation to the revolving surface, designed the shape of the propellers, and ascertained the required elasticity of the material. He then displayed a toy that was a clockwork prototype. 'But it's already been done,' they tell him. He started to swear and for two days he was livid and liverish. 'It was invented by Sikorsky in 1909.' 'Who's this Sikorsky?' he asked. Accetto wanted to calm him down, 'Above all, don't swear; Feltpad might learn.' 'Yes, but the propeller is my patent,' he argued. 'No, John Ericsson invented it,' Rasorio replied. 'But when?' 'In 1837.' 'Hah,' he said, 'son of this and son of that.' And he indulged in his verbal intemperance. One night, he disassembled several pairs of glasses, put the lenses in a tube on top of a tripod, and said, 'This is a telescope.' They didn't even

Chapter Q

bother to call Rasorio; Accetto took him aside and said, 'Galileo Galilei invented it in 1609.' He didn't want to believe it: 'Who says so?' 'Everyone knows it. They make you learn it by rote in school.' 'So I'm supposed to be an ignoramus? Nothing I invent ever counts for anything!' and he started to shout that it was all a mafia, that freelance inventors are treated like dirt. They count for nothing, while those in charge are the mafia who produce encyclopaedias. They're the ones who sow the tares and spread false rumours; who knows what shameful interests lurk beneath?

"One night, for instance, a cooking stove blew up, but according to him he had written down the formula. 'It's another invention,' he declared and everyone came running. He repeated the experiment and the door blew up. 'Now you believe me,' he said, but Rasorio put him right, 'That must be dynamite. Nobel invented it in 1862.' 'What do you mean?' 'I mean that you're a bit late. Dynamite already exists.' 'To hell with it! Why does something always have to meddle with things? Who is this Nobel anyway? He must be some loafer, a gangster who exploits the simple-minded and bribes the ministers to provide him with propaganda in books and dictionaries.' 'He's dead.' 'Serves him right.' And the whole business took its usual course: endless swear words, rambling diatribes against encyclopaedias, an unseemly chaos and reprimands for Feltpad because he wouldn't get off his camp bed."

Chapter R

We got there just as the director invented the electric motor. It was a table fan. Accetto, his assistants and other people were crowding round in a circle. Perhaps they were employees and readers, as some were in uniform and others in pyjamas or threadbare and seedy-looking clothes. The fan spun at a great speed creating such a draught down the entire corridor that those present kept their jackets closed and had the red eyes of a motorcyclist. Santoro and Fischietti were all excited and their hair stood up on end. An incredible number of feathers and a great deal of dust floated in the air. Seated in front of it on a chair buffeted by the current of air, Rasorio was explaining at that very moment, "... the electric motor working on alternating current was invented by Tesla, an American engineer, in 1892."

"What's that? What's that? Engineer, you say?" said a choleric little man whom I immediately took to be the director Perbeni. "This time you're just making fun of me! An engineer! But who ever heard such nonsense?"

Accetto was listening to the conversation with a fierce expression, while his two assistants put their faces near to the blades so that they could watch them turning close-up and prod them with pieces of straw which were noisily chopped up and sent flying in different directions. Then Santoro, at Fischietti's instigation, tried putting his finger in, but he removed it immediately. He then studied it carefully, before showing it to Fischietti.

"You just want to make fun of me," the director repeated, while he increased the fan's speed to everyone's admiration, "but I would say that it works outstandingly well."

"There is no doubt of it," said Rasorio, "but if you ask me whether it has already been invented, I have to tell you in all honesty that it has."

Chapter R

The director was indignant, "Give me your proof, because I have provided proof of my part." He switched it on and off, to the enormous satisfaction of both himself and his witnesses.

"The proof," replied Rasorio, "can be found in just any encyclopaedia."

When he heard these words, the director's bony and obstinate face quivered. "Let's see it then," he said, and the assistants echoed him, "Let's see it, let's see it." They were very happy with the direction the conversation had taken.

Thus, after a little more scurrying about, an enormous volume was produced and Rasorio set about thumbing through the pages, while keeping it inside an open drawer in the desk to shelter it from the proof-providing draught, which was blustering and unrelenting. "Here we are," he said, "Nikola Tesla, an American of Croatian origin, and so on... high-voltage currents... carried out research... created the first electric motor..." On hearing these words, the director, who had stood next to Rasorio to peer at the book, suddenly closed the drawer on the professor's hands and kept them hermetically sealed in there by putting his whole weight sideways against it, and in that instant Santoro and Fischietti grabbed the fan, as though that was all they were waiting for, and placed it at full speed next to one of his ears, so that the blades just brushed against the ear, while making the noise of a salami-slicer.

Rasorio shouted and protested, "I shall never adjudicate again. From now on, no more adjudications."

"You belong to the encyclopaedia mafia, and it's time you confessed," screamed the director; "you're an international menace. You want to lay down the law, but not to me, you won't." In the meantime, you could hear the fan brushing the ear at various speeds, and all the bystanders were shocked and a little frightened by the offensive power of a fan and its improper use on human beings. The readers were more frightened than the others. Then Fischietti said he wanted to shave him and he passed the fan along his cheeks like a mower. Santoro pushed, so that he would shave more deeply and against the growth of the poor man's beard.

"This is what always happens," said Bisolfo with a slight tone of disgust, "if Feltpad doesn't get all the blame, then poor Rasorio does."

Eventually someone tripped on the cord or perhaps the two assistants pulled on it too much, and the plug came out of the wall. During the ensuing turmoil, Rasorio freed his hands, and he wandered off with an offended and urticated face, while gingerly pressing his auricle and grumbling that he would no longer give either judgements or marks. The others continued to tinker around.

I glanced into the director's office, which had a neon light. It was not an office as you would normally imagine it. It contained all manner of things piled up on the floor, chairs and two tables, and also attached to nails in the wall or hooks on the ceiling. There were open drawers spilling over with stuff, and the long and contorted items were poking out from under a bed. A small glass cabinet, which probably should have contained books, was packed on each shelf with a tangle of junk. Everything was covered with slimy filth and either dull or rusty. There were dismantled parts that no one could even name. If they had a hole or a ring, they were tied together with wire. On the floor there was a path that led to a table and to the bed, but it was strewn with cogs, springs and washers.

There was someone in the room, lying on the bed and smoking. I inferred that this must be Accetto's son. His face and person resembled a celery stick, diaphanous and white tending towards light green, with hair and ears splayed and tasselled like celery leaves.

"This place is a midden!" I said. "What is this room supposed to be? Isn't it supposed to be the director's office?"

"It is," he replied.

Chapter R

I stood there. I had trampled on glass and touched an old piston which had dirtied my sleeve. He had lifted himself up a bit, and was looking at me quizzically.
"Well then," I said, "how did all this happen?"
He put out his cigarette and said something along these lines: "When all you do is pile up a whole lot of words and names on one side, as in the case of a library, then somewhere else you have to create a whole lot of trash. I'm not the only one who's saying this: you go for a little stroll around the city and open the dustbins, which are all over the place and always overflowing and foul-smelling. Just go ahead and open those bins and have a good rummage around inside; and all you'll find is things with no identity, things that have no name. You are unable to call them anything other than rubbish. They are the remains, whereas their names – the lustrous ones they had in the past when they were specific, nicely coloured and recognisable objects – continue to exist elsewhere and on their own inside books. Oh yes, you can find them all shiny and in perfect order in a dictionary, and there they remain indifferent to time, acids and atmospheric agents, even when the things from which they were taken are battered and completely corroded, or buried in grass until they have entirely dissolved away."
I listened. I leant against a small table, but coated my hands and pyjama bottoms with black grease. On shifting away, I tore the bottoms on a nail. I was trying not to tread on some needles with my naked foot.
"Well," he continued, "Perbeni, the director, says that to invent he needs not words but things, and nothing can be excluded *a priori*. So he sends me to a place around here – not far from the library – where there's an enormous tip that has been piled up against the city wall, and there I pick up anything that comes to hand. If he can, he too comes secretly when it's still dark to root around in that great mass of rubbish. He has a preference for things made of tin, gears, pipes, but also bottles with dregs of acid, turpentine and zinc sulphate. Lorries come every day to

dump tons of unserviceable stuff. Then we discovered that many of these academics are collectors; in other words, they gather stuff from the rubbish within bins, on the ground and in skips. Some things meet with their approval and they keep them in their pockets. The director proposed that they should come and hand in what they have found in exchange for perks and special privileges such as a place reserved for them in the library, the right not to be woken up or as compensation for damage they have inflicted on the books, chairs and fittings.

"Occasionally I find a partially completed and badly battered invention at the tip, like a broken and disassembled motor; indeed something that is no longer recognisable as a motor. I take it to him, and Perbeni is immediately enthusiastic; no one knows what this is, what invention this could possibly be, and so he studies it night after night with an unflagging passion. He disassembles it, reassembles it and runs some tests on it in accordance with his own whims. Occasionally he ventures into the unknown and improvises some kind of fuel, which either explodes or remains inert and silent; or perhaps by some miraculous happenchance it actually starts to work. When he invented the internal combustion engine, no one could have known that that piece of rusty cast iron could have started running. It was a single-cylinder engine with valves at the top. I found it without any wheels or fuel tank; it could have been a radiator or a gas ring. But our director examined it so carefully, in terms of both theoretical and applied science, and worked on it so hard with his hammer and file, that eventually it started up. Of course he had to turn the carefully positioned crank again and again and again, but he got there in the end. It was a four-stroke engine; full of pride and contentment, he would run it at top speed, which created a tremendous din because we hadn't invented a silencer. The walls and tables vibrated, and everyone came running to see, and he kept the throttle wide open to demonstrate, he said, the theoretical power it was capable of. The noise and exhaust gas immediately

Chapter R

gave me a headache, and when it was discovered that another, a German, had already invented an internal combustion engine quite some time ago – Rasorio said in 1885 – he took it out on me because my lying in bed showed that I was a pessimist and gave in too easily. But I'm not interested in these matters: who was the first to invent something, and whether there has been deceit and false pretences in books and encyclopaedias. I am not interested in proper nouns and progress."

While he was talking I realised that there was a little door. "And in there?"

"In there we have a storeroom."

I went over clambering amongst and getting entangled in the scrap iron.

"Don't open it, for Christ's sake!" he said leaping to his feet.

But I had already turned the handle and opened it. A whole lot of stuff poured out, an avalanche of odds and ends no different from those in the first room, but here in an incredible variety. Fortunately the door was small and low and it soon became obstructed. "It is the director's private collection. He is very protective of it; he says it is a complete universal museum from A to Z."

Some letters had also fallen out: I saw an "A" of oxidised copper, which possibly came from an inscription on a marble. Then I saw an abacus for the very first time; it had been broken in two. I picked it up and dusted it, and there was a terracotta abbot at my feet – the height of a little finger, without a nose and tied with a piece of string to an abbey used as an ashtray. We tried to push back into the storeroom the snarl-up of brake linings, ballcocks, bathtaps, bearings, binnacles, binoculars, blades, blinkers (vehicle indicators), blow torches and bolts of all descriptions, just to mention a few things that fell out together.

"The director will be angry," said Feltpad.

We pushed the door to shut it and almost succeeded in going all the way. Then Feltpad tied it up with rope to the wall.

Naturally this had to be the moment in which the director came in: he let out a scream, as though I had desecrated an altar, "But what are you doing? Now you are spying on my desk?" There was a piece of squared paper on the table with some scribbles and numbers, and half covered with screws, clock hands, washers and a shiny and well-kept barometer. Perhaps it was the current invention. I hadn't even seen it. "You're not here to steal something off me, are you?" he asked.

"No, of course not; I was looking for directions. The library is so large," you could tell that he was already irritated by the direction of my argument, "and everything is in such a mess."

He became very agitated, "The management is not responsible! Let me immediately make that clear."

"I know, I know, I wasn't saying that. I was not trying to attribute blame."

"But you should be. Let's be absolutely clear," he said in a lower voice as he drew me out of the office. "Do you want to know the truth? Then here it is! I'm not afraid of telling you this or even saying it in public. A library could go on forever on its own accord and without need of anything beyond its own resources. It doesn't even need a director. But hanging around here somewhere is a prankster, a mindless joker, and I know who he is. Do you want to know his name? Vincenzo Gallo.

"He is an employee I recruited for the conservation department simply because I felt sorry for him, and he turned out to be malicious beyond all description. He is the one who changes the positions of the books, removes the pressmarks, and deliberately replaces pages and covers. He does it out of revenge, and he hides who knows where in these cellars. What can I do? I would have to read the entire library before I could put it right, but have him arrested first. Even if I had the time, do you think that

Chapter R

possible? Do you think that reasonable? Think about what he gets up to: he glues pages together or cuts them into little squares so when you open them you just get confetti; he erases every second heading or word with acid or cuttlefish ink, which look like mould stains; in place of a book he often leaves a card with a puzzle on it, because he delights in these inanities – riddles and anagrams that send you off to another shelf in another room, and so on in an exasperating circle that makes you curse the inventors of libraries, books and the alphabet. After this wild goose chase, you perhaps end up with just a cover with nothing in it, or simply straw or white polystyrene or glass wool. Now wait, listen."

He was getting warmed up, and pulled at my sleeve to make sure that I paid attention. I did, and was becoming a little bewildered.

"Listen to what he gets up to. He puts little jokes with spring mechanisms in the books so that they jump in the air in front of the reader who opens a page. Hardly very amusing! And what does it mean? He makes ones that look like grasshoppers from bits of paper; or like frogs or puppets with berets and their tongues sticking out, which whistle as they leap, so that the public can no longer take books and libraries seriously. If it just happened very sporadically, one might be inclined to laugh. I would be the first to do it, because laughter is an integral of being a human being, is it not? The occasional joke is always very welcome, and I myself did a few in my youth. We used to put sugar in the salt pot; you should have seen how we laughed in my family. And then there was salt in the sugar bowl: it was a hoot, good fun amongst friends, it really was. But his are ridiculous pranks that never change and go on and on and on: he puts sneezing powder in some books, itching powder in others, so readers scratch themselves and their respiratory tracts become congested, causing them to lose their concentration. They think they might have fleas, and those who are allergic turn red and get covered with thousands of very unsightly spots. They practically skin themselves alive as they furiously scratch themselves. Readers, as you know, are percentagewise very sensitive and unsettled souls. He also uses pepper, paprika, sulphur dioxide, which produce sores on the hands, the tongue and the conjunctivae. He applies powders or gelatines of his own invention so that when a book is opened you can smell faeces or putrefaction which send everyone running off in search of fresh air, while someone else is probably accused of having broken wind on the quiet. You must know that readers are easily offended and how they never admit to a moment of weakness on this point, be it only very occasional or even unique in an otherwise eminent career. Thus there are tiresome squabbles between the different tables during the ensuing attempts to identify the culprit and even between tables that are very distant. And they exchange such biting and veracious insults on each other's excessive sedentariness, the lack of reciprocal esteem and the trade that the other would have been best advised to follow, that the whole tenor of the library is negatively affected, so that even the person who was sitting in the remotest dark corner immersed in careful study of some book runs over, because the foul smell is poisoning the air over there too. Incompatibilities hitherto dormant suddenly come to the surface. For instance, they all take it out on a single individual, who in reality is just another victim and fellow sufferer of that book's nauseous smell. 'You smell like a sewer,' the other professors and colleagues shout at him. 'It wasn't me,' he replies. They send an emissary to check it out, and he arrives at his diagnosis when he is still a metre away: 'Here there's something persistent and all-pervasive.' 'It's the book,' he says. 'Shame on you!' the other join in; 'you've mistaken study for stomach disorders. There are more appropriate places, you know – places where you should be locked up for good.' But it can happen – and it has happened – that other books are sprinkled with a powder which, in my opinion, is a laxative, a powder with powerful purgative effect, once more for the sake of a

Chapter R

prank. So it ends up that amongst those who have made the unfair accusations, there is one person who has the foible of wetting his fingers before turning the pages. First of all his mouth turns black; this is a sign I have learnt to recognise. Then what follows can only be defined as a despicable crime. The accuser turns pale, and everyone looks at him. He struggles in vain against himself, and would prefer to die than offer up such a miserable spectacle, but inevitably the spasms and convulsions bring him to his knees on the floor, and there follows a release that creates both confusion and consternation in the whole room and all the adjacent ones. This of course amounts to self-incrimination in relation to the other crime he did not commit. Once the initial moments of dismay have passed and the criminal and his crime have been removed from the scene, the party that has been unjustly accused is readmitted to the academic community with a few faint apologies, although there remains a suspicion of his collusion and covert collaboration with the principal culprit. So in conclusion, there is no peace, and the books that should provide it have become instruments for removing it: they induce anger, shame, slander and gossip, and faint-heartedness. But this is not all. Although I cannot be absolutely certain of this, I do have sufficient evidence to assert that something impalpable and volatile is being spread on the books, which can suddenly remove all sexual restraint. When it is inhaled, it produces the venereal concupiscence and carnal pleasure that are so inimical to learning and academic endeavour. Here it is dark, and there are very few staff. Let me tell you that I have seen books on logic, mathematics and calculus interpreted as romantic novels and read and reread with watery eyes and those cretinous smiles born of ugly thoughts. This is the most insidious of his pranks, because no one is willing to admit it, but you cannot fail to notice certain forms of behaviour, a lot of toing and froing, even amongst people who are getting on a bit, with many years of teaching behind them... Some faces, looking downwards, betray some persistent ideas, perverse misinterpretations and frenzied imaginations applied to all the surrounding people: women, men, objects, attendants – so much so that it would be best to call the police and have them do a roundup to prevent the resulting scandal, extreme consequences and the improper and unnatural use of books.

"I'll tell you this: the lavatories are full and you should see the shameful behaviour! A great crowd of them there in a queue and knocking on the doors. 'Come on! How long is this going to take?' they shout at the first to get in. After a while this person comes out goggle-eyed; he is perhaps the head of faculty, an academic or an ageing researcher. He holds the book under his jacket to avoid making a fool of himself, but his face displays a pervert's moronic grin. You must understand that in this way our library stock is gradually ruined: there are bite marks and other signs of violence, because these venereal substances that emanate from the books overheat the academics' heads, and they are not accustomed to it, they have no experience and they mistakenly let their passions rip on the inanimate things that come to hand. I have seen three of them shut themselves up in a cubicle with a footstool. Now you tell me what could be less seductive and titillating than a footstool! And then there are the pens, ink pots and notebooks, which they are always sniffing and sticking in their mouths. They unscrew light bulbs and carry them away while they are still burning hot. When two people sitting close to each other suddenly experience erotic desires, they argue over a pencil rubber or look at each other's books with the concealed covetousness of an adulterer. Then one of them puts out his hand and touches the paper; the other screams that the first academic should be ashamed of himself. His speech adopts a moralistic tone, but as he inhales more of this gaseous aphrodisiac, he fondles the cover and puts his fingers under the spine. Being inexpert and not content with the effect, he spies on his neighbour to see what he does. Sometimes they

Chapter R

actually exchange books, which is absolutely forbidden in the library, because everyone must keep the book they chose, for which they take sole and rightful responsibility in accordance with the law.

"But this is not all. This Vincenzo Gallo puts whistles that produce birdcalls in draughty cracks, and when the wind blows, it makes a sound that resembles a flock of dangerous and hungry birds. He also has these special little trumpets which, when the wind blows, sound like the charge of a herd of enraged elephants. I don't know what he does with the keyholes – whether he uses ordinary wax or sealing wax – but they hiss like snakes, and he smears some kind of corrosive substance on the door hinges so that even a slight movement produces a horrible squeaking sound like that of a pack of hyenas. All this just to discredit me and my library, terrorise the readers and those who make sacrifices, and stir up the staff against the management."

Chapter S

"So there isn't anything there?" I said to the director, "there are no predatory and poisonous animals, no cobras, no hyenas, no horses, no ants and no birds?"

"Who told you this rubbish?"

"Professor Rasorio; he told me this on his word of honour. But I also heard them when I was over there on my own – I heard all those animals screaming."

"Never believe what Rasorio tells you. He belongs to the mafia; I am now certain of it. He tries to terrorise ordinary people. He even tries it with me. He wants to close my mouth for good. He follows orders and obeys the encyclopaedia and his bosses. He doesn't see what is really going on."

"So it is all just pranks? Even the books?"

"All pranks! All the work of Vincenzo Gallo! It is his vendetta against me. I am a practical man; I like facts and not words, but they reported to me that he – who would have thought it? – claimed that he was just fading away in the office and every night he faded a little more. But these are just the same old excuses to avoid working. I know these devil-may-care types when I see them. I have long experience, but when I hear such illogical claptrap as 'fading away', I get very nervous. Then he was saying that if nobody looked at him, he was capable of becoming transparent. 'I can do that too, when no one's looking at me,' I had him informed through the official channels, 'in fact, everyone can do it.' In any case, they saw very little of him at the office – indeed, hardly at all. I didn't want him to give a bad example to the other and above all I didn't want him to make a fool of me. He said he had been a conjurer and knew many tricks. He might perhaps have done it in the provinces, before I took him on out of the kindness of my heart. Everybody in here knows this story and many believe it. He uses this to his advantage.

Chapter 5

He persisted so much in his claim that he was fading, that he became convinced of it himself: he actually believed that he had in some ways become invisible, but I can assure you that he was not. Reality was very different: he was fat, he was obese. I wanted him to retract his idea. Do you think an employee should be allowed to hold such an idea, when he is supposed to be accountable for his actions to the management and the public? It is also a matter of propriety?

"I started to speak to him. 'Sit down,' I said. 'Now let's see; you say that you are transparent, and yet you are a temporary, category-four worker recruited in accordance with Law 480. How can these two things be reconciled?'

"'How can they be reconciled? Yes,' he said, 'that's what I keep wondering.'

"'Besides here you are in front of me,' I said, 'and I can see you very clearly. And you've put on a lot of weight recently; I can see it with my own eyes, but if you want, I can show it to you on the scales. So, how come a transparent person can get fat, and I can see it?'

"'Yes,' he said, 'it is strange that you see me as fat and actually I do to some extent feel fat. I don't deny it; it is strange. I'll have to think about this one, and I'll give you my reply tomorrow.'

"The following day I went to see him in his little room on the second floor, after the anatomical theatre and the Rare Books Collection and the Unclassified Books Collection, because otherwise he would have failed to turn up, having his own entrance at the back, which only he knew about.

"'Right! Have you thought about it?' I said.

"'Yes, you are too close when you look at me.'

"'But what is that supposed to mean? Why? Are transparent things no longer transparent if seen up close?'

"'You want to have an argument,' he said, 'which I don't like.'

"'What argument is that? You're the one who says you're transparent. I say you aren't!'

"'That's up to you; I don't care. I'm not forcing you to believe.'

"Who can blame me if I got a little heated at this stage? 'This is not an opinion,' I shouted, 'it's a fact. I'll show you you're not transparent: here you are seated and fat. Take a look at yourself, you must weigh a hundred kilos. You seem puffed up, even your face. You look like a stuffed pig. You look like half an ox. Well, what have you got to say for yourself?' I stood up, 'Well then?' and I said many more hard-hitting things, in part for his own good and appearance. My anger boiled up with increasing ferocity and impatience. I went up to him and muttered, 'You don't reason; you offend me,' and seeing him there so fat and argumentative, I slapped him. That was wrong of me; one should not slap one's employees. Besides, what reason did I have? He was right: his being transparent or not transparent was not my concern. He trembled in his corpulence, and the poor man's cheek was red, as was the back of his neck, which I also hit repeatedly. I pulled his ear as hard as I could, almost tore it off. I pulled it almost under his eyes, so he could see it, as though he were a schoolboy. I pinched his nose and twisted it, while shouting, 'Is it transparent?' I twisted it with pleasure and great force as though I wanted to unscrew it, and insulted him nigglingly, without knowing how to contain my anger to the smallest degree. He defended himself weakly.

"At some stage he said, 'What difference would it make if I were thin?'

"These arguments were repeated not every day, but very often, because when I was alone in my office I remembered – who knows why? – that he was down there in his room and convinced of being transparent, while in fact he was a hundred kilos of lard bundled up in those grey and worn trousers of his. I remembered this cock-and-bull story devoid of any sense, and I imagined him down there sitting peacefully in the midst of this error perhaps a little smugly. Then I was seized by anger and this need to convince him of his folly. I ran up stairs and along corridors and through

Chapter 5

reading rooms and up a small, out-of-use stair that served as a short-cut and across a terrace and down a tiny, dark hallway and finally entered his room, not with bad intentions, but to make him aware of his obvious mistake. It was this lack of logic that made me so free with my fists. At the same time, however, I could not say that he had done anything wrong. I was brought up with the principles of liberalism, and why then did I have to get involved? What had I to do with another person's beliefs?

"I entered without knocking to catch him out, and there he was behind his desk and entirely visible. He gave a start, because from the very beginning his wonderful theory was having to measure up to reality. I sat down and spoke to him as a friend, 'It's very nice up here. I thought I would pay you a little visit. Well then? Have you got rid of those silly ideas?' I put my hand on his shoulder and spoke in a tone of fraternal jocularity, 'Okay, so you got there in the end!' He recoiled and did not answer – in either the affirmative or the negative. He merely got on with the job of wrapping up a half-eaten roll and a chocolate bar and putting them back in a drawer.

"'... oh, don't tell me you're still a little transparent? Is that it?'

"He made a small gesture of apology, but my voice had already started to change in tone. Inevitably an argument broke out.

"'What is this transparency of yours supposed to mean? You're not made of glass, by any chance?'

"'No,' he said, walking backwards to the corner as a precaution, 'no, it means that one is not opaque.'

"When I heard such expressions, I just lost my powers of reason. There was nothing to be done, and I wanted to extort his retraction, for while the errors of this world are many, as are the deceits, as is only natural, his arguments would have turned the world into a Babel of wasted words, if they were ever allowed to spread.

"'You might,' I replied, 'get away with such talk when you speak to others, but not to me! Opaque! But where?

Who?' I got so carried away with my cause that I ran at him. He covered his head with his arms and tried to disappear into his jacket, but I took him by his cheek and pinched it. Through his clothes I pinched his chest, his stomach and his hips, in part to demonstrate my arguments and in part with the clear intention of covering him with bruises and giving him an extravasation of blood that would bear witness, in the days to come and also in private, to the absurdity of his claims.

"'So you've got it at last,' I cried, 'you're not made of air.' He massaged his bruises, and settled back in his chair.

"'So we're back to square one,' I followed up my argument. 'In your opinion, is all this fat something or is it nothing?' and my fist came down with threatening force on the table, causing the pens, rubbers and glue bottles to bounce up on the table, and increasing the disorder that was already considerable – on the verge of being intolerable in an employee. But I would have liked to really give vent to my feelings: smash up his chair and the table, hurl him and the furnishings about, tear up the books, throw them against the wall, hit him over the head with them and then climb up on him with my feet until he was finally persuaded. Bodies are heavy and broad, and are provided with considerable mass, both of us included, and one cannot go on forever using words illogically and randomly without them rebelling, and then there's no telling what will happen. I was very restrained, to avoid putting myself in the wrong; I only threw as hard as I could a pencil, a screwed-up piece of paper and some paper clips. Then I went off, but for the rest of the night I was on edge and continued in my mind to argue with him and hit him. I couldn't get any more work done.

"I believe that following my attentions he started to be more circumspect and to keep out of my way so as not to have any arguments, which would have meant giving in to the evidence. He obstinately wanted to cling to his antiscientific persuasion. I asked myself: is he here at the moment? Or is he not here? Who knows? Does he come in?

Chapter S

Does he leave? It appeared so. It was his duty, and his signature in the register confirmed that he was here. He always left the light on in his office, but it was now impossible to find him in there. Sometimes towards the morning, I would think about those ridiculous and misplaced claims, which were so irritating and contemptible, and I could resist no longer. I would run over to his room and, to tell the truth, I wanted to surprise him, to catch him out and reason with him, to find out whether he had reformed and finally given in to common sense. I would find the office open and the radio on, which frankly was not a sign of due diligence. I also found mess and dust, a complete chaos of overturned chairs, a table with a wobbly leg near to collapse, papers, scraps of paper, labels, paper clips, rubber filings from erasing, cuttings partly on the floor, open and crumpled books, bottles of dried glue and bottles of God knows what, certainly nothing to do with office business. Well, what else do you think I found amongst all this Babylonia, which was only a tiny part of the laxity and neglectfulness found everywhere he was responsible for, including the corridors? I found breadcrumbs, salami skins, chicken bones, roast-meat leftovers, sauces, pickles and the remains of drinks in a flower vase – not coffee, which would have been permissible, but beer and wine. There was the unmistakable smell of cooking. Clearly he is not only eating but also bivouacking in his office or in the immediate area around it. There is oil and vinegar in the ink pot! And thus his wastepaper bin contains not only those modest objects any conscientious clerk will throw away – rejected writing paper, carbon paper, pencil shavings – no, in his wastepaper bin I have found rotisserie wrappings, tablecloths, napkins, dirty cutlery, plastic plates, greasy packaging and pizzas that were still warm. I know that he is not far away. In that area, the library is primarily a warehouse. There are converted rooms with implausible layouts, low ceilings and plenty of twists and turns. Everything is so contorted and uneven that a fat man – even a man twice as fat as he is – could certainly pass unobserved if he stood still in a corner, between two bookshelves, in a broom cupboard or up a passageway that has been blocked off, particularly because of the bad lighting. I then started to wander around, walking very quietly because I wanted to see if he was working and in what manner, find out if he still had that absurd idea in his head and remove it once and for all. I looked up and down the corridors and occasionally caught a whiff of hot soup, which is his typical smell, and I searched the surrounding area, behind the doors and in the window openings. I took a ladder and inspected the beams and the highest bookshelves, because he is evil and capable of anything. I have even looked in the cupboards and underneath them. Even though he is fat, he is capable of flattening himself out and slipping through a slit, simply in order to avoid being answerable to me for his conduct. I heard the calls of game birds and wild animals: that is him with his devices designed to spread fear and humiliate me. A rabbit or a clutch of turtle doves can suddenly appear, because he has created a private poultry pen amongst the books. He knows where to go to collect the eggs. He has ingratiated himself with the hens by giving them dried bread and leftovers. So the chickens are proliferating and there are more of them than there are books. The library has become his kingdom, his vegetable garden, and the hens are everywhere. He has encouraged them, because he cooks them, makes soup from them, and has them roasted."

The director Perbeni said these words with a furious intensity that made his voice hoarse. As he spoke, he plugged the fan back in and stood next to it with a proud expression, like an artist next to one of his creations. Meanwhile the table drawer was open and the pages of Rasorio's *Very Modern Encyclopaedia* were flapping about.

When he felt that he had spoken long enough, he looked at his watch and pushed a button in the wall. In that precise moment it struck seven o'clock: it appeared that he had caused the bells to chime with his finger, but he had

Chapter 5

in fact pressed a buzzer, because a tiny attendant came running up, breathless and full of zeal.

"Put that back in its place," the director said, indicating the encyclopaedia with evident distaste, "we work in here; we don't fool around."

The attendant seemed fearful of the director, as though expecting him to be free with his fists, and he never looked him in the eyes. I seem to remember that his name was Caper, or perhaps I just imagined it after having looked at his face. I thought that the encyclopaedia could actually be very useful. Why didn't I think of it beforehand? I said, "Just a moment! Couldn't I take a look at it, seeing that it is already here..."

The director looked very unhappy; he said nothing, but turned his back on me. While I was settling into the chair with great solicitude, the director had retrieved from under the table with the listless assistance of Accetto's son an enormous and battered sheet of metal with some traces of paint still on it, perhaps a car bonnet or a plane fuselage. He sat it on the table and started to pummel it with a massive blacksmith's hammer, which produced a deafening noise. And perhaps because it was not taking the shape he intended, he swore and cursed the type of iron used, accusing it of being some vile aluminium alloy of little worth, which only made him pound it more violently with increasing anger and bitterness. In the midst of this infernal racket, whose source was but a metre away and spraying me with shards of paint, the letters of the alphabet became all jumbled up in my deafened brain, so I ended up flicking backwards and forwards through the book on a rather random basis. The attendant bowed down to hide himself behind me, as though to shield himself. I could feel his tremulous breath on the back of my neck and it did not smell nice. It was like a gas leak. I was, therefore, caught between two fires, and on top of that, there was the cold wind from the fan that I found very unpleasant when it came my way. For a second, I saw what I was looking for, the twentieth century, but then a shard went in my eye and a hammer blow came down close by, so I probably got confused about which page or turned over several unintentionally. What I read, in the midst of all my difficulties, was this:

Cycle paths in purgatory

During the Bordeaux-Parigi bicycle race, the automatism of the Englishman Mills was such that he had to be grabbed at the end of each leg, and placed on a stretcher with his legs in the air. He would continue to pedal in the air and to see the road and dust in front of him. They gave him water and a restorative syrup to drink with a pump. Then they put him back on the saddle: four men attempted to hold his legs still and a fifth one quickly strapped his feet to the pedal cranks. This was a perilous moment both for the men and the bicycle.

Then they launched him off on the road once more.

He would occasionally regain consciousness and look to the left and the right, and if there was nobody there, he would shift to the side and, still pedalling furiously, answer the call of nature. Immediately afterwards his automatism would once more take over, and he would maintain the same identical rhythm both uphill and downhill. In general, he tended to go in a straight line, but he was able to predict the bends through an unerring sixth sense, and he took the bend on a fixed radius, as though he were calculating it and seeing it, but he never altered the force of each pedal stroke.

After the finishing line, they lowered him into a bathtub full of water and covered his head with snow. Then he appeared to wake up and stopped pedalling. The contracture of his muscles ceased, he smiled and he said a few kind words to his friends and his trainer.

He could not remember anything. But on just one occasion, he said he had often dreamt of purgatory where everyone was on a bicycle, but the dream was so full of dust and rubble that he could not say anything very definite about the landscape.

Chapter T

The page I had just read was yellowish, a few millimetres narrower than the rest – perhaps a photocopy – and not bound into the book, but fixed there with a rusty pin. I had no sooner thought it might be one of Vincenzo Gallo's interpolative jokes, or one perpetrated by someone working on his behalf, than the director smashed the book in two with a blow of his hammer. I feared that he was going to hammer me as well, such was the passion and the frenzy that had taken hold of him. But the two or three blows that followed only struck the drawer and the book glancingly, as though it were an enemy whose ostentation he could no longer put up with.

But he did pick on me, "So you too are giving in to the mafia! You too have signed up! Away the lot of you! Clear out, you delinquents and counterfeiters, you swine." He seemed completely mad, and there was good reason to be frightened. He went out to see Feltpad who, being more accustomed to his boss's behaviour, carried on smoking his cigarette and leaning lethargically against the door jamb.

Caper and I withdrew hastily. "Now look what you've done! You've made him angry," Caper said.

"If a person can't read in a library," I retorted, "where in the world can he?"

"He's got other ideas in his head, and you should not provoke him or hang about in front of him in an insolent manner. That's the way it is." He was carrying the sorry remains of the encyclopaedia under his arm; it was Volume X, the letters "s" to "t".

"I would like to consult it in peace," I said.

"That's all right, sir."

However, I could not get out of my head the idea of a Vincenzo Gallo, a fat man in hiding who hissed, roared, had imitation flies and bats flying around the place, sprinkled erogenous powders that caused horrible blunders, possibly gnawed at books, muddled up papers and deliberately spread misleading information, so that we can no longer be very sure of anything. "But could a man ever become transparent?" I surprised myself with the thought. Incautiously, I had actually said it out aloud.

"Who?" Caper immediately replied, "Vincenzo Gallo?" He saw that I was not denying it, and went on, "One would should really consult a doctor or a vet... Very well then, it's rare, but it can happen."

"Impossible," I said in order not to encourage further learned disquisitions. I wanted to read the encyclopaedia; it was my last hope and I tried to take it from under his arm. But I must have touched on a delicate subject, which perhaps for him was a real thorn in the flesh, because his eyes opened wide and became clearer, and he started to talk. Instinctively he moved his arm away with the book under it, and brought his mouth closer with its gaseous breath that acted as his own bell jar, a shield. In the meantime, the hammer blows were off again, and they reverberated behind my ears like acute otitis.

"It is never daytime here and we become depressed," said Caper with conviction. "If someone has a happy youth in the open air, in here they become disheartened. And then, yes, it can happen. It can happen that a man in particular conditions of stress, subjected to constant psychic pressure which in the long term can build up to tens of tons per cubic centimetre, eventually desires with all his body and all his soul to escape, but at the same time undergoes an equal and opposite force within his heart of hearts that immobilises him in the exact spot he currently occupies – for example, the desk in his office. And if that man is repressed and vilified, and particularly if he is fat, then it can happen that one fine day he can no longer stay within his skin, he loses his unity as a human being and he is dispersed into the environment in unidentifiable forms. His organism loses all cohesion, and his organs, like autonomous, responsible beings capable of locomotion, slip stealthily away, some go one way, some

Chapter T

the other: the spleen over here and the kidney and bowels over there, and so on with the thyroid, coronary arteries, oesophagus, pylorus, tongue and teeth."

"This is all rubbish," I said, "will you put a stop to it."

"No," he said, "if you want to understand the phenomenon, then you have to start with the idea that a human being is a cluster of animals that live one on top of the other in a state of absolute contiguity. I would have liked to study medicine, and I say this with some knowledge of the subject. When well-being reigns, they too are packed together in a harmonious embrace, as in a nest, but if the life becomes ugly, some of them become irritated, agitated and angry enough to bite. For example, the heart starts to give an occasional kick, the lungs deflate and become depressed, and the bladder will not listen to reason and spill water in protest. None of them want to stay in their proper place: initially there is animosity between them all, but then there is a general stampede. It's rare, I admit, from a histological point of view, but it does happen. In such cases, we do not talk of the person's disappearance, but rather of the diaspora of their entire being. Nose, throat, tongue, soft palate and uvula all fly off and mix with the sparrows, barn owls and bats. You can hear them singing on a branch, if there is one, or on a gutter or an exposed nail. They imitate all sorts of birds and after a bit, they are on friendly terms and love to go on excursions together. Ears go off in pairs and look like hummingbirds hovering together. An eye can be lost on the ground, and withdraws into its eyelid, timid as a snail. Nerves spread out all over the place, very fine and insubstantial like a spider's web: on the spines of books, from one bookshelf to another, on the floor between the tiles, so that you get entangled in them. The heart, on the other hand, follows its own particular nature and runs off like a hare, leaping as far as it can go. Once it is out in the fresh air and feels itself free, it makes a tremendous leap and no one can hold it back any more. No one knows where it goes, except when it darts between the director's legs or his secretary's, with its ears erect, and then it loses itself in the distance, where you can only hear some thuds. The lungs are mammoths whose muffled roar is cavernous. They go in search of air or they will die out. If it is cold, steam comes out with their breath. Glands look like toads and salamanders. They lie under stones and secrete mucus and poison. And the bowels? Well, the bowels slip out of a person's backend and go downwards; they're looking for dampness and maybe pass an old latrine or find an old disused sewer, and there they reign like the royal python at the mouth of the Brahmaputra, swimming in the black mud and feeding on rats, frogs and tadpoles, but going up to the surface at dawn to enjoy the view.

"What about the head, though! Its case history is the most unpredictable. During the period of pain and stress, when sufferers are convinced that they are about to explode but haven't exploded yet, it appears that their heads exude some kind of liquid – an acidulous, spirituous product of the pressure in their brains – through the pores of the forehead, temples and neck, and they can smell like a kind of yogurt of millions of micro-organisms fermenting within it. Then one night this so-called human brain goes outside, like leaving an anthill, and its contents swarm on the pillowcase and initially remain within a small radius. Then they gradually explore further afield but still in the area: the bedstead, the wall and the bedside table. Sufferers have the sensation of being in a wonderful, spacious and evanescent dream that lightens their load, and in the meantime their brains are wandering off in single file, as though they were ants going up an electric wire. Thus the lamp is giving off a tiny amount of light, in spite of being switched off. Even the brass knob on the chest of drawers, the iron one on the bed, the hinges and handle of the door are also giving off this very weak light, like so many brushstrokes of phosphorus. When these myriads of insects dry, they leave behind minute silver husks, which at the slightest breath of air lift up in a cloud of fine dust like icing sugar, but the sufferers' heads are left empty. The insects move away in swarms that are increasingly rarefied, variable and free from any obligation to be intelligent. Finding themselves in the open with a generous food supply, these insects can grow up to visible dimensions. They grow legs, wings, wing cases, and occasionally pincers or aculei, according to what they have specialised in. They spread and reproduce. They can easily be mistaken for normal insects, but a naturalist would not know how to classify them, even though they resemble better-known species. If they gather together under the bark of a tree, in a hole in a piece of wood or within a hollow, and if they are also in large numbers, tightly packed together and a little syrupy, then they can still produce a glimmer of intelligence, perhaps some vague childhood memory, which cannot however express itself, except through a faint, luminescent dream isolated from everything else.

"At the same time, all the skin sags like a paper bag, but remains within the person's clothes, which however are carelessly thrown in the dirty-clothes bag to be sent to the laundry.

"These cases are extremely rare. Perhaps the only one was that of our ex-employee, Vincenzo Gallo. In any event, they elude clinical observation because they occur when there is no one around. In bed at home, on the chair in the office or behind the desk in school, all that is left is just a few flakes of cutaneous tissue, the odd chewed nail, a fluffy hair or two, a shirt, a jacket and little else. They say all that remained of Vincenzo Gallo was his complete skin on the coat stand along with his clothes, always supposing it isn't a rubber joke or a very modern diver's suit.

"It could be said that Vincenzo Gallo is still in the library's employ, but scattered all over the place under various animal guises. It is highly unlikely that they will all come back together again: they are frightened of the director Perbeni, and besides they have now gone wild. They are taking their revenge: they gnaw the books and the shelving, they frighten the staff, and they sting and torment those who fall asleep, but not just them. Perhaps one day the whole place will come tumbling down and here will be open country again with the appropriate fauna, and when people look at a grasshopper, a worm, a chicken flea or a spider, they will never know whether or not they were once part of Vincenzo Gallo."

While Caper was talking, I managed to penetrate the barrier of natural gas that surrounded him and take the book off him. There was a door open, and we entered a long and narrow box room. There, to my surprise, was Iris – yes, none other – and she was looking in the mirror, combing her hair and preparing, it would appear, to go out.

"Are you talking about Vincenzo Gallo?" she said on hearing Caper's last words.

I didn't want to take any notice of her and lowered my head, because in my opinion she most certainly had been an accomplice of Albonea Bucato at great cost to myself. Instead I had opened the encyclopaedia and had placed it on the only chair, which had an overcoat on it. There were other coats hanging from hooks on the wall, and umbrellas in the umbrella stand.

"You, my little Caper, do not know everything," Iris told him.

I wanted to study the twentieth century and was leaning over the book as I thumbed my way through it. I suddenly found, "Twentieth Century, Chronicle of". But on one side I had Caper whose sickly breath forced me to turn the other way, towards Iris. I was between them, and their words had to pass through me. Iris was as lovely as ever. "Ah! If only I didn't have this exam," I thought. Instinctively I cast a furtive eye on her mouth which was soft, pink and glabrous – if anything spring-like. And her voice was a fox trap.

Chapter U

"You, my little Caper," said Iris close to my ear, "don't know the celebrated story of Vincenzo Gallo's childhood, when he was thin and could pass through a keyhole."

"I did once know it, I did," said Caper close to my other ear.

"If you don't know it, then I'll tell you: Vincenzo Gallo, at the age of four, was a skinny and delicate little scamp, who drove his nanny crazy. At the age of five he started to upset people. He used to attach lighted catherine-wheels and stink bombs to their clothes as they were passing by and, while they were screaming and struggling to put out the flames that were spreading across their clothing, he would steal their hats, gloves and purses. He did this in response to a congenital instinct of his."

I stared at the encyclopaedia in despair, with time inexorably beating its rhythm in my epiglottis. I pretended to be reading in order to reclaim a little silence, but my eyes could not get past the title, because Iris's voice was permeating my ear and left cortex like a hemiplegia. "God willing she will get this over and done with quickly," I said repeatedly to myself, having noticed that she had started this story from the man's childhood.

"When the time came for Vincenzo Gallo to go to school," Iris continued, "there was this teacher who was supposed to educate them; he never stopped talking from the moment he entered the class in the morning, but on the whole no one listened to him because they didn't want to be distracted from their principal occupation, which was stealing. The older children set an example and educated the smaller ones, so that the class made enormous progress in the arts of dissembling, nimbleness and sleight of hand. There was a hive of activity under the desks, with recourse, where necessary, to sneezing powder and itching powder. They even practised on the teacher, but mainly for the spectacle this produced: for instance, they would hurl flies towards his mouth, which interposed themselves between his words, buzzing as they did so and altering his phonemes, and then suddenly flew off like incorrect consonants. This was a little frightening for the poor teacher, who started to stammer. He thought it was a weakness of his own, a sign of his advancing years.

"Anyway Vincenzo Gallo was one of the most accomplished pupils before three months were out. He could hide small objects in his teeth, nose and folds of his eyelids, and what he hid were needles, drawing pins, breadcrumbs, threads, nibs, tiny strips of paper, tissues and blotting paper. He hid other objects between his toes, under his tongue or between his cheeks and his gums. Under his armpits, for example, he would keep salami, bread and two fried eggs; he had a locker in his ear. His hair was very long and thick, and in a sense acted as a strongbox. If everyone in class fell asleep during the siesta period, the janitors would come in creeping along in complete silence, and rummage around in pencil boxes, folders and dust jackets, but their hands were like air, so light and cautious were they, and even if someone woke up, they did not notice. They stole off Gallo a watch that he had swallowed, and a tooth that looked as if it were made of silver off another boy, and their takings included fountain pens, money, pencils, combs, elastic bands, laces and even shirts and other items of clothing that were being worn at the time. The fact is, however, that these janitors were never caught in the act, and no one ever saw them. All this was mere speculation, because some objects, especially the minuscule ones, disappeared never to be seen again. For this reason, the janitors were looked up to at school as the supreme ideal of perfection, everyone's shared aspiration to become invisible.

"One day at the school gate, Vincenzo Gallo was going about his business of attaching smoke and flashes to a group of virtuous ladies, when two policemen saw him and gave chase. In a single movement he was hidden under one of their skirts, for he was still very short and as thin as a

Chapter U

stick. But the policemen could see his feet, and to avoid capture, he set fire to the skirt. In the ensuing melee, he just managed to make his escape, taking with him a soft tulle ribbon and shoe buckle. With the policemen at his heels, he leapt on a tram which came by at high speed. But his mania for matches caused a fire to start on one of the seats. The passengers screamed, as did the driver because he couldn't find the brake pedal. At the bottom of the hill he was caught at a roadblock set up by the police and fire brigade: he was found hidden in a briefcase with two locks under a gentleman's arm. This is just to show how skilled he was even then. When they brought him out, four policemen were holding him as tight as they could. They took him to the chief of police, but all of a sudden he slipped up a trouser leg of one of the officers who had brought him in, because the officer was busy with the exacting act of standing to attention. Another officer caught sight of Vincenzo Gallo's clever move and had grabbed the first officer's knee, thus neglecting the decorum required by good discipline. The disorders occurring in chief of police's office were turning him red in the face. But Vincenzo Gallo did not want to come out. They pulled from above and pulled from below, and eventually a fire lit from behind forced him out of the trousers. It seems unbelievable, but you have to remember that he was as thin as an anchovy and besides, these were just trifles compared with what happened later. While the chief of police was writing Gallo's personal details in the register, the nib disappeared, then the pen, then ink from inside the ink pot; they searched him, but found nothing. They wanted to ascertain his height with a measuring tape, but in the meantime the register had disappeared. They sent for another one, but now there was no measuring tape. The chief of police was beside himself with anger, and he still could not get his hands on the boy."

Iris spoke well, like someone reading aloud, and all the time, she carried on combing her hair and looking at herself in the mirror. I gawked at her lips and almost forgot my own existence.

"Once he had started down this road, Vincenzo Gallo inevitably spent his teenage years going in and out of prison and institutions for young offenders, but as the years passed, it became increasingly difficult to apprehend him, put him inside and keep him there. To tell the truth, the justice system is completely impotent when it comes to characters like this, because there was no padlock, no bolt and no window that he could not open. He could escape when and how he liked, and could always avoid capture by camouflaging himself in a fraction of a second or by actually disappearing in front of policemen's eyes. He often just did it for practice or amusement. He was twelve. He was impudently lingering so that they could surround him with ten or twenty men – the number made no difference – who would handcuff him and attach those handcuffs with a double chain to the wrists of two massive officers of the law, one on each side. Two more officers went ahead and four followed behind. These latter four were champion runners, swordsmen and lassoers. The two on either side were wrestling instructors. Those ahead of him were consummate sharpshooters, and they were armed. Vincenzo Gallo waited for a crowd to be formed, as he had already developed an instinct for the theatrical: passers-by stopped to take a look, the shopkeepers ran into the street because his name was becoming famous, and then people gathered at the windows – whole families with children, aunts and a grandfather who took up their positions in the front row. And then it happened: quite suddenly Vincenzo Gallo was gone and all the athletes and wrestlers were quite superfluous, because they never saw him escaping. People simply turned to look at each other, and they realised that he was no longer where he had been. You have no idea: the applause! And the tricks he used always changed and were invented in the very moment they were implemented. You might say that on each occasion he produced a work of art: handcuffs, padlocks and chains, it

Chapter U

was as if they didn't exist. He slipped them off like someone who had no bones, and then he simply disappeared. For example, he would make a feint as though to escape and the policemen would close their ranks around him, but he was no longer there. They speculated that he had escaped down a manhole, that he had entered a hatchway down a tube, or that he had dressed up as a policeman and was still there amongst them. They came up with the most absurd and unlikely hypotheses: that he could make himself small, dry himself out and get into someone's pocket, or that his capture had been an optical illusion, all smoke and mirrors. They even thought that the real Vincenzo Gallo was remotely operating a rubber puppet that looked like him to deceive people, then at the appropriate moment he would deflate it. The police officers wrote in their reports that there was a piece of bowel left over on the ground, some nylon threads, and they found clothes pegs, a smear of methylated spirits, and threads from his jacket. Sometimes his hat was left on the ground, sometimes a shoelace and they were irrefutable evidence that he had been there, and that for a short while they had caught and tied him up. But no more than that.

"When he reached the age of fourteen, a magistrate, who thought himself more astute than the others, summoned him for trial and swore that no one would lay a finger on him until the sentence had been read. Gallo promptly went to sit down at his place in the dock. But then the clerk of the court's pen disappeared, sheets of paper flew off, ink was spilt on the floor but then got back into the ink pot or on the judge's chair. A lawyer's wallet vanished and was found in another man's pocket, causing mutual recriminations and police charges. Eggs and chicks appeared amongst the legal papers. Chickens were flying about the place and the court officials were unable to catch them, and everything was turned topsy-turvy in the pursuit, which the public, witnesses and prosecutors joined in. At some stage, it then appeared that another

Vincenzo Gallo in ermine was seated in the presiding judge's chair and the presiding judge was handcuffed and seated in the dock. The jury were all wearing the three-cornered hats of the *carabinieri*. The confusion was at its climax: no one could find their own jacket, hats were floating in the air, quite possibly on invisible threads with hooks; the owners of the hats were attempting to leap in the air to retrieve them, and they clambered up on table or one would go on another's shoulders forming human pyramids. The ushers were required to form the base, but the poor fellows could not hold up that weight and the whole thing collapsed and crashed down on benches, crush barriers and onlookers, from which Vincenzo Gallo's innocent and ironic face popped up. At this stage the public prosecutor went back on his word and screamed, "Hold him still! Arrest him! Handcuff him!" The *carabinieri* stopped running after the hens and sought him out in the midst of that crush of bodies and pile of chairs. Thinking they had seen him seated and barefoot in the public gallery, they rushed to grab him, but it was the judge who was wearing Gallo's meagre jacket and started to squawk like a magpie calling for help. Meanwhile Vincenzo Gallo appeared and disappeared, producing smoke as he did so – smoke from which he would re-emerge on each occasion stupefyingly transformed: he looked like an old lady, a bishop, a swimmer, the man-in-the-street, the king, queen and jack of hearts. In the end, when the hunt had also been joined by the lawyers, witnesses, judges, typists and jurors, he shot into a drawer like a rocket or so it appeared. They immediately opened it, but there was no sign of him. On such occasions, all they could expect to find were an egg, talcum powder or smoke bombs.

"As a training exercise, he would allow himself to be taken to prison. And to escape he exploited the smallest imperfections in the security system, using his mimetic, acrobatic and contortionistic arts. First of all, locks had no secrets for him. He could open them with the nail of his little finger, which was long, slightly hooked and had seven

Chapter U

kinds of notches. Or he would have recourse to the fillings in his teeth, which were in fact very delicate instruments: scalpels, small screwdrivers, picklocks and tiny band saws. His starting point was the theoretical principle that everything can be dismantled and any place you go into you can get out of. Or he would slip through the inspection hole or seep through the wall or floor in some inexplicable manner, as though his body was not made of flesh or he could dematerialise. In actual fact, he was just using artifice and deception, or in other words, his natural inclination and his training.

"This reputation for being a great escapologist did have its drawbacks. When he was walking down a street, a queue of people would form behind him, and they wanted perhaps to shut him up hermetically in a barrel or a milk churn or a tank made of reinforced concrete. He accepted with good grace, but said that this was not much of a challenge for him; he wanted the barrel to be put underwater and the churn hung from a rope, and as for the tank, he insisted that he should be handcuffed before he went in. On other occasions, they would pay him a thousand compliments and invite him home for lunch or dinner, and then without warning they would lock him up in the icebox or on some pretext they would push him into a wardrobe or safe and immediately turn the key in the door or using another pretext place him in a suitcase or under a large bell jar together with stuffed birds, mosses, leaves and dried twigs. He unfailingly found the weak point and succeeded in freeing himself, but without leaving any visible signs of forcing the locks or breaking his way out. It is undeniable that in the long term these attentions and infatuations started to weary him. While he was peacefully dining at a restaurant, they would tie him to a chair, put a noose round his neck, and wrap him up in gauze like a mummy. Once the chair had a device that, when triggered, trapped his hands and feet in metal clasps. He never had any difficulty in freeing himself; he darted out like an eel and opened padlocks with a toenail and rapidly loosened the screws holding down a chair or opened the way out as one might open a door. Usually waiters, cooks and customers would applaud heartily and the restaurant owner would have a plaque engraved, 'Here Vincenzo Gallo freed himself from a garrotte', 'Here Vincenzo Gallo escaped from an ancient Chinese torture chair' or 'Here Vincenzo Gallo unfastened fifty-two knots and opened twenty-seven locks'. But the excessive frequency of these encounters became a source of annoyance. They bundled him up like a sausage and threw him in a well full of knives and water; while he was out walking, four dog-catchers snared him and laughing and joking attached leather fetters for horses to his feet; they locked him in a cage and in a coffin which they then buried. They invited him to smell the roast in the oven, and then pushed him inside and shut the oven door, while turning up the heat as far as it would go. They could hear him singing. Five minutes went by, then ten and then half an hour. Someone was worried and opened it up. There was a bundle and it was black, carbonised and smoking. Screams of consternation and the lady of the house fainted. They ran to the bathroom to get the smelling salts, but the bathroom was locked. Who could be in there? They knocked. They knocked again. They smashed in the door. There was Vincenzo Gallo under the shower, who said laughingly, 'You must excuse me, but I was a bit sweaty. I took the liberty...' How he did it remained a secret."

"This is never going to end," I thought, rousing myself from some kind of hypnosis. I wriggled around in my chair as though some demon was tormenting me. I rustled the pages of the book to show my agitation, I nodded my head over the writing and pretended to be driving away some flies, but Iris, undeterred, carried on talking and combing her hair.

"That was his childhood. Then one day it happened that a dove – by some strange chance, perhaps because it was

Chapter U

migrating and could not stop or perhaps to satisfy a mad and inexplicable predilection – laid two eggs in one of his pockets. He was very surprised, but also a little pleased with himself. He put the eggs under his armpit and after a little time two little doves were born. This gave rise to his intimacy with birds and other animals. As they grew these fledglings became very fond of one of his shirt pockets, even though it was a little cramped. They looked on it as their home, their childhood nest. In the morning they flew away and all day long they went in search of grain and drink and to develop their relationships with other pigeons, as was only natural, but half an hour before the sun went down they returned home. They knew how to find Vincenzo Gallo wherever he was, because of the unfailing sense of direction peculiar to all doves, but especially carrier ones. They slipped under his jacket and into his shirt pocket, where they flattened themselves out like pieces of paper and passed the night in blissful contentment. It has to be said that you could no longer notice the very slight bulge: the jacket lay perfectly smooth on his front and his back, and his perfectly white and starched shirt didn't have and had never had a crease, bagginess or any other unsightly defect.

"Then came the arrival of this rabbit, which would become a distinguished figure in many theatres in the years to come. It was a white rabbit with white and orange eyes. When Vincenzo Gallo and the rabbit met each other, there was a natural attraction between the two. They were two lonely beings in this world; Vincenzo Gallo was an orphan and the rabbit was fearful and newly born. Moreover Vincenzo Gallo had a smell of earth and the woods which had a magnetic power over animals. Vincenzo Gallo bent down slightly and the rabbit stood up on its hind legs and sniffed. He stretched out his arm by only a fraction, and the rabbit, responding to a sudden inspiration, was up the inside of his sleeve with just two leaps. In the early period, the rabbit lived at his elbow. It went out to eat and stretch its legs. To ask permission it made a scratching sound. Vincenzo Gallo would then lower his sleeve and it came out like an arrow, and resembled a hare, because it was young and happy. It dug holes in the ground, ate grass and roots, and gnawed just about everything here and there. This was what Vincenzo Gallo wanted: the animals were to be unrestricted and autonomous, free to come and go, and to have their own life outside. They were in any case self-sufficient when it came to their primary needs. He loved to feel them on top of him and safe at home, but also to know that they were off flying or running in the midst of life's diversity. Then the rabbit ceased to feel so at ease: either the sleeve was no longer suitable or it was going through that intermediate age before adulthood, which is full of aspirations and discontent. It probably felt miserable and lacked many comforts. One day after having run about and grazed in the meadow – but clearly not enough – it returned full of cravings to his sleeve. Vincenzo Gallo was not interested in this psychological malaise. He happily provided accommodation, but didn't want to go beyond that. The rabbit set off to explore: it climbed up over his shoulder, crossed his back and his chest, and then looked out from the buttons of his shirt. It climbed up once more, stuck its head out of his open collar and an irrational impulse drove it up on top of his head. Here some birds which were nesting there took fright and started to squawk. There were also some snails, fleas and a cuckoo, and all of them were irritated by this invasion and the disagreeable bulk of this rabbit. Then its eyes fell on a top hat on a table, upside down and uninhabited, and in no time it had jumped into the hat and turned it into its apartment. The hat was spacious. It lay concealed inside, and when Vincenzo Gallo travelled, he carried it on his head. The rabbit could position itself propped up against the sides of the hat and just above the top of his head. It would then fall asleep between the felt and the lining as though on a silk hammock. The white rabbit was happy with this respectable accommodation, which in the living quarters constituted by Vincenzo Gallo took on the role of a

Chapter U

tower or belfry, far from the irritatingly close confines of communal life below.

"By now – and this is the nub of the matter – Vincenzo Gallo was home to an enormous number of animal species, particularly those with the powers of flight, simply because he did not know how to say no to silent requests and unauthorised settlements. When evening came, all these birds would circle dizzily in the air around his head, and gradually one by one they would go to their nesting place: they slipped under the collar of his shirt, up his sleeves and into his pockets. The minuscule birds of Patagonia lived in the turn-ups of his trousers, but many birds made their nests in his hair, using woollen threads and loose hairs. A chicken scampered on seeing dusk falling over Vincenzo Gallo and leapt with a flap of its wings onto his knee which acted as a perch. It then entered his trousers through an open pocket and took up its position just above the crotch. It occupied very little space because it only gave the impression of being large, created by its enormous quantity of feathers. At more or less the same time the bats and nocturnal birds of prey were on their way out. Actually there was only one bird of prey, an owl which lived between the padding and the lining of the right-hand side of his tailcoat. There was a hollow there that suited it very nicely. It was dark and protective when it returned just before the first light of dawn.

"Three fleas lived in the middle of his hair. They were very clean and rather earnest, and came from an equestrian circus. They knew how to do an act consisting of leaps and vaults on a miniature trapeze, which were simply but always perfectly executed. Apart from that, they lived in a small encampment at the foot of a specific hair, and they were no bother to anyone. Vincenzo Gallo had great respect for them, and they were enormously grateful to Vincenzo Gallo. He had taken them away from the circus and out of the control of a vicious and exploitative tamer and horsebreaker, a man called Ferguson, who never tired of swearing and forcing them to do what they didn't want to do. He made them leap through rings of fire, which did not suit their temperament, and the tamer was dirty, sweaty and of bad blood, and their lives lacked hygiene, security and satisfaction. They were slaves at that time, by day and by night, always working, emaciated and skeletal. Their mood was always dark and pessimistic. They slept in a pigsty – the only way to describe the dark, filthy and fetid area close to the tamer's earlobe, from which wafted the insalubrious stink of seborrhoea.

"At this point, one can comfortably assert that Vincenzo Gallo had become by fate or by nature an accomplished conjurer and illusionist. He had no art, in the ponderous sense of the word, but everything was going in accordance with his intimate nature.

"The show that he put on at the theatre in response to unanimous demand, was distinguished by clarity and simplicity, and was slightly autobiographical. The curtain came up on an empty stage, and for a moment it remained empty and silent. If there was some impatient joker in the audience, he was quickly told to be quiet by the many who kept coming back to see it again and again. Then an attendant came in wearing a blue circus uniform, with frogging, epaulettes, borders and gold buttons. He held a very small aluminium briefcase in his hand – very small but visibly heavy. He placed it flat on a stool in the middle of the stage, and then went back behind the scenes. Then the briefcase came alive and started to vibrate. It rocked from one side to the other, and a lock came undone, and then the other. The lid flew open and something black unrolled out of it. It took no time to go from its deflated state to its full volume. It was Vincenzo Gallo in top hat and tailcoat. He finished adjusting his collar, bowed and made a grand gesture to greet the audience. The applause never failed to be very warm and extremely welcoming. Then he started his act, which he always did absolutely on his own, by which I mean no other human beings came to assist him.

Chapter U

"He immediately started to pull out all sorts of things from his pockets, and likewise from his mouth, his ears and his teeth. He pulled out pencils, penholders, nibs, rubbers, paper clips, pins, drawing pins, compasses – whole or in parts – biro caps, ink cartridges, dampers, felt pads, pincers, and stamps. It was not however the mundane and rather scholastic nature of the objects that was so striking, but their scarcely believable quantity that steadily built up into great piles that started slipping from the stage into the stalls. Then came elastic bands, pieces of string, ribbons, strips of adhesive paper that stuck to just about everything, and kilometres of cord that appeared to come out of one ear, and as he pulled and pulled, it just kept coming, like a spider spinning its web. Eventually you could see an enormous sticky tangle that cluttered the stage and the proscenium. The astonished audience was almost fearful that this pile would grow like a disorderly ball of wool until it exploded or exploded the theatre. At this stage it was a kind of thriller – an almost anguished one – and the more fainthearted members of the audience started to mutter: That's enough! Think of an amorphous lump of things rolling around an abandoned stationery shop. There was something about it that was both portentous and comical, which unnerved you and made you laugh. Vincenzo Gallo's talent consisted in exactly that: a kind of incomprehensible turmoil. Then, just like snow, this great vorticose knot started to loosen and disentangle itself; a top hat appeared and then so did he, extricating himself with one easy movement. He took off his hat by way of greeting and the sparrows flew out: there was early morning light and they chirruped as they flew. The audience were happy and the spotlights shone as though spring had replaced winter and the weather had brightened up. Out came the doves in pairs, then the turtle doves, blackbirds, chaffinches, carrion crows, hummingbirds, hoopoes, woodpeckers, and they came out of his collar, revers, lining and who knows where else. He resembled a tree swept by the wind, a poplar shaken and enlivened by having more birds than leaves. It was the wildest and most unheard-of thing that every happened in a theatre; it was a kind of wonderment. Every now and then a huge peacock leapt on his head and flared out its feathers as in its courtship display. The audience was enraptured. Then chickens started wandering about, as did ducks, ducklings and an enormous goose distinguished by its intelligent behaviour. He would open his jacket slightly and out flew a kingfisher; then raise his tails and there would be a flight of swallows. This part of the act was always considered impossible, because swallows never obey anyone. And then we had the rabbit which jumped with a somersault and appeared to laugh. Members of the public who came equipped with opera glasses could see the fleas on his nose and whiskers, doing their acrobatic manoeuvres while the rabbit acted, as it were, as their circus ring. When the lights slowly started to fade and it felt like dusk, to the unanimous screams of the ladies, the bats came out accompanied by a splendid owl, which flew over the stalls in silence and landed on the velvet parapet of one of the boxes.

"By the time the show was nearly over, the theatre was swarming with birds: they sat on the chandeliers, stuccoes and parapets of the upper and lower-tier boxes, and flew in vast numbers under the ceiling painted sky-blue with clouds. They chirped and sang together like an orchestra, while the audience gave a standing ovation. The rabbit, which had almost become a little actor, stood straight-backed beside its boss, and with its ears performed an action that from a distance resembled a bow. The fleas jumped from one ear to the other as though possessed and drunk with success. There was never any need for Vincenzo Gallo to whistle, call out or clap his hands; the animals, even if distracted or playful, never took their eyes off him. As soon as he looked as if he were about to turn and go back towards the briefcase, they all plunged headlong towards him like a reverse whirlwind, as though he were sucking them back down. They disappeared under his jacket, waistcoat or hat, and each to its allocated place. Given the crush and the lack of entrances, there might have been some momentary altercation and some bully pecking with its beak. One or two might have shone with metallic light, as a nib or penknife might do; one or two might have appeared to be made of felt, sponge or blotting paper in the instant they came to land, but it was only a moment of misapprehension. Within a few seconds, he was standing alone on the stage just about to leave, and there was complete silence: everyone was standing entranced by the sight of that great flurry of activity. Then came a second thunderous applause: Vincenzo Gallo stopped and turned in each direction, while the public shouted frenziedly and threw flowers and confetti. Vincenzo Gallo smoothed his jacket with an elegant gesture, removed a stray feather from his nose and adjusted his cuffs; he was as smooth and elegant as an eel while he made the appropriate bows to the audience. Like a pianist after his recital, he looked meagre and alone, and everyone felt a little uncertain about the reality of that zoological garden they had just witnessed. In that final moment, he himself seemed to be a suit without anyone inside, and that serene and clean-shaven face of his looked like a bladder held up in the air. This just shows how he had the conjurer's art in his blood. He turned and put first one foot and then the other inside the briefcase; he bent down with his back towards the audience, shrank and miraculously went back inside like a deflating bag. That was him and his illusions. He closed the lid from the inside. Next you heard two clicks of the locks, and then perfect silence. The attendant came back in and picked up the briefcase with two fingers. There was more applause and shouts of encore, but Vincenzo Gallo would not reappear, and the curtain came down. The whole show was unbelievable, and no one ever worked out how he did those tricks. Some people said that the briefcase contained secret mechanisms and inside it was incredibly spacious, like a furnished room. Others claimed that the animals were not alive, but merely reflections from a kaleidoscope. Even the stationery, they said, was merely tissue-paper and dry ice. Still others suggested that Vincenzo Gallo was actually the attendant, and the tailcoat was empty and concealed a hole in the floor. There was even the odd person who said it was all spiritism and Vincenzo Gallo was a spirit raised from the dead or, at the opposite extreme, that it was all just a 3-D cinema production. To which others replied, how come maddeningly material bird droppings kept falling on the spectators?"

Caper blinked and sighed. I shifted away from the infernal breath this produced. Iris had not yet finished; it seemed that she never would.

"Well," she continued, "it occasionally happens that childhood is something glorious and the rest of one's life is exactly the opposite. This is what happened when Vincenzo Gallo started to put on weight. Initially he tried to prevent this: he ate bran, chicory and hayseed, but with such an appetite that it was all absorbed, included wood fibres. The rabbit, duck and doves looked on as he swelled up almost in front of their eyes. His clothes were tight, the stitching ripped and the buttons popped off his waistcoat, trousers and jacket. He could no longer do up his shoes. Even the birds – blackbirds, chaffinches, hoopoes, etc. – abandoned their accommodation, because there was no more space and they didn't want to die. They perched on the chairs and wires, and studied him sullenly. He went on a diet, but that was not the point, because getting fat was now his destiny, and in the absence of anything else, he grew fat on air and the smell of roast meat. Only the fleas found room to stay, but then even they started to be fearful and went to live above his ear, because they could hear the clothing splitting and sense that his skin was incredibly taut. They felt pity for him. He said to people, "Tie me up", and then lay there all tied up like a salami. He had himself put in a box, and said, "Handcuff me." They waited ten minutes or half an hour, and reopened the box. He was still there, red in the face with just the strain of thinking about it. He would mutter, 'I can't do it anymore.' He had himself tied up and thrown in the sea, but he just floated like a boat and was in no danger. Some children swam out, climbed on board him and started to row.

"Yes, all this will sound a little over the top, but it was Vincenzo Gallo himself who told me it in strictest confidence. As he was now too fat to pursue the career of conjurer, he was shut up in here to work as a clerk."

Chapter V

When Iris got to this point, it was as though I was coming round after a period of unconsciousness, because a piercing siren was ringing and a great crowd of people were coming through the door. They were looking for their coats and umbrellas; it was going-home time for the employees. Time was up and I had to get a move on. It was eight o'clock and it was daytime. I had achieved precisely nothing, and all night I had been continuously distracted.

My anxiety and torment returned, and I quickly tore five or six pages from the encyclopaedia. I looked up: there was the head of the arbitrator Pantani sticking out of a small window in the ceiling just above me. He was looking at me and said, "Not that!" but there was already such a crush that the chair was knocked over, and the encyclopaedia fell and was trampled underfoot. I too was caught up in the midst of the crowd. Caper was entirely swallowed up by it and could no longer be seen. On the other hand, Iris and I had become pressed one against the other, face to face, and completely adherent in all our other parts, like sardines in a tin, so that I became intimately aroused. In the crowd, I could see Accetto, Tiraboschi, Rasorio, Santoro, Fischietti and Guastalamenti. I also saw Natale being manhandled and squeezed like a cork, and the director Perbeni who, being smaller, tended to disappear below people's shoulders. I nearly brushed Iris's mouth, but she did not respond. Next to me, Feltpad whispered, "I've such a headache!" I held on tight to my pages under my armpit and inside my jacket. But in that throng, there was someone pinching me, someone pulling my hair and someone sticking straws in my ears. Someone was tickling me and fumbling with fingers that felt like feathers. I had the taste of salt in my mouth, and my naked foot was constantly being trodden on. We were pushing each other, but staying in exactly the same spot. Once again I was about to be slave to my senses.

Chapter V

Then I saw Pantani in the distance, followed closely by Mrs Bucato. He was floundering about in the middle of the crush and trying to open a path in my direction. He was making some threatening gestures, but I couldn't hear what he was shouting over the hum of voices and the shuffling of feet. Perhaps he was saying, "Thief, stop thief!" I knew that I would never get out of there, even though everyone was looking at me with benevolent expressions. I made a supreme effort and managed to detach myself from Iris and force my way through the crowd. I was in fact breathing laboriously – in fact I was snoring.

I pushed so hard that I eventually found myself outside and in front of the door to my own house. Strangely, no one else had come out of the library.

I went in. The bed was unmade and I was a complete mess: dressed like a beggar, covered in dust, feathers, threads and spider webs. I had no buttons, my pockets were torn and my elastic broken. Flying insects were caught up in my hair, and the sole was off one of my shoes. My mouth was numb and swollen with the residual toothache. However, I did have the pages torn from the *Very Modern Encyclopaedia*.

I lay on the bed, opened them, and tried to read them in the little light there was in the room.

Twentieth Century, Chronicle of

1901 marked the beginning in the Great Book Explosion. Up to that time, the average time per capita devoted to reading in Europe was below 0.05%, which means just 43 seconds every 24 hours. Between 1900 and 1910, the figure leaps up to one hour and 22 minutes per person per day. The further progression was vertiginous: in 1911 one hour and 40, in 1912 two hours, then steady growth up to 1935 (7.15 hours) and slower growth until the highest ever result of 8.49 in 1959. As the figures were arithmetical averages, this means that some sections of the population were reading for 14 or 15 hours per day between 1950 and 1959. With a slight delay the other continents followed the European pattern, the first amongst them being North American and Japan. It could be said that this was the most striking feature of the Modern Era.

In the evening during the fifties, very few people would be seen in the streets because the majority were at home reading, and even the very few who were wandering around in the night carried small paperbacks. Social habits were changing rapidly: families ate in a hurry, and then rushed back to their books, one family member on the sofa, another in the armchair, another on a chair in the kitchen and yet another perhaps on the lavatory seat. The maid curled up under her bedclothes would read the books already read by the lady of the house, who would pass the small hours with the bedside lamp on. The gentleman of the house, on the other hand, would spend the whole night in the drawing room, only falling asleep at dawn with his face down on the last page of a crime thriller. These were the follies of the time. But the same was true of daytime on the building sites, on the trams and in the offices: everyone had their book ready with its bookmark, and as soon as there was a break, everybody picked up their book and returned to their reading, and there was a general sigh of disgruntlement when the end of the break period was signalled. This illustrates very well the moral climate of the time.

You could not say that political meetings and conferences were either successful or a failure, because attendance was very good when they coincided with working hours, but it was clear that there was little interest in the matters under discussion, as everyone was distracted by some book hidden under a newspaper, in a folder or stuck to the back of the chair in front. The members of the government, the party's central committee or whatever body was involved, would keep one eye on a book held on their knees, while continuing to take part in the panel and nod their agreement with their heads, and the speaker, irritated himself by the sheer volume of his own words, would stand in silence behind the microphone reading some novel with the excuse that he was looking for a quotation, while all around everyone was happily reading. The sound engineer, the translator, the personnel director and the staff on duty at the doors, they were all reading. Eventually there would be complete silence in these political meetings, like the reading room in a library, and occasionally it would continue for a considerable period to everyone's great satisfaction.

Then came the famous crash of 1959: in the space of a few days everyone had stopped reading, indeed people felt a certain repugnance for books and they all wanted to get rid of them.

To give an idea of the gravity of this situation, suffice it to say that some 54 million writers suddenly found themselves without employment, and on top of that there were more than three times that number who were economically dependent on writers (3.4 individuals for each writer). It has been estimated that during the fifty years of unprecedented and quite insane growth, Italy reached a density of writers out of the total population of 6%, about 1,800,000. The figures were similar in France and Germany. In England they rose to 7% and 8% in Ireland. The European average settled at about 5.5% with highpoints of 12% in the cities of Prague and Vienna. The rural percentages were much lower for Austro-Hungarian writers, close to 0.3–0.2%. The phenomenon was equally widespread and extreme in Asia, which, it's true, had extensive areas that were still empty of writers for climatic reasons, such as the Turanic Plateau, the Sub-Siberian Steppes, the Salt Desert of Takla Makan and Karakum Desert, but this was more than compensated for by the very high figures for India, Japan, China and Siberia. The same can be said of South America, Australia and Oceania: there were islands – the Solomons, the Fijis and the Marquesas – which produced the unique phenomenon of an overwhelming majority of writers from ethnic minorities (70%), who during that fifty-year period imposed themselves on the local population, which was often illiterate and resistant to continuous reading. Part of this local population fled to the mountains, taking refuge in volcanic craters and in the dense tropical vegetation, and part of them accepted literacy, schools and books, and like the rest of the world, ended up slaves to this extreme mania for reading. Having forced reading of their books on that 15-20% of the indigenous population, these writers also imported the diseases typical of sedentary life and the inhalation of stuffy and stale air: arthritis, colitis, ulcers and luxations caused by decubitus, not to mention ophthalmological and cerebral illnesses. Following the recession and overcome by a pernicious neurasthenia and a sense of insecurity, writers started to migrate, driven by rumour and hope, and pour into Italy and the Mediterranean area. German writers, along with Dutch, Swedish, Finnish and Czech ones, went up the Rhine, the Meuse, the Danube and the Elba, and crossed the Alps at Brennero or Tarvisio on foot or by car. 50% travelled with their family, 10% with one or two pupils who were not yet writers however, 20% with a sexual partner, and the remaining 20% on their own or with a companion. The French, English, Basques, Spanish and Moroccans, who gathered in the Rhone valley, came over the San Gottardo, Sempione, Moncenisio, Frejus and Tenda passes. Many of these then set off in the direction of Rome. Bands of ragged and half-starved writers terrorised the course of the Tiber. You came across some yellow faces that looked like they had come straight from prison; these people with foul-smelling hair could be seen tearing up wild chicory and rocket, and cutting a slice of bread with a penknife. Many slept or lived in their cars, and many others in the Colosseum, the Caracalla Baths and the ancient Forum, where they had little sanitation and few means of support. It is startling to think that within a few months the population of Rome rose from three to thirteen million. These are estimated figures, given both the impossibility of any precise quantitative verification of this flood of immigrant writers and the progressive abandonment of the city by its previous residents. By the beginning of the

Chapter V

summer holiday of 1959, the immense and vociferous horde of writers had taken possession of the city and its suburbs.

The fact is that the critics too found themselves unemployed and in a state of unrest. It may seem incredible but there were even more critics than writers, but they were less visible and more respectable. As a rule of thumb, the growth rate of critics in normal times has an average coefficient slightly higher than the rate of growth of writers. If, for example, the writers' coefficient is an annual +1%, which means that in a hundred years their number has been multiplied by a factor of two, the critics with an absolute coefficient of 1.01, or in other words 0.01 higher than that of the writers, will double in just 92 years. This is true if the rate of growth remains unchanged over a period of time, which in reality does not happen: there are periods in which there are demographic explosions for critics while writers undergo a decline, or vice versa. There can also be joint fluctuations at the same rate with sudden rises and falls which can, in particular conjunctures, reach 2.8%. During the fifty years of vertiginous growth for writers, the rates for critics were initially below those recorded over the last 120 years, as though the critics were behind their times. But then they made up for it and overtook the writers' European and North American record by 0.04.

The critics usually have a more non-migratory temperament, but their abnormal numbers did put pressure on the administration of public services, mortgages, public transport and subsidised canteens, and this created widespread intolerance, but also a sense of shared responsibility: "We allowed this growth to happen," people would say, "we cosseted them, we treated them as the jewel in the crown, and now we find that we don't have the resources to pay for them." Others, like ecologists and environmentalists, said that it could have been predicted that this insane and irresponsible growth would eventually reach the point where it would seriously compromise the future viability of our planet. Several thousand tons of critics needed to be disposed of (this was the expression used at the time) without causing damage to existing human settlements. Large-scale retraining proved impossible, because senior office workers refused to work with them. The few that were recruited proved to be lazy, gossipy, bad at spelling and always smelling of onions. The majority – and the figures are staggering – stayed at home or on the stair landings spreading false rumours on the expenses for the joint maintenance of apartment blocks. Or they would crowd into the periodicals room at the library or the waiting rooms at bus and railway stations. There were always some seated at bus stops, on the underground, in the shopping arcades and reading the newspapers and playbills pasted to the walls. They were always arguing and questioning the price of things with a phraseology that the normal population found extremely wearying. There were, it's true, those who continued to joke about it and did not see the first sign of the coming war. "Be careful, or you'll find a critic in your soup," used to be said with excessive frivolity. No one could do anything without a small crowd of critics forming around them and then starting quietly or loudly to pass judgement, give advice, shake their heads and then after a while to needle each other, divide into factions, and inevitably down came the slaps, fists, curses, shoves and stones, as is easy to imagine in the case of idle good-for-nothings. A few statistics will help: the greatest concentrations of critics were in the large conurbations, where the figures rose to 13.3% (Turin, Milan and Genoa), 12.2% (Bologna, Piacenza, Rome and Naples) and 11% (Catania, Lecce and Venezia). There were lower levels in the small cities with populations of less than 200,000, but went up again in small towns, occasionally with percentages higher than those of the large metropolises (Sanremo, Imola and San Severo). This is to restrict ourselves to Italy, but the situation was similar in the rest of Europe and the four continents, which excludes the Antarctic where only very few forms of animal and vegetable life can survive.

Chapter V

The first skirmishes and warnings of the war to come occurred just before Ash Wednesday in 1960, when 140 writers on two coaches were passing through the town of Vimercate, bare-chested, chanting loudly and waving their flags. They passed a bar under whose canopy there was a small group of critics displaying well-developed sneers of disapproval, and as they had some tomatoes in an advanced state of fermentation, they did what any writer would have done if they came across a critic with that typical expression crying out for a well-aimed slap or, supposing some are handy, tomatoes. More critics ran out of the bar, others came to the windows, others were wandering about or watching the television. As it was a sleepy little town, the shouting could be heard everywhere. 140 writers were surrounded by 502 critics, who were all they had in the town (6.3%). How it all ended is terrible to recount: the two coaches were burnt and everyone inside died, including the drivers.

There was another version of this first incident: a writer was travelling the hills of Chianti on his motorbike. It was the first Sunday of Lent and there were three critics on a hay cart, on which they had got a lift. They were eating cherries and on seeing the writer behind them blowing his horn and screaming that he was in a hurry, they though it amusing to spit their cherry stones at him. Naturally the writer was overcome by a wave of anger and indignation. But what could he do? Being the reckless fool he was, he took out his lighter and set fire to the hay cart. The only survivor was the tractor driver who was pulling it.

Whether there is any truth in either story, or whether they were simply rumours that came out of nowhere, there was a succession of vendettas, assaults and massacres throughout Italy. In Milan, 15,000 critics were drowned with their children. In Genoa the critics were masters of the city, but four thousand writers landed on the coast and did another Saint Bartholomew's Night. A column of Hungarian and Bohemian writers was stopped at Treviso and massacred under a motorway flyover. Other militarily inexpert writers were lured into the marshlands of the Po and there they were gunned down like woodcocks.

In other words, all Italy was in flames, and shortly afterwards France, Great Britain, Austria and the German lands. The conflagration spread beyond the Danube and the Bosphorus, and then like wildfire throughout Asia as far as the Bering Strait, the China Sea and Ceylon. And in Africa, even in the forests of Zambia, the Congo River basin and the deserts of the Ténéré, you could see critics and writers battling it out.

The war lasted fourteen months, but those fourteen months were the equivalent of an apocalypse. All kinds of things were used as arms but, particularly in the early stages, fire was used where the enemy had amassed large forces. Gas was the favoured weapon of the writers, and they released it wherever there was a smell of critic. They walked around with canisters on their backs and rubber tubes for flamethrowers. In this way they burnt entire neighbourhoods and tens of thousands of critics. If they suspected that just one critic was hidden in a wheat field, they would burn the lot just to flush him out, and thus immense tracts of arable land, woodland and pastureland were destroyed by fire, resulting in the slaughter of cattle, horses, sheep, goats and birds, with the subsequent scarcity of supply of butter, cheese, eggs, wool and meat; such was the collapse of civilisation. Propane and methane were used in car bombs against the critics' conferences and other gatherings.

In Paris, when the entire population was at home to stay out of danger and there were only armed critics on the streets, the underground network was filled with an odourless gas and this was one of the most heinous crimes, because 600,000 people died like rats down there. The few thousand survivors were left to die of hunger in the court of the Louvre. After just two months, there was no longer a single critic in Paris.

The writers set off with a large liberation army along the railway line that goes from Lyons to Marseilles. They were singing as they marched along in single file, when a whole train driven at full speed by a critic surprised them from the rear and crushed many of them horribly over a distance of ten kilometres. There were 22,000 dead. The survivors, confused and terrified, scattered in small groups around Bourgogne and the Franche-Comté, where they were easily overcome and butchered. The estimated figure is 1,200,000, of whom 125,000 were women and camp followers.

The critics defended themselves with fire-extinguishers. Initially they were just used for putting out fires, but then it was noted that carbon dioxide in particular could lead to suffocation if used in sealed environments. It was used as a weapon, and we can only guess at the resulting massacres. They used extinguishers based on both powder and foam, and this created panic amongst the crowds of writers, with deadly consequences for all involved. They learnt to spray copper sulphate, sulphur, pesticides and fungicides, which enter the body through pores or inhalation and paralyse the central nervous system. They did also use conventional weapons, although they were never typical of this conflict. Principally they resorted either to means of extermination, as one does with mosquitoes, fleas and moths, or to hand-to-hand fighting and bare fists in an undignified scrum.

But enough of anecdotal evidence; we can divide the campaign into three phases: the first was characterised by large-scale massacres on both sides, and lasted from March 1960 to the end of June, leading to the formation of territories under the control of one side or the other. The second phase was more sluggish but still a very bloody war across battlefronts. The third phase commenced in November and can be defined as one of mutual genocide: the final invention was the so-called bacteriological warfare. The critics captured a writer, injected him with meningitis, scarlet fever, whooping cough and hepatitis, and then sent him back amongst his own people. Given those miserable times of famine and indifference to human life, epidemics broke out with fatality rates running at fifty to sixty or even seventy per cent. The European example was imitated around the world: a black and purulent plague spread amongst the writers, and it lasted three months from December to February, leaving very few alive. The critics were hit by cholera which proved more virulent than ever before: it dehydrated them, squeezed their stomachs and left them like dried-out entrails. It was the greatest scourge that ever hit mankind. However, the civilian population was miraculously unaffected. They were incredulous onlookers who tried to contain the damage to themselves and their property.

So no armistice or peace treaty was signed, partly because there was no principle of representation. The more authoritative or, perhaps one should say, the more vicious of their leaders died in the first week of the war, victims of gas. The survivors suffered from delirium, jaundice, scurvy and stereotypy.

By the end of March of 1961 in the northern hemisphere with the sun entering Aries, a generally milder climate deprived the few critics and writers still alive of every last remnant of vitality. The season was a kind of universal antibiotic. In the other hemisphere there were still some lingering cases of leprosy, distemper and even the odd brawl, but they were now overcome by hunger. So what was the result of the war? The percentages went back down below their historic levels, and there were neither victors nor vanquished. The dead were close to one hundred million, with equal numbers on each side. There were horrifying piles of partially buried skeletons near all the capital cities, but every city and every town had its so-called literary cemetery, an ossuary without writing and without names, in which the bones were all mixed up together and no longer belonged to any flag. Critics and writers lie in these artificial mounds like ants and flies.

The more serious problem were the maimed, crippled and shell-shocked, who altogether number between thirty and forty million, with a prevalence of mentally disturbed and atrophic writers (16% more) and a corresponding prevalence of critics who had gone blind, lost limbs or suffered third-degree burns to 40–50% of the body. They

Chapter V

were a pitiful sight: in enormous hospitals for the chronically ill, you can still find them today seated alongside each other with vacant and stuporous expressions, like pieces of dried wood, and nearby critics promenade to the sound of the mechanical joints and wheels of which their prostheses are made. Arguments occasionally break out, but very rarely. In a hospital in Dortmund, four writers covered a critic with a nylon bag and let him suffocate. In Lille the writers, who were the majority, got their fun from swelling up some asthenic critics with a pump and throwing them into a fountain to see them float. In Krakow a critic systematically poisoned the writers' soup with lead oxide, causing several deaths. There was an inquest and the critic was put in isolation. It appears that he was not convinced that the war was over. But these were isolated incidents.

The outcome was that during the first few years after the war, writers were almost nowhere to be found. In the whole of Europe, there were only thirty who were able-bodied and capable of rational thought (i.e. 0.00001% of the population). Some states were entirely without writers: Belgium, Austria and North America, where the war had been at its most ferocious, and descended in the final month into a daily round of hand-to-hand fighting through the entrance halls of houses, in the lifts and up the stairs. The race of critics was also nearly lost: there was a report of a few in Bermuda, and one on an atoll in the Coral Sea, who was however debating the literary concerns of fifty years earlier. Still others, but very few, lived silently in the countryside, feeding on vegetables.

Chapter Z

It was after eight o'clock. "Perhaps Perbeni was right," I thought, "you cannot trust encyclopaedias: they're in the hands of the mafia." I was outraged.

The window was open to let a bit of air in. But dawn seemed not to have arrived that morning, or at the very least it was late, because outside it was still dark. Anguished and perplexed, I put those useless pages down on the bedside table. My head and my teeth ached; I closed my eyes for a second.

I don't know how much time passed; perhaps half a minute or perhaps a whole one. When I felt a puff of air, I opened my eyes and suddenly there was broad daylight, which I found quite astonishing. That was not the day's only incomprehensible surprise. The light bulbs were working normally and producing their usual brightness. I looked on the bedside table, on the floor, inside the drawer, under the sheet and under the pillow, but the pages torn from the encyclopaedia were nowhere to be seen. It was as though they had disappeared into the ether. There was a dusty notebook. The alarm had gone off some time ago. And what day was it anyway?

Other Vagabond Titles Other Vagabond Titles Other Vagabond

www.vagabondvoices.co.uk

Alessandro Barbero's **The Anonymous Novel**

About the book

Set in Gorbachev's Russia, this complex but highly readable novel not only provides a portrait of a society in transition, but also fascinating studies of various themes including the nature of history and the Russian novel itself. Barbero uses his skills as a historian to study the reality of Russian society through its newspapers and journals, and his skills as a novelist to weave a complex plot – a tale of two cities: Moscow and Baku. And throughout, the narrative voice – perhaps the greatest protagonist of them all – represents not the author's views but those of the Russian public as they emerged from one dismal reality and hurtled unknowingly towards another.

Comments

"In the depiction of these changing times, Barbero's political intelligence is apparent. So, however, is his skill as a novelist, for he contrives to integrate the socio-political analysis in his story of imagined characters. It never obtrudes itself; yet you can't ignore or forget it... If you have any feeling for Russia or the art of the novel, read this one. You will find it an enriching experience." – *The Scotsman*

"He writes in a bright and breezy, satirical style ... which leads the reader to believe that some Russian master has been leaning over his shoulder, guiding his hand... It is a deeply rewarding pleasure to be lost in this novel." – *The Herald*

"Barbero uses the diabolic skills of an erudite and professional narrator to seek out massacres of the distant and recent past. The Anonymous Novel concerns the past-that-never-passes (whether Tsarist or Stalinist) and the future that in 1988 was impending and has now arrived." – *Il Giornale*

Price: £14.50   ISBN: 978-0-9560560-4-7   pp. 464

www.vagabondvoices.co.uk

Allan Cameron's **Presbyopia**

About the book

Cameron's collection of bilingual poetry is introduced by an essay on the distinction between myopic and presbyopic poetry: the former focuses on the self, its emotions and its immediate vicinity, while the latter focuses on what is distant in space and time. Poetic myopia is not as negative as the name might imply, nor presbyopia the only desirable form of poetry, but now that two centuries have passed since Wordsworth, whom Heaney has described as the "an indispensable figure in the evolution of modern writing, a finder and keeper of the self-as-subject", the time has perhaps come to put aside our prejudices against the presbyopic. In reality, all poetry reflects a mixture of the two, and Cameron's poetry is no exception. He writes on politics and philosophy, but always with the passion that comes from a humanist sensitivity.

Comment

"Cameron confesses to a weariness with poetry's old forms and old concerns, particularly the perennial Romantic subjects of love and exploration of the self. As a corrective he steers clear of personal topics, turning his presbyopic gaze outward in a sequence of poems that takes in eco-vandalism, press barons, George W. Bush and death. One admires this determination to reject ... pretension and obscurantism ..." *The Sunday Herald*

Price: £10.00   ISBN: 978-0-9560560-3-0   pp. 112

Bond Three Vagabond Three Vagabond

www.vagabondvoices.co.uk

Allan Massie's *Surviving*

About the book

Surviving is set in contemporary Rome. The main characters, Belinda, Kate (an author who specialises in studies of the criminal mind, and Tom Durward (a scriptwriter), attend an English-speaking group of Alcoholics Anonymous. All have pasts to cause embarrassment or shame. Tom sees no future for himself and still gets nervous "come Martini time". Belinda embarks on a love-affair that cannot last. Kate ventures onto more dangerous ground by inviting her latest case-study, a young Londoner acquitted of a racist murder, to stay with her.

Allan Massie dissects this group of ex-pats in order to say something about our inability to know, still less to understand, the actions of our fellow human beings, even when relationships are so intense. It is also, therefore, impossible or at least difficult to make informed moral judgements of others. This is an intelligent book that examines human nature with a deft and light touch.

Comments

"Massie is one of the best Scottish writers of his generation. *Surviving* – sympathetic, unsentimental, atmospheric – is an overdue reminder of how good he is." – Alan Taylor, *The Herald*

"… an impressive novel which poses moral and philosophical questions but works equally well as a compelling thriller." – Joe Farrell, *TLS*

"… an excellent little novel." – Ben Jeffery, *The Guardian*

"The dark brilliance of Massie's style … *Surviving* may be an instant classic in the alcoholic literary canon." – Patrick Skene Catling, *The Spectator*

Price: £10.00   ISBN: 978-0-9560560-2-3   pp. 224

www.vagabondvoices.co.uk

Allan Cameron's **In Praise of the Garrulous**

About the book

This first work of non-fiction by the author of *The Golden Menagerie* and *The Berlusconi Bonus*, has an accessible and conversational tone, which perhaps disguises its enormous ambition. The writer examines the history of language and how it has been affected by technology, primarily writing and printing. This leads to some important questions concerning the "ecology" of language, and how any degradation it suffers might affect "not only our competence in organising ourselves socially and politically, but also our inner selves."

Comments

"A deeply reflective, extraordinarily wide-ranging meditation on the nature of language, infused in its every phrase by a passionate humanism" – Terry Eagleton

"This is a brilliant tour de force, in space and in time, into the origins of language, speech and the word. … Such a journey into the world of the word needs an articulate and eloquent guide: Allan Cameron is both and much more than that." – Ilan Pappé

I like *In Praise of the Garrulous* very much indeed, not only because it says a good many interesting and true things, but because of its *tone* and style. Its combination of personal passion, observation, stories, poetic bits and serious expert argument, expressed as it is in the prose of an intelligent conversation: all this is ideal for holding and persuading intelligent but non-expert readers. In my opinion he has done nothing better." – Eric Hobsbawm.

Price: £8.00   ISBN: 978-0-9560560-0-9   pp. 184